REBEL

Are You Brave Enough to Join?

JOSEPH IAQUINTA

Author Photo by Bridget Barrett
Plot Consultant: Paul J. Militello
Editor: Amelia Beamer
Editor: Gerard J. Senick

Archway Publishing books may be ordered through booksellers or by contacting:

Archway Publishing
1663 Liberty Drive
Bloomington, IN 47403
www.archwaypublishing.com
1 (888) 242-5904

ISBN: 978-1-4808-4451-3 (sc)
ISBN: 978-1-4808-4452-0 (hc)
ISBN: 978-1-4808-4453-7 (e)

Library of Congress Control Number: 2017903241

Print information available on the last page.

Archway Publishing rev. date: 03/09/2017

CONTENTS

ACKNOWLEDGMENTS

Amelia Beamer
Gerard J. Senick
Paul J. Militello
Edward T. Ellis
Margherita G. Lombardo
Michelle W. Wegori (Sticky)
Ewa Markiewicz
Trader Joe's #674 management and crew
Pearl M. Iaquinta
Tony Militello
Bruce Lee
Tony Nolan
Senator Bernie Sanders
Michael Moore
To all of my family and friends

PHASE 1

Family and Friends

December 1999, Michigan

Ten-year-old Nickolas was watching television in his bedroom. As he flipped through the channels, he found a martial arts movie titled *Enter the Dragon,* starring Bruce Lee. Nickolas was amazed by what he saw. He couldn't take his eyes of the TV as Bruce would take on several opponents at once. The art of combat drew Nickolas in like a magnet. Nickolas began to jump on his bed while kicking both feet in the air, falling back onto the mattress. He mocked Lee with a high-pitched scream. His mother, Lena, rushed into her son's room from the living room.

"What are you doing in this bedroom, Nickolas?" she asked.

"I want to learn martial arts, Mom," Nickolas replied, staring at her intensely.

"Calm down, Nickolas," said Lena. "We will talk with your father about it tonight at dinner. Please let me do most of the talking though. You know how your father can be when it comes to something he doesn't understand or relate to."

"Okay, Mom," Nickolas replied. He thought, *I will be the next Bruce Lee.*

Nickolas Leader was bigger than most ten-year-old boys. With black hair and brown eyes, he resembled his mother and favored her Italian heritage. The Leaders lived in a suburb on the west side of town. Their large home had six bedrooms and a few bathrooms on the upper level.

The home had a large, formal dining room, a family room, a study on the main floor, a state-of-the-art kitchen, and two guest rooms with their own bathrooms. They had a small house staff, including a chef and a housekeeper. Nickolas's father, Michael, had to have a spectacular home in order to impress his circle of wealthy family members and business associates.

Later that night, Nickolas and Lena waited for Michael to arrive home from work.

While Nickolas was watching television in the family room, he asked, "Mom, is Dad home yet?"

Lena walked into the family room. "Your father is running late … as usual. You know how his work is. He may not even make it home for dinner."

"I know, Mom," Nickolas said.

An hour later, the chef asked, "Would you like me to hold dinner any longer, Mrs. Leader?"

"No, Stephen. You can begin to serve," Lena replied. After asking Nickolas to set the table for dinner, she said, "We are going to have to start without your father … as usual."

"Okay, Mom," Nickolas replied with a look of sadness.

About twenty minutes into dinner, Michael showed up. He was a burly fellow, just over six feet tall, with a balding head and a frown tattooed on his face. Michael always wore a well-tailored suit and kept himself clean-shaven to maintain a professional image. Michael's family was from the United Kingdom. He was third-generation American and had been raised with very conservative values.

"Sorry I'm late, Lena. Busy day at the office," Michael took his seat at the table.

"Sure, honey. We understand," Lena replied.

Nickolas waited patiently for his mother to bring up the topic of him taking martial arts lessons.

Halfway through dinner, Lena finally said, "Nickolas was watching a martial arts movie today, and he would like to learn, Michael—"

"Mom said I could learn martial arts, Dad!"

Disturbed by his son's behavior, Michael asked, "Nickolas, why are you interrupting your mother?"

"Sorry, Mom," said Nickolas, turning to his mother with a look of embarrassment.

"Michael, Nickolas is just very excited about learning a new art form. Please be patient with him."

Michael began to eat his dinner again while leaving Nickolas in suspense. Finally, Michael asked, "So, why do you want to learn how to fight, Nickolas?"

"There are these two boys in my class. They are much bigger than the rest of the other kids, and they are always picking on someone," Nickolas said.

"Have they bothered you yet?" Michael asked.

"No, but I feel a little scared sometimes when they look at me. They haven't said anything to me yet, but I don't like it when they bully the smaller kids."

"So, you feel intimidated? That's only natural. Violence is not the answer though. If they bother you, report them to the teacher," Michael said.

"I understand that, Dad. I want to learn martial arts so I won't feel scared anymore. I'm not gonna start a fight."

"So, you just want to feel more confident?"

"Yes, Dad."

"I guess you have a point."

Nickolas smiled, thinking that he had convinced his Father. "Do you know who Bruce Lee is, Dad?"

"Of course I do. Everyone knows who Bruce Lee is, but Chuck Norris was the best," Michael said.

"I've seen Chuck Norris before, but I really don't like the way he fights. His style looks too easy. I like Bruce Lee better. Can I please take martial arts lessons, Dad?"

"Sure, if it will relieve me of any more questions," Michael said in an insensitive tone. Nickolas did not say another word, fearing that his father would change his mind.

Nickolas's mother knew that his cousins went to the boys club. Her sister-in-law, Pearl, had said her boys were taking martial arts classes there. Nickolas's parents would allow him to join the boys club with his cousin Paul and his two older brothers, Rob and Frank.

"I'll call Pearl after dinner to ask her when they go to the club," Lena offered.

"Thanks, Mom," Nick said. He was very excited to start training with his cousins.

Nickolas's father was the owner and CEO of a large Fortune 500 company, which he had inherited from his father twenty years earlier. Michael Leader was a cold man who did not care how people perceived his actions. All he wanted was to become one of the wealthiest men in the world. As a result, he did not spend much time with his son or any family for that matter. He was a businessman first and foremost.

Lena Leader was Michael's college sweetheart. She was beautiful and had a classic curvy figure and long, black, silky hair. She would spend time at the health club and was very mindful of her health and conditioning. Her family members were blue-collar factory workers. Michael's family didn't approve of Lena's family, but they were civil toward them. Lena's family would visit for holidays and birthdays.

The evening after Michael agreed to let Nickolas take martial arts training, Nickolas and his parents attended the company Christmas party at Leader Industries.

They were driven in a limousine to the business district of downtown Detroit where Leader Industries had its headquarters. Nickolas stared out the limo window at the dilapidated inner city. He was aware of the irony as he glanced at the fine clothes he and his parents wore for the Christmas party. He looked out at the boarded-up buildings, vacant lots, and shady dudes hanging out on the street corners. It seemed as though there were two worlds, created unequally.

The business district housed the most impressive buildings in the city. Within minutes, Nickolas and his parents arrived at Leader Industries. The shiny glass building stood an impressive twenty stories tall.

After entering from the indoor parking structure, the family went to the banquet hall on the top floor. It had a seating capacity of a thousand people, and his dad's parties were always packed. Michael liked to show off his accomplishments, and the balcony wrapped around the entire hall. His dad made sure the hall would impress even a king.

The hall was full of employees, their families, and business associates of the corporation. There were other children at the party, but Nickolas had met all of them at similar functions and parties at their homes in the past few years. He was not interested in socializing with the other rich kids because he couldn't relate to them. Nickolas sat at a table by himself, feeling bored. He couldn't help but to distract himself with thoughts of Bruce Lee and becoming a martial artist.

A tall, handsome man with salt-and-pepper hair and a very expensive suit walked up to him and said, "Hello, my name is Giovanni Grimaldi." He pulled out a chair and sat down.

"Hi, my name is Nickolas Leader. Do you work for my dad?"

The band began to play on the stage.

"No, your dad and I met back in grade school. I have my own company. Your father and I have done business together for years now."

Nickolas asked, "How come I've never seen you before?"

"I usually only see your father during business functions, but he is always inviting me to these parties. I decided to attend this one because I had no plans for the evening."

"What kind of business do you own?" Nickolas asked.

"Mostly military-related," Grimaldi replied.

"Do you make martial arts weapons?" Nickolas asked.

"No, but maybe I will look into that." Grimaldi smiled. "Are you a martial artist, Nickolas?"

"Not yet, but I just saw my first Bruce Lee movie last night. I will be just like him one day!" Nickolas said.

"Sounds like you are ready to get started," Grimaldi said.

"Yes, I think next week," Nickolas replied.

A couple of Grimaldi's business associates interrupted their conversation for a minute. Once they had moved on, Nickolas asked, "How do you get along with these people?"

Grimaldi looked around the room. “Not so well, most of the time, but I have learned to tolerate them over the years.”

“I like you, Mr. Grimaldi,” Nickolas said with a smile.

Nickolas’s father walked up with a drink in his hand. “Giovanni, how are you tonight?”

“I am very well, Michael. I was just getting to know Nickolas. He is a very bright boy.”

“Yes, he is. He has been asking about training in martial arts recently.”

Grimaldi said, “He was just telling me about that. You should bring him by the simulator facility. He would love it.”

“Yes, I remember visiting when you first opened. What’s it been now—three years since you opened that to the public?”.

“Yes, three years now. We have added a couple of new simulators since. It is growing very well,” Grimaldi said.

“So what kind of simulations do you have?” Nickolas asked.

“We have small and large weapons simulators in an interactive setting. It’s like a video game—but with the actual feel of the weapons firing on their targets. Also, we have vehicle and aircraft fighter simulators with the same realistic simulations. Let me know when the two of you would like a personal tour. I will set something up for Nickolas to experience each of the simulators.” Grimaldi smiled at Nickolas.

“Sounds like fun, Nickolas,” said Michael. “Would you like that, son?”

“Yes, I would love to!” Nickolas replied. “When can we go, Dad?”

“Well, I have to check my calendar. I will call you, Giovanni, so we can set this up soon,” Michael replied.

“No problem. Just let me know when, and I will make the arrangements,” Grimaldi said.

“I can’t wait!” Nickolas said.

“I am glad we met. I hope to get to know you better in the future, Nickolas. Have a good night,” Grimaldi said.

“I’m happy to have met you too, sir.” Nickolas stood up to shake hands. “Good night, Mr. Grimaldi.”

The following week, Nickolas joined the boys’ club.

Nickolas walked into the club with his mother and his cousins. His mother signed him up, wished the boys a good time, and exited.

The cousins gave Nickolas a tour of the club. In the first room, children were shooting pool. In the next room, children were playing ping-pong. Other groups were playing basketball and baseball. In the martial arts room, the boys introduced Nickolas to the trainer. The trainer's name was Salvario.

Salvario set Nickolas up with a gi, and there were about twenty boys and girls in the room. Rob was the best fighter among his brothers. He was the oldest and the biggest, and he was very fit after training for several years. Rob had long, dark hair and a rugged demeanor. He took Nickolas aside and said, "You need to be focused if you want to do well."

"Okay, Rob. I'm ready to do this."

Nickolas's cousins grew up in the city of Detroit and wanted to test his toughness. His cousins couldn't have him being pushed around while they were responsible for him at the club. Frank, the second oldest, had brown hair and was just a couple inches shorter than his older brother. He was about the same size as Nickolas, and they would be matched up with each other in sparring. Frank roughed up Nickolas pretty well in his first face off, almost breaking his finger.

Salvario checked his hand for a break. "Are you okay to continue, Nickolas?" the trainer asked.

"I'm fine," Nickolas replied.

Paul walked over to Nickolas and said, "Are you okay, Nickolas?"

"No problem. Let's keep training." Nickolas was focused on learning every move. The hurt finger didn't bother him while in that state of mind. He went home pleased with his first day at the club. He and his cousins would soon fall into a comfortable routine.

A few weeks passed by. Nickolas was fitting in very well at the club, and he enjoyed participating in most of the activities. He really liked shooting pool and playing basketball, but he focused on his martial arts training. Nickolas trained three to four days a week at the club with his cousins after school and was excelling at a very fast pace.

Eventually, Michael got around to setting up the appointment at Grimaldi's military-simulator facility. Michael and Grimaldi agreed to meet on a Saturday afternoon.

Grimaldi's building was in a suburb of Michigan and was designed as a military facility with camouflage-painted walls inside and out. There were several simulation stations. People would pay to enter and then line up to experience the weapons and vehicles.

Grimaldi greeted Michael and Nickolas at the entrance. "Welcome, gentlemen. Let me show you around the place."

"Thanks again for the invite, Giovanni," Michael replied.

"I've been asking my dad to bring me here every day since we met," Nickolas said.

"Your father is a very busy man, Nickolas. Be grateful that he is taking the time for you," replied Grimaldi.

"I am, sir. Thank you for inviting us," Nickolas replied.

Grimaldi walked them over to a simulator that featured handguns and pointed to the shelf of weapons. There were also vests so that the players could feel the results of gunfire when they were hit.

"Choose one, Nickolas."

"I'm not sure which one to pick," Nickolas replied.

"Whichever feels comfortable in your hand, for starters," Grimaldi said.

Nickolas walked up to the shelf and viewed his choices. "I think I'll try this one." He picked up a Walther PPK like the one from the James Bond movies. "This one feels comfortable."

"Good choice," Grimaldi said. "You must remember you will not be firing real ammunition. There is nothing to worry about. Once you enter the simulator, the system will begin. Targets will pop up for you to take aim at and fire upon. The trigger will feel completely natural—as if you were firing a real weapon with actual recoil motion."

"What is recoil?" Nickolas asked.

"Recoil is the motion of the weapon when fired. It's also referred to as the kick after pulling the trigger. You will be scored at the end … so take your time and focus on your targets."

Nickolas said, "I'm ready to start, Mr. Grimaldi."

Nickolas put a vest on and proceeded to the simulator. Just as Nickolas walked through the maze, one of the targets popped up. A man wearing a mask and aiming a gun appeared. Nickolas quickly reacted by firing three rounds at the object. He missed every one of them because he was nervous. He felt the vibration through the vest as the assailant hit him. Even though it was just a simulation, it seemed very real.

In the next area, another target jumped out. This time, he took a deep breath, aimed, and fired. He hit the target with one shot. This triggered a bell to signify that the target was eliminated. Nickolas felt much better when he realized the importance of being patient. He completed the exercise and anticipated his results.

Grimaldi greeted him at the exit and handed Nickolas a sheet of paper with his score on it. "Very good for your first test, Nickolas," Grimaldi said with a smile.

"Thanks, Mr. Grimaldi. That was cool." His results revealed a score of 70 percent. Nickolas turned to his father. "Look, Dad. Mr. Grimaldi says I scored great for the first time."

Michael looked up from his cell phone. "Oh, sure, son. Great job."

"Are you ready for the next simulator?" Grimaldi asked.

"You bet!" Nickolas replied.

Nickolas tested the assault rifles, the all-terrain vehicle, and the stealth fighter. He scored very well for his age.

"You may have a future fighter-pilot here, Michael," said Grimaldi.

"You think so, Giovanni?" asked Michael.

"Yes. Nickolas has great focus and anticipation. I am very pleased with his scores."

"Can we please come back again, Dad?" Nickolas asked, turning to his father.

"You may have to ask your mother to bring you back, Nickolas. I am very busy this time of the year."

"Whenever you would like, Nickolas. Have your parents call me, and I will be happy to have you back," said Grimaldi.

For the next few weeks, Nickolas trained at the club a few days a week and visited the military simulation facility a couple of times. Nickolas was beginning to feel very confident in his new surroundings.

One day at school, he walked with a young classmate on the playground. "Hey, Skylar, how are you today?"

"I'm okay, Nickolas," she said. "How are you?"

"I'm great!" Nickolas replied. "I've been training in martial arts with my cousins. I'm practicing with military weapons and jet fighters at my friend's military simulation facility too. I'm learning a lot of cool stuff."

"Wow, that sounds exciting!" Skylar said. "I play for the basketball team at school. I would like to learn martial arts too."

"Ask your parents if you can join the club with us," Nickolas said.

"Okay. I will," she replied with a smile.

Suddenly, Nickolas heard a cry for help. Raymond was in trouble. Two bullies were picking on him.

"Hey!" Nickolas yelled. "Leave him alone!"

One of the boys turned to see who was approaching them, "You wanna make somethin' of it, punk?"

Nickolas drew closer to the boy and said, "Maybe. Now let Ray go!"

"Mind your own business, dude," the other boy yelled.

"He *is* my business!" Nickolas said. "You have two choices: walk away or deal with me."

The first boy let Raymond go and backed off.

The second boy said, "Come and make me, punk!"

Nickolas rushed to break the boy's grip from his friend. His actions would convince the bully to release Raymond.

"Okay, okay, man. I didn't know he was your girlfriend," the boy shouted.

The two bullies laughed as they retreated.

"Smart choice," Nickolas replied with a scowl. "And don't let me catch you picking on any of my friends again—or else you'll have to deal with me!"

"We'll let you slide this time, dude. Be careful how you talk to us though. We're feeling generous today," the bigger bully said.

As the boys went their separate ways, Nickolas asked, "Are you okay, Ray?"

"Yeah, I'm fine. Thanks for the help. They were about to cream me."

"You don't have to worry about them anymore. I've got your back from now on," Nickolas said.

"Those martial arts classes are paying off for you," said Raymond.

"You bet, buddy. You should join the club too."

"Maybe I will," replied Ray.

"I'm definitely going to join now!" said Skylar.

Nickolas smiled at Skylar and felt the spotlight on him. He liked the way it felt to be able to help his friend and impress the girl. Nickolas liked Skylar but he'd never had the confidence to approach her. Nickolas felt a sense of pride and accomplishment. He was growing tremendously in a short period of time.

PHASE 2

A Boy Finds His Way

February 2003, Michigan

Nickolas and Paul were at a wedding reception for a member of Lena's family. Being from a large family, they would attend a few weddings per year. The enormous hall belonged to a family with whom his mother had grown up. Everybody was dressed in suits and gowns.

Nickolas walked up to his cousin and asked, "Did you tell your mom and dad about that martial arts school we heard about?"

"No, I forgot to ask them," Paul replied.

"We need to ask them while we have them all together."

Nickolas grabbed Paul by the arm, and the boys approached the table where their parents were talking.

Paul said, "Mom, Dad, we have a question. Can Nickolas and I join a new dojo?"

Both boys were smiling.

"Where did you boys hear about this school?" Lena asked.

"One of our classmates at the club was talking about it yesterday," Nickolas said.

"We are going to have to visit the school first," Paul's father replied. "We'll make sure that they are running a legitimate operation. I have heard that some of these schools are all about the money. I don't believe that anyone should pay to advance. You must earn your advancement."

"I agree, Tony," Michael said with a sarcastic look.

Michael thought, *What does Tony know about this?*

"We'll do some research this week and visit with the trainer to see what he's like," Pearl said.

"Thanks, Mom," Paul replied.

The boys high-fived each other.

Nickolas shot Paul's mom a big smile. Pearl was very short and had black hair and a few extra pounds. She was always cooking and cleaning and was very dedicated to her children. Pearl was always harping on the boy's manners. She would constantly stress that they reply with "please," "thank you," and "you're welcome." The boys understood the difference between right and wrong—not just what they could or could not get away with.

Pearl researched the martial arts school. A couple of weeks later, Nickolas, Paul, and Skylar joined the Jeet Kune Do School of Martial Arts. The three children walked into the new dojo and looked at the posters of different Kung Fu legends on the walls. There were a few different areas—one with mats for exercises and drills, another for punching bags and exercise machines, and another with a kickboxing ring for sparring. The training was intense, which was the style that Nickolas wanted.

The owner and sensei walked up to Nickolas, Paul, and Skylar. He was Chinese, stood about five feet seven inches, and weighed 145 pounds. He wore a black gi, and his students wore white gis. "Hello, my name is Sensei Lee. You will address me as Sensei. Please head to the locker room to dress in your gis," he said.

The twenty students went through basic beginner drills.

About forty-five minutes into the training, Nickolas said, "May I please spar with someone, Sensei?"

"You are feeling unimpressed with my class?"

"No, Sensei. I would just like to compete," Nickolas replied.

Sensei Lee pointed to one of his more experienced students in Nickolas's weight class.

"Please enlighten our new student," Sensei said.

Nickolas climbed into the ring and squared off in front of his opponent.

The student was a year older and more experienced than Nickolas, but he was the same height. Nickolas was not worried. He was eager to show off his abilities.

Nickolas stepped to the line with great confidence. Showing no fear in front of the entire class, Nickolas bowed to Sensei and then to his opponent. His opponent did the same—but with a look of disrespect toward Nickolas.

Sensei Lee put his hand between the two boys and commanded them to fight.

Nickolas moved forward and then quickly back. His opponent struck first but missed. Nickolas struck with great timing, following the boy's retreat, and scored the first point.

Sensei Lee halted the match to grant the first point to Nickolas.

The boys squared off again. This time, Nickolas rushed in from the go, striking with a lead kick to the chest. His opponent tumbled backward into the ropes, which was an automatic point.

Frustrated and embarrassed, the boy balked, staying in his corner.

Sensei looked at him, demanding that he continue.

Reluctantly, the boy faced off with Nickolas again.

Sensei yelled, "Begin!"

The boy cautiously circled the mat, confused about how to time his attack.

Nickolas took advantage of his opponent's fear by aggressively smothering the boy with several combinations. His opponent was knocked into the ropes a second time, and Nickolas gained another point.

"That is enough for today," Sensei Lee said.

Everyone dispersed into the locker room.

Paul and Skylar grabbed Nickolas.

Paul whispered, "Wow, you were awesome, Nickolas."

"Thanks, cuz. That felt great! I can't wait to come back," Nickolas replied.

"That was awesome, Nickolas!" Skylar said with a smile.

"You know that they are going to make you fight someone way better next time," said Paul.

"I hope so. I'm not here to take it easy. I want to get better," Nickolas said.

"You're crazy, Nickolas," Paul replied.

Nickolas was developing a crush on Sky.

Skylar's mother picked her up, and Pearl picked up Nickolas and Paul.

Tony and Pearl lived in a small, modest home on the east side of Detroit. The two-story house was in good condition, with a full basement, but the two younger sons had to share a bedroom. Tony was too proud to have his wife take on a job since he was raised to be the breadwinner of the family.

Tony Perisi was an assembly-line worker and machine operator with General American Automotive. G. A. Automotive was the largest automotive manufacturer in the world. Tony was an old-school type with large shoulders and chest. He could be very intimidating with his deep voice and heavy beard.

While sitting at the table for dinner, Tony asked, "So how was the martial arts training today?"

"You should have been there, Dad. Nick asked for a match, and the sensei looked at him like he was crazy."

"It wasn't that big a deal," Nickolas said.

"Are you kidding, Nickolas? You knocked that guy into the ropes—twice. He was so embarrassed, Dad."

"Sounds like you boys are gonna enjoy the dojo," Tony replied.

"I can't wait to go back!" said Nickolas.

"I'm glad to hear that you boys like it," said Tony. "How would you two like to help me fix the brakes on my car after dinner?"

"I wanna learn!" Nickolas shouted.

"Good. You should learn how to maintain your own vehicle." Tony repaired and maintained his own vehicles and home as well as those of his family and friends when he had the time.

After dinner, the boys joined Tony in the garage. Nickolas focused on every step of the brake repair. His uncle was very patient and even let the boys use some of his tools to remove the old parts.

Paul bragged about how he had learned how to change the brakes last year.

Nickolas enjoyed the experience and was happy to spend quality time with Paul's family. He felt great admiration for his uncle and aunt and appreciated everything they were willing to teach him.

Nickolas and Paul were waiting in front of the dojo for their ride.

Nickolas asked, "Is something wrong, Paul?"

Paul sighed and shook his head. "I don't know how to tell you this, man, but I can't train anymore."

Nickolas asked, "Why?"

"My dad is going to be laid off from work for the first time in seven years."

"G. A. Automotive sucks!" said Nickolas.

"I don't know what's gonna happen." Paul replied.

"Maybe I could ask my mom if she could pay your way for a couple of months?" Nickolas said.

The next night, Nickolas talked to his father after dinner. "Dad, Uncle Tony was just laid off, and Paul can't train with me at the dojo until his dad goes back to work."

Michael said, "This country is made up of two kinds of people. America and Americans. We are America—the elite class that rule. The rest of the population are just Americans—the workers who are below us. People choose to live like the masses of the world. Your uncle should consider going back to school since he is always being laid off. If people would just get an education and work hard, they could have the American dream as well." Michael never had to pay a dime to attend college. He was born into money, and he could not relate to the struggles of most Americans.

"If the workers show up for work every day, if they do a good job, and if the company is making money, why should they be laid off?" Nickolas asked.

"Maybe the company is losing money and has to make cuts."

Nickolas walked out of the room, shaking his head. Even at thirteen, he felt that his father's reply was wrong. He could not agree with his father's philosophy.

Not too long after joining the dojo, Sensei Lee approached Nickolas after class. "I feel that you are ready to enter a tournament, Nickolas."

"I want to compete, but are you sure that I'm ready so soon, Sensei?"

"Absolutely. You are one of my most focused students."

"Okay. If you think so, then I'm ready."

"One of the most important elements that a fighter must possess is self-confidence. Having belief in oneself is half the battle."

"I understand, Sensei. Thank you."

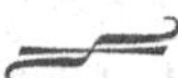

At the dinner table that night, Nickolas said, "Mom, Sensei Lee asked me to enter a tournament."

Lena said, "Why don't you invite everyone to the tournament?"

"Yeah. That would be great, Mom."

On the day of the tournament, Lena, Tony, Pearl, Paul, Skylar, Rob, Frank, and Mr. Grimaldi showed up to see Nickolas compete. Lena decided to surprise Nickolas by inviting Grimaldi too.

Nickolas was preparing for battle. After warming up and stretching, he began to look around the gymnasium for his family and friends, but he could not find his father anywhere. He noticed Mr. Grimaldi and was happy to have him show up for his first fight.

Nickolas would be called for the third fight of the evening. His opponent was in the same age group and weight class, but he had already fought in three tournaments. Sensei was not concerned and told Nickolas that he had the utmost confidence in him.

The gymnasium was buzzing with excitement. Nickolas looked

around at the crowd, and a bit of nervousness began to set in. He quickly shook it off and squared off with his opponent. He and his combatant bowed to the official and then to each other. The official ordered them to begin.

The boy rushed Nickolas with several attempted strikes to the chest, but Nickolas was very light on his feet. He evaded the attacks and landed a spinning back elbow to the boy's shoulder.

The boy dropped to the canvas with great force, and the official stopped the match. The crowd cheered loudly, but Nickolas stayed focused on his objective. The boy was not getting up. His sensei attended to his student and asked him if he was hurt. The boy could not continue, and his sensei threw in the towel.

The official walked over to Nickolas's corner to explain. Both boys lined up in the middle of the ring. The official raised Nickolas's hand and called the match for him.

The crowd was impressed with the newcomer bringing such a display of talent and power. The spectators were not accustomed to that type of outcome in a point-fighting contest. Boys rarely were hurt in the matches.

Nickolas had won his first match with ease.

In the second round, Nickolas would have a much better challenger. The boy was even more experienced, and Nickolas would be very cautious in his approach.

The boys were directed to begin, and Nickolas attacked first.

The boy slipped Nickolas's right hand-strike and countered with a kick to the stomach, throwing Nickolas back a few feet.

The official stopped them and awarded the point to the boy. The crowd groaned. Nickolas gathered himself, and the official directed them to begin again. Nickolas's competitor went for a quick lead-kick strike, but Nickolas slipped the attack and countered with a perfectly timed right hand to the chest, sweeping the boy off his feet and to the canvas.

The official stopped them to award Nickolas a point. The majority of the patrons cheered for Nickolas. The official lined them up again and gave the order to begin.

Nickolas's opponent was intimidated by the last strike, and Nickolas took advantage by quickly faking a low kick and changing it to a high kick to the head. He followed it with a right-hand strike to the abdomen. The official stepped in again, awarding Nickolas the point. Nickolas would strike fear into his opponent, scoring the remainder of the points to advance to the final round of the tournament.

His last opponent had competed in ten previous matches, but Sensei Lee looked at Nickolas with confidence. The audience was eager to see what Nickolas would do next.

The boy stared at Nickolas, but Nickolas was not fazed. They faced off, and the official asked if they were ready. The boys bowed to the official and then to each other.

The command was issued, and Nickolas's opponent rushed toward him. He circled the ring, avoiding every strike and showing discipline and patience. Nickolas decided to frustrate his opponent, waiting for the right opportunity.

The boy was unable to land a clean strike while Nickolas waited for an opening. He finally found one, struck with a drop-kick to the stomach, and knocked the wind out of the more experienced competitor. Nickolas landed a vicious strike directly to the liver, and the boy fell to the canvas like a ton of bricks.

The official jumped in front of Nickolas, turned to the hurt fighter, and asked if he was okay. Nickolas's opponent could not reply while he attempted to regain his breath.

The boy's sensei was called over to check on his student. He asked the boy if he could continue, but the boy was still recovering. His sensei asked the official for a minute, but the official warned that he only had fifteen seconds to continue or else he would be disqualified.

The boy said that he was okay, and he and Nickolas lined up again. Nickolas wasted no time in attacking his prey. He led with a scissor-kick to the chest, fooling his opponent by faking a strike with one foot and throwing his other foot, landing on his opponent's chest. The boy was knocked into the ropes and left dazed, scoring another point for Nickolas.

Nickolas was awarded the match, and the crowd cheered. Nickolas couldn't have asked for a better result.

Nickolas went to celebrate with his family and friends after the tournament.

Grimaldi said, "I am very impressed with you, Nickolas. I cannot believe that this was your first competition."

"Thank you for showing up, Mr. Grimaldi," Nickolas said, looking around the gymnasium for his father. "I wish my dad could have seen me compete."

"Your father wanted to be here, but he had a very important business transaction," Lena said.

"I'm very impressed with you too, Nickolas." Uncle Tony extended his hand for a fist-bump.

"Yeah, Nickolas, that was awesome!" Paul put up his hand for a high-five.

"You were great, Nickolas!" Skylar hugged Nickolas.

"Thank you all for coming to my first competition. It means a lot to me," Nickolas said.

When he and his mother headed toward the parking lot, Nickolas said, "I wish Dad could have come."

"I know, Nickolas, but you know how your father is—always working."

The two remained silent for the ride home, and Nickolas went to bed early.

The next day, Nickolas walked in to his father's study after dinner. "How come you weren't at my tournament yesterday, Dad?"

"I am sorry, Nickolas. I had a very important business deal to be completed. I will try to make it next time."

"Everyone was there except for you, Dad."

"I promise to be there next time, Nickolas."

"Don't make promises you can't keep, Dad." Nickolas quickly walked out of the room.

PHASE 3

Becoming a Man

October 2006, Michigan

Nickolas continued to win tournaments and became the best student at his dojo. Nikolas also earned the spot of starting point guard on his basketball team. He spent more time with his cousin's family as well as with Grimaldi at the military-simulation facility.

During the summer, Nickolas would sleep over at Uncle Tony's house quite a bit. Tony kept firearms in his home for protection.

Tony walked up to Nickolas after dinner and said, "You're having a birthday this month, Nickolas. Sixteen years old. Wow, a young man."

"Yeah. I feel very confident and enthusiastic about the future," Nick said with a smile.

"That's good. It's about time you begin learning how to use the weapons in our home. If something happens, you may have to act quickly. The neighborhood isn't getting any better with all of the job losses in the state. Do you think you can handle that?"

Nickolas smiled. "Yes, sir. I want to learn."

"As long as it's okay with your parents, we will be training this weekend out in the hunting grounds."

"Great! I'll ask my parents tomorrow at dinner."

"Well, I have to call unemployment now," Tony said.

"What's going on with work, Uncle Tony?" Nick asked.

"Oh, nothing much. Not to worry, Nickolas. Everything will be fine."

The following night, Nickolas said, "Uncle Tony asked if it was okay if I went to the hunting grounds this weekend to learn how to fire weapons."

"Weapons? What kind of weapons?" Michael asked.

Lena said, "My brother has a few handguns and a shotgun for protection. Nickolas has been spending quite a bit of time there over the past few years. He should learn to use these weapons in case something happens."

"Have you used the weapons before, Lena?" Michael asked.

"Well, you know that I grew up in the city."

"How come you never told me?"

"Well, it never seemed to come up," Lena said. "Besides, this isn't about my past. This is about Nickolas becoming a man."

"I don't know if this is such a good idea. Let me think about it," said Michael.

"Dad, I have been training with Mr. Grimaldi for years. I am ready to learn with the real thing."

Lena said, "I will go with them to be sure they are practicing proper gun safety."

"As long as you are willing to attend, Lena, I am fine with it."

Nickolas walked in to the kitchen and saw his father eating lunch. "Hi, Dad. How you doing today?"

"I am fine, Nickolas. What are you up to today?"

"I just picked up my driver's license. I was hoping I could have a car for my sixteenth birthday."

"What do you need a car for, Nickolas?" Michael asked.

"I'm sixteen, Dad. All the kids my age at school have a car!"

Nickolas's father walked out of the room.

Nickolas found his mother in the living room. "I asked Dad for a car, and he ignored me. Why can't I have a car, Mom?"

"We didn't want to worry you, but the economy is taking a turn for the worse. Your father's company is losing money, and Uncle Tony keeps getting laid off from work." Lena turned on the news.

The next day, Nickolas went to see Tony.

Tony said, "Things have been getting worse over the last six years since the new president took over. He has allowed the transfer tax to be decreased. As a result, jobs are being outsourced and automated. Families are being torn apart, people are losing their homes, and very little tax is being paid to the federal government. This has resulted in police departments, fire departments, and public schools laying off employees. Millions of families are struggling. Three of my coworkers were laid off permanently. Their wives divorced them and won full custody of their children, leaving them decimated by the greed of corporations."

"Oh, I had no idea things were so bad," Nickolas replied.

"Manufacturing facilities are being closed across the country. I don't know how exactly this affects Leader Industries, but you should get a job this summer and save your own money to buy a car."

"Forget about the car." Nickolas said. "I'm more concerned with what is going to happen to you and Aunt Pearl."

"Nickolas, you are not to worry about these issues at your age. Just focus on getting your education and enjoying life while you're still young."

"Okay, Uncle Tony. I trust you to give it to me straight. I will get a job this summer and save every penny to buy my first car."

Once Nickolas returned home, he searched for news about his father's corporation. He focused on corporate income over the past ten years. Leader Industries was showing gains over the past decade—not decreases like his mother said. He wondered if his father had lied to his mother. Nickolas searched for the number of employees at Leader Industries over the past decade. The search showed that the number of employees had decreased. Nickolas could not understand why the revenue increased while the workforce was depleted.

For weeks, Nickolas stewed over his findings. He went about his routine, but he said nothing to his father.

Nickolas explained his situation to Mr. Grimaldi. "I could use someone who knows what's going on—and will be honest with me."

"I probably shouldn't get in the middle of this. Please do not mention to your parents that we spoke about the matter," Grimaldi said.

"Of course not. I would never put you in a position like that. I just don't understand all of it."

"I don't know how to explain this without giving you an awful impression of your father. If what you say is true, your father is lying to your mother. I have done business with Leader Industries, and I know the corporation has been growing in recent years. As far as the employee situation, I am afraid they are using the downfall of the economy to take advantage of the situation. It is a shame that people are being asked to do more work while understaffed. The majority of corporate America is following this business model."

"My father is taking advantage of his employees. The whole system is a mess. Thank you for being honest with me, Mr. Grimaldi. I appreciate our friendship, and I trust you."

"Thank you, Nickolas. What are you going to do?"

"I won't say a word to my father about any of this. I will do what most people do when they need something—I will go to work and earn it."

"You never fail to impress me, young man. I am proud of your decisions." Grimaldi put his hand on Nickolas's shoulder.

"Thank you, sir. I appreciate everything you have ever done for me."

"You are welcome, Nickolas. It's been my pleasure," Grimaldi replied with a smile.

Later that day, Nickolas called his cousin to ask if he could get him a job as a busboy at a restaurant. Paul talked to his manager, confirmed that they were hiring, and told Nickolas to go see the manager. Nickolas got the job.

The restaurant seated about one hundred people and could get pretty crazy at times.

Paul trained Nickolas, and the manager said, "Very good, both of you. I like the way you teach, Paul—and I like the way you listen, Nickolas."

That summer, Nickolas saved every penny he earned. "Hey, Uncle Tony. Can you help me find a car?"

"Why don't you ask your parents?"

"They have no idea how to get a good deal on a used car. Neither of them has ever bought a used vehicle."

"Makes sense. Okay, we will search the Internet for used cars in our area. What kind of car do you want?"

"I only have two thousand dollars—so whatever you think is best for that amount."

"Okay, then, let's see what we can find," Tony said.

After an hour, they came across a car Nickolas was interested in: "Get it while it lasts.
1969 GTO. Body needs work. In decent condition. With a rebuilt engine and transmission. Runs like new. Backyard mechanic special. Twenty-five hundred dollars."

"That's the one, Uncle Tony!"

"Yeah, but he wants five hundred more than you have."

"Come on, Uncle Tony. I remember the last time I went with you to buy a car. You always talk them down."

"Okay, but don't be disappointed if we can't get it."

"I won't. But I know you can get him to take less."

Tony called the number. "I saw your ad, and my nephew is interested in looking at your car."

"Okay. I actually have had a couple of offers this week, so you better hurry."

"Great! Give me the address, and we'll be right over."

Josh's house was a couple of miles north of the city.

When they pulled up, Tony said, "There it is. Let's look it over before he comes outside to meet with us."

"Why is the paint so dull?" Nickolas asked.

"That is called primer. What did you expect for twenty-five-hundred bucks?"

Josh came outside and popped the hood.

Nickolas was happy to see the clean engine and shiny valve covers.

"So, can we take it for a spin?" asked Tony.

"Of course. Who will be driving?"

"Nickolas is the buyer. You can hand him the keys."

Nickolas accepted the keys from Josh, and they all climbed into the GTO. Nickolas fired it up. The engine purred like a well-oiled machine.

Nickolas headed for the expressway to test the engine on the open road. Once he was able to find an open patch of road, Nickolas floored the gas pedal. He was not impressed with the performance of the car though.

Josh said, "Slow down to about thirty miles an hour—and then drop the gearshift into low one."

Nickolas shifted into low gear and floored it. Suddenly, the GTO's front end lifted as it reached ninety miles per hour within a few seconds.

Josh yelled, "Shift into low two!"

Nickolas followed his orders, and the GTO reached 120 within seconds.

Uncle Tony yelled, "Let off, Nickolas!"

Nickolas shifted into drive and allowed the car to drop down to the speed limit.

They returned to Josh's house, and Tony asked for a moment alone with his nephew.

"Nickolas, I'm not sure that this car is safe enough for a first-time driver."

"Uncle Tony, I have been practicing driving for a couple of years now. Between you taking me out to the parking lots and the simulators at Mr. Grimaldi's, I'm ready for this car."

"You must be careful if you buy this car. You can get into a lot of trouble with a race car."

"I promise to be careful, Uncle Tony."

"Okay, let me do the talking," Tony said.

Tony said, "Josh, Nickolas wants the car, but he only has two thousand bucks. I would help him out, but I have been laid off from work more times than I can keep track of over the past few years."

"I understand. We're all struggling right now. Nickolas, how bad do you want this car?"

"We have been searching all day, and I know this is the one!" said Nickolas.

"Okay, you've got a deal," Josh replied. "When I bought my first car, I couldn't afford much either. You seem like a good kid."

Nickolas shook Josh's hand, thanked him, and screamed, "Yes!"

Just as Nickolas was pulling up to his house, his father was getting home.

"Where did you get that car?"

"I just picked it up from this guy on the Internet."

"How much did you pay for it?"

"Two thousand bucks."

Michael laughed. "Does it run?"

"Would you like to race?" Nickolas said.

"Sure. I'll go warm up my Corvette, but don't tell Mom." Michael pulled out of the garage, stopped next to Nickolas's new car, and laughed. "Do you think you have a prayer?"

"Try to keep up, Dad!" Nickolas replied.

When they arrived at the racetrack, there wasn't much of a crowd. They were able to pay for the track time and enter the track within ten minutes. The men lined up at the starting light and began to rev their engines.

As the green light struck, Michael came off the line faster than Nickolas. However, once Nickolas reached thirty miles per hour, he dropped the gearshift into low one. The GTO launched and caught the Corvette halfway down the track. Once Nickolas reached ninety miles per hour, he shifted into second gear, passing his father for the win. Nickolas won by two car lengths.

As they parked, Michael asked, "You only paid two thousand dollars for that car?"

"Yes. The man who sold me this car was a mechanic. He built it to be faster than most new sports cars. He recently built a faster car for himself and wanted to make room in his yard. He gave me a first-time-buyer discount."

"He must have put all of his money into the engine and transmission because that thing looks like a piece of junk. You better be careful with that type of power."

"I will, Dad."

"Remember, don't tell Mom about this."

The next day, Nickolas went over to Uncle Tony's house and explained what had occurred at the racetrack. Tony, Paul, and Nickolas began to laugh.

Paul asked for a ride in the GTO and was impressed with its speed. After that, Nickolas and his cousins had all kinds of fun racing on the weekends. All the boys had fast vehicles. They were quite the daredevils and would race on the expressways at 150 miles per hour. Nickolas loved the thrill of going fast and developed his skill over the next few summers. He decided that he would begin to race for money once he gained more confidence in his racing ability. He also took Skylar out on their first official date.

Nickolas yawned and took a sip of his drink. His dad's Christmas party was just getting started.

Mr. Grimaldi approached and said, "Hello, Nickolas. How are you doing?"

"I'm doing great, Mr. Grimaldi. How are you?"

"I am well. When is your next tournament?"

"In two weeks. Are you going to be there?"

"For sure. I love to watch you in action!" Grimaldi said, putting his fists in the air.

"Have you added any of those martial arts weapons to your arsenal yet?" Nick asked.

"I actually have been working on a few new weapons in the last year. I think you should come over to my shop after the holidays to test them out."

"I would love to!" Nickolas replied with a big smile.

"I was speaking with your father earlier. He explained that you have been learning to use weapons with your uncle."

"Yeah. We've been going out to the hunting grounds every other weekend for the past three months. I'm improving each time."

"That's good, Nickolas. I think you should continue to practice with your uncle."

Nickolas said, "I've watched you over the years at these parties. I've noticed the way you treat everyone with respect—even the help—and how you acknowledge strangers. I am not sure I understand why the other corporate owners will not even acknowledge them—or even each other at times. When they come over to the house for parties, they are not very friendly or sociable with the caterers either."

Grimaldi nodded and said, "Unlike most of these businessmen, I was not born into money. My father was a factory worker like your Uncle Tony, and I had to earn my opportunities in business. No one handed me a family company when I graduated from college."

"I think I understand where you're coming from now. I wish my dad was more like you!"

"I hope one day, if you decide to join your father with his company, that I can be a positive influence on you in the business world."

"Thank you, Mr. Grimaldi. I would respect any advice that you would be willing to pass on to me."

The two of them spent the rest of the evening talking.

PHASE 4

Us against Them

October 2007, Michigan

The G. A. Automotive plant produced three different vehicles. In the past, they had three shifts running, twenty-four hours a day, with four thousand employees. Now, the plant was down to one shift.

The factory floor was noisy and hot, but Tony didn't mind. He was just glad to be back to work. He and Pearl had burned through all of their savings during the last layoff. They'd almost lost the house to the bank as well. Things weren't going well at the plant, and he wondered when the next unemployment notice would be handed to him. Tony was given his assignment for the day.

Tony eyed the machine in front of him. "Has this machine been fixed yet?"

The supervisor replied, "There is nothing wrong with that machine. You better just get on the job and quit complaining."

Tony reluctantly agreed, though he was nervous as he prepared to fire it up when the shift began.

This machine was seven feet tall and cut down the tubing that encased the brake lines on the underbody of the vehicles. The machine was loud. Oil dripped from the lower-back casing, which smelled like burnt popcorn. Tony's job was to load the machine with the metal tubing while it was cut down into different sizes for the assembly line.

At break time in the lunchroom, one of Tony' coworkers walked up to him and asked, "How is that machine running today?"

"Not too good. I had to call maintenance two times already," Tony replied.

"I was on that machine yesterday, and I had to call maintenance four times to fix it."

"I'm going to call the union steward after lunch to see if we can get something done about that machine once and for all," Tony said.

After lunch, Tony returned to work and began to run the machine again. The machine made a grinding noise that scared Tony. He turned the machine off, but an ear-splitting screech drowned out the ambient noise. A sharp pain shot through Tony's spine, causing him to gasp and clutch his back. He became dizzy and fell to the ground, passing out. The machine malfunctioned again and shot a tube into Tony's back. A coworker contacted the supervisor, and he called for an ambulance. Tony was rushed to the hospital.

Nickolas went over to Tony and Pearl's house after school, but no one was home. Nickolas found out from a neighbor that Uncle Tony had been severely injured at work and was in the hospital.

When Nickolas got home, his mother was crying at the kitchen table. "Mom, what's wrong?" Nickolas asked.

"Uncle Tony was in an accident at work today. He's in surgery."

"What happened?" Nickolas yelled.

"I don't know, but it must be serious."

Nickolas ran out to his car and raced to the hospital.

He parked his car and ran to the front desk. He pleaded with the receptionist for some information. She explained that Tony's family was in the waiting room. Nickolas rushed over and saw that Aunt Pearl was crying. Nickolas could barely contain his emotions as he walked over to Pearl, clasping her hands in his. "I'm so sorry," he said. "What happened?"

"No one will tell us anything. We have no idea what happened," Pearl said with tears running down her cheeks.

Moments later, the doctor entered the waiting room. "My name is Dr.

Domonico. The surgery went well, but Tony is going to have to stay in the hospital for at least a couple of weeks. He should be fine. Tony will have to be in a wheelchair until he is able to rehab his back. With the proper rehab, he should be able to make a full recovery."

"When can we see him?" Pearl asked.

"As soon as he wakes up, I'll have the nurse come get you."

"Thank you for everything, Dr. Domonico," said Robert.

Pearl said, "Short-term disability only lasts for six months. I may have to get a job. Oh, my God. I haven't worked since Robert was born—twenty-one years ago."

"Don't worry, Mom. We will pick up the slack in the meantime," Robert said. "I'll drop most of my classes and get a full-time job for now."

Frank put his hand on his mother's shoulder, "Yeah, me too, Mom. We'll do what we have to."

Paul was speechless. He seemed broken up over the situation.

When Tony regained consciousness, Pearl explained what had happened.

Tony said, "The machine I was assigned to had been malfunctioning on and off for the past few months. Management was aware of the problem, but instead of having a repair company come in that specializes in fixing these problems, they kept patching up the machine with their own maintenance department. I had a bad feeling about the situation."

"I will call Mr. Grimaldi to see if his lawyers can help. We'll see what they can do for you," Nickolas said.

"Wait a minute. Please don't do that!" Tony clutched Nickolas's arm. "We have to wait and see what happens."

"Sounds to me like they don't really care about their employees. I think they're gonna try to screw you, Uncle Tony."

"Okay. I get it. They have neglected other employees in the past, but I want to see what they are going to do for me first."

"Okay, if that's what you want. Please let me know if you need any help, though."

Once Tony was released from the hospital, he went with Pearl to speak with management. The human resources director explained that Tony's medical costs were going to be covered—and there would be an investigation into his part with the accident. Until the investigation was complete, he would not be paid for any time off. Pearl was infuriated and complained to the director. The director asked them to leave, and they exited the building in disgust.

Before they could get out of the parking lot, Pearl called Nickolas. "Nickolas, can you please call Mr. Grimaldi for us?"

"Absolutely," Nickolas said. "Are you okay, Aunt Pearl?"

"No, dear. You were right. They are not going to pay your uncle until an investigation is completed."

"You don't worry about anything, Aunt Pearl. I'll get right on this!"

Nickolas called Grimaldi immediately and explained the situation.

Grimaldi said, "I will have my team of lawyers go to G. A. Automotive right away and see what they are going to do for Tony."

"Is there anything you can do to help speed up the process?" Nickolas asked.

"I will have the lawyers take action as soon as possible."

"Uncle Tony can't afford to be without income for too long."

"I will have them get right to it."

Later that week, the lawyers went to G. A. Automotive.

The director explained that the procedure was for Tony's drug test results to be recorded first. A full investigation would have to be performed before any decision could be made.

Grimaldi went to see Tony and Nickolas. "These are the best lawyers in the state, and they will do their best for you, Tony. My lead counsel is Annette Grassi. She will contact you personally."

"What do think the end result will be?" Nickolas asked.

"This is a large corporation with lawyers to spare. They will most likely hold this up in court for years." Grimaldi replied.

"We will be fine, Nickolas," said Tony. "We'll have to play the game and let the chips fall where they may."

Nickolas and Tony thanked Grimaldi and gave him a hug.

Tony received a phone call from Annette Grassi.

She said, "The good news is that the drug test came back negative. However, the corporation is claiming that you were not supposed to be anywhere near that machine at the time of the malfunction."

"They are lying. I was on my assigned position."

"The manager claims that he did not assign you to that machine. It appears that the company is manufacturing a lie to remove the blame from themselves."

Tony said, "What can you do about the situation, Annette?"

"We will file a lawsuit with the courts, but it could take years to fight a corporation like G. A. Automotive. We will not give in though—I promise."

"Thank you, Annette."

"Keep your chin up, Tony. I will keep in touch."

Nickolas could see the pain in his uncle's face. "I will go to my father and ask for help!"

"Don't bother your father with anything," Tony replied.

"Don't worry, Uncle Tony. I will take care of everything."

That night, Nickolas went to his father and said, "Uncle Tony is being denied income for his accident. Paul and his brothers are going to have to drop out of school to support the family. Can you help them in any way, Dad?"

"No! Those boys need to stay in school and focus on their education. G. A. Automotive will take care of Tony. You don't worry about it."

Nickolas ran out of the house, jumped into his car, and peeled out of the driveway. He burned rubber and left a trail of smoke.

Nickolas went to speak with Paul. "I cannot believe this is happening. You never know when something like this could happen. I have been thinking about what I want to do with my life. I don't want to have any regrets before my time is up."

Paul said, "If you do what you're passionate about, it doesn't feel like work—and you will not have any regrets in life."

"Yeah, I agree," Nickolas replied.

The boys dropped out of school, and Paul could not afford to pay for his dojo training on his own. Nickolas missed his cousins and would visit them at their house a few days a week, but it wasn't the same. The boys were on different schedules. Nickolas would spend most of the time with Skylar, Uncle Tony, and Aunt Pearl.

Nickolas helped his uncle with the rehab. He decided he wanted to become a professional fighter, but he couldn't find an avenue that could lead him to making a living at it.

Nickolas went to talk to Rob. "How can you make a living in martial arts?"

"The Ultimate Fighting Championship is not paying much, but boxing sure is."

"I don't really want to just box. It is so one-dimensional," Nickolas replied.

"I don't know where else you can go to fight in mixed martial arts and make a living, Nickolas. I know that some boxers make twenty million a fight. That sounds like a living to me. Go down to Cannon Boxing at Finney High School. They train amateur fighters there."

"Thanks, Rob," Nickolas said. "I'll go check it out."

Nickolas started boxing at the high school his cousin attended. Nickolas walked into the office and met Ducky Meeks, a middle-aged man who was a former professional fighter.

"Hello, sir. I would like to learn to fight."

"Okay, kid. How old are you?"

"I'm seventeen."

"I don't personally train fighters, but we have some trainers come in with their teams all the time. You can talk with one of them if you're serious. This program is set up for inner-city youths, so it only costs five dollars a year."

Nick felt bad about taking advantage of a program for poor kids, but he didn't know where else to turn. The old gym reeked of sweat and mold. The place had poor lighting and meager equipment.

Ducky introduced Nickolas to everyone. Nick found several heavy bags, and a few speed bags. The gym was older and run-down, but Nickolas was not concerned about the condition of the place. He just wanted to become a professional fighter.

After his first day of training, Nickolas said, "Mom, since Uncle Tony's accident, I have been thinking about what I want to do with my life. I would like to try to become a professional fighter. I know it sounds crazy, but it is what I'm passionate about—and life is too short."

"Oh, my God! If your father finds out about this … I don't know, Nickolas."

"Mom, you don't have to tell Dad. I just need your help to pay for my car insurance. I will not have time to work in the summers anymore. I have to dedicate all of my time to training. Besides, Dad has never made it to any of my tournaments. He'll never find out."

"Are you sure that you want this, Nickolas?" Lena asked.

"No regrets, Mom. That's my new motto!"

"Okay then, but not a word to your father about this. He would be against this idea."

Nickolas trained five days a week. He did well enough that a trainer from Kronk Boxing would eventually take him on. Tommy Bolan was another former professional fighter. Tommy would bring his team down to Cannon because Kronk was too busy most of the time. Nickolas joined the team and became an amateur boxer.

Training with Tommy really toughened him up. It included full-contact sparring with other amateurs, retired professionals, and occasionally some active professionals.

After a couple of months, Paul decided to join him. Paul did not have much time to train because he had a full-time job at the restaurant to help support his family. However, Nickolas loved when they could train together.

Michael called Lena into his study. “I am sending Nickolas away to school for college in the fall.”

“I don’t think that is such a great idea, Michael,” Lena replied.

“I am not happy with what I am seeing. Nickolas is becoming just like your family. I will not have him working in a factory one day, struggling to make a living.”

“What do you expect, Michael, when you’re never around to influence your son? He has maintained excellent grades in school and will be able to attend any college he wishes to. Nickolas is just being a rebellious boy.”

“No, I do not think so. He is developing into a lower-class person. I will not allow this to happen.”

“What are you going to do?” Lena asked.

“He will go away to college—whether he likes it or not!” Michael pounded his fist on the desk.

“Calm down, Michael. We will talk with Nickolas later,” Lena said.

Michael called Nickolas into his study. “Nickolas, you are going away to college next fall, and you will be majoring in business management. I will pay for everything. You must be able to take over Leader Industries one day. My father gave me the opportunity to take over a billion-dollar corporation, and I will help you take over a multi-billion-dollar corporation.”

Nickolas refused to respond to his father’s demands and walked out of the room.

“Just let him enjoy the rest of the summer,” Lena said. “He will be fine with your plans when the time comes.”

“He has no choice in the matter,” Michael said.

Skylar met with Nickolas for lunch. “My family has to move out of the state because my father is being transferred.”

"Do you have to go with them?" Nick asked.

"I have no choice, Nickolas. My parents won't let me live on my own. I'm only seventeen."

"Yeah. I guess not." Nickolas replied.

"I'll miss you, Nickolas." She reached for his hand.

"I'll miss you too, Sky." Nickolas kissed her as they said their good-byes.

When the summer was nearly over. Nickolas went to see his uncle. "How are you feeling today, Uncle Tony?"

"I'm okay, Nickolas. My rehab is going great, and I'm feeling stronger every week."

"I'm happy to see you feeling better," Nickolas said. "I don't think I want to go to college."

"What do you want to do with your life, Nickolas?"

"I want to become a professional fighter and help people like you in the workforce."

"Most people don't have the finances to get a great education like you do. If you really want to help people, you will have to be in a position of great power and influence. You are a terrific basketball player and should be able to play for a college team. You should take advantage of this opportunity if you really want to help others who are less fortunate!"

"I'm not sure about going to college. I really would like to give this fight thing a shot."

"Nickolas, you're not going to be able to help many people as a fighter. If you take over the family corporation one day, now that's real influence, Nickolas."

"I trust you, Uncle Tony, and I agree with you. Thank you for everything. I love you."

"I love you too, kid," Tony said as they hugged.

Tony convinced Nickolas to take advantage of the opportunity to go to college. Nickolas respected his uncle's opinion and agreed to continue his education in the fall.

⁓

Nickolas received an acceptance letter from UCLA. As he finished reading it, his mother walked into the living room.

"Congratulations, Nick. I'm so proud of you."

"Thanks, Mom. I think what with everything that's going on with Uncle Tony and the economy, I'm ready to make a difference in this country."

"I'm sure whatever you decide, it will be to help people." Lena gave him a hug.

"I want to advocate for real change and help those who are powerless to do so themselves. I will major in business management and minor in economics."

"Are you ready to make the big move?" Lena asked.

"I'm as ready as I'll ever be. Mom, I have a request though. I would like to be called Nick from now on!"

"Okay, Nick. You are a very special young man. Most children who grow up in this type of environment do not really care about others like you do or have respect for those with lower incomes. I am very proud of the man you are becoming. I love you."

"I love you too, Mom."

"Are you going to take the GTO with you or do you want to fly out to California?" Lena asked.

"I'll bring the GTO with me. I'll need something to remind me of home."

"I understand."

"I don't know how to word this question, Mom, but how can you be in love with a man like Dad?"

"Your father was a much different person when I met him in college. He was very attentive toward my needs. Once he joined Leader Industries, he followed in his father's footsteps … unfortunately. He has been consumed by success ever since. He loves us in his own way. You can't understand how I grew up. We were poor, and I cannot go back to that lifestyle. I want the best for you, Nick. That is all I have ever wanted."

Nick hugged his mother and told her again that he loved her.

Nick met with his uncle, aunt, and cousins for dinner at his favorite Arabic restaurant. The higher-end restaurant had low lighting, curtains draped over the booths, and excellent food.

Tony raised his glass and made a toast. "Congratulations, Nickolas, on being accepted to UCLA. I know you will be successful in school and whatever you decide to do with your future. We will miss you."

"Thank you, Uncle Tony. I will miss you too. Please call me Nick from now on."

"I'll miss you too, Nick," said Aunt Pearl. "I think of you as my own son!" Pearl stood up and gave Nick a hug and kiss.

"I'm going to miss you too, Nick!" Paul said.

"I'm just going away to school—it's not forever. I'll be back to visit in the summers."

They decided to stop talking about school and enjoyed the rest of the evening. The waitress brought out platters of Lebanese food. They reminisced about their experiences together. The evening would come to an end. Nick said good-bye. As he drove home, he realized how important his uncle's family had been to his development—and he appreciated everything they had done for him.

PHASE 5

Off to College

August 2008, Los Angeles

Nick drove through the city for hours to get a feel for the it, including a visit to the Hollywood sign.

Nick then made his way to the campus and explored his new home. The large campus was a little overwhelming. The main entrance was grand, and Nick was fascinated by the artistic design and unbelievable construction. He did not feel comfortable going away to college, but the road trip helped change his perspective. Nick began to anticipate the next chapter in his life.

Nick found his dorm. In his room, an athletic African American man was unpacking. He stood about six foot four and was wearing shorts and a tank top.

Nick knocked on the door. "Hello, my name is Nick Leader."

"Hey, man. My name is Isiah Thomas. How you doing, Nick?" Isiah smiled and extended his hand.

Nick accepted with a smile of his own. "I'm good … just adjusting to campus life. Where are you from, Isiah?"

"I'm from Chicago. I'll be trying out as a shooting guard on the basketball team."

"Cool, I actually will be trying out for point guard. I knew I recognized you from somewhere."

"Yeah, your team beat us in the semifinal round last season." Isiah shook his head. "That was one hell of a pass you made for the winning bucket. You're a throwback player, like Magic Johnson."

"Oh, yeah, I remember you. Man, you're a great defender and shooter. That game could have gone either way." Nick smiled, "Actually, my favorite all-time player is Isiah Thomas of our Detroit Pistons."

"No way! My parents actually named me after him. Isiah was from Chicago, you know. We weren't even born when the Pistons won their 1989 championship. So how could he be your favorite player?" Isiah asked.

"Classic Sports Channel—what a great source of basketball knowledge!" Nick laughed. "I'm also from Michigan, man."

"So, what do think about this dorm room?" Isiah asked.

"I see five bedrooms, one kitchen, and one living room. It's gonna be a little tight in here, but overall it's not too shabby," Nick said.

"I can deal with it too. So you wanna practice later?" Isiah asked.

"Yeah, definitely. What time are you going?"

"Around six. Let me get your cell number in case I get too busy."

"Okay. I've gotta sign up for classes in about an hour—and then I'll give you a call."

"Cool. This is gonna be great. I'm glad we ended up in the same dorm, Nick." Isiah smiled.

"Yeah, me too, Isiah."

They shook hands again.

Nick's routine was go to class, study, work out on the heavy bag, weight train, and play basketball.

While Nick was working out on the heavy bag, a student walked up to him. "Hi. My name is Zack." He put his fist up to tap Nick's glove. "You're an awful good striker."

"Thanks," Nick replied with a smile. "I fought amateur in Michigan."

"Yeah, I could tell you have experience. There's a mixed martial arts gym not too far from campus. You should definitely check it out."

"Thanks, bro. I think I will." Nick decided to visit the gym.

When Nick entered the gym, he saw a woman at the front desk. "Hi, what's your name?"

"My name is Sarra," she replied.

"Who owns this gym?"

"Conor McGregor."

"That's awesome. He is one of my favorite fighters. How much are the fees?"

"Are you a student?"

"Yes, I just started at UCLA."

"That's great for you. It's only fifty dollars a month for students. Do you have any experience or do you need to enter a beginner's program?"

"I have amateur status in Michigan as a boxer as well as five years with the Jeet Kune Do School of Martial Arts."

"Great! What belt do you have with the dojo?"

"We don't use the belt system in my dojo. We advance through challenges and with experience."

"Oh, okay. You can grab a schedule for advanced classes on the right side of the desk."

"Thank you very much, Sarra."

Nick decided to join the gym that day and began training in Brazilian jujitsu. This martial art was primarily ground fighting, like wrestling. Nick had never grappled before, so he felt that he should work on his weakness first.

The dojo was very clean, and the equipment was like new. Nick took a deep breath, anticipating that typical gym odor. Instead, it was pleasant. It definitely didn't remind Nick of Cannon Boxing.

The trainer walked up to Nick. "My name is Mark. I'll be your trainer for today. Here's your gi. Head to the locker room and change, Nick."

"Thank you, sir," Nick replied as he went to change.

While sparring, he would find himself in many compromising positions. He had to tap out quite a bit since he was not used to being dominated. Nick loved a challenge and enjoyed the training experience. Nick improved with every visit.

He was tempted to forego his education and become a professional fighter, but he didn't want to let down his Uncle Tony. Nick would stay focused on his education and his commitment to helping others.

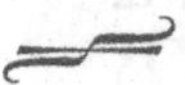

The following week, Isiah knocked on Nick's bedroom door. "You awake, bro?"

"Yeah, I'm up. You ready for tryouts today?"

"Man, I can't wait to get in the gym. I've been busy scouting our competition. It looks like you're a lock for starting point guard, but I don't know if I'm gonna beat out the starter from last year at shooting guard. He's a beast!"

"I got you. Don't worry about it," said Nick.

"What can you do to help me get that spot?"

"I'm gonna be your agent on the court. When I get the ball, your number will be called."

"You would do that for me, Nick?"

"Of course, bro. You are one of the best players on the squad. You deserve as many looks as I can feed you. Just keep playing that killer defense—and I won't have to justify anything to the coaching staff."

"No problem," said Isiah. "Thanks, man."

The coaching staff was happy with what they saw from both young men. A week later, Nick ran into the dorm room. "Isiah, are you in here?"

Isiah replied, "Yeah. What's up, bro?"

"We made the team! I just saw the post on the gym wall."

"Whew. I was so worried at first, but whenever you had the rock, it was like we had been running together for years. You're the best, Nick!"

"I told you I had your back," Nick said.

The two friends high-fived.

Nick called Uncle Tony and said, "How are you doing?"

"I'm good. Rehab is going well. I feel better, but I still can't work. I'm taking it one day at a time."

"Great! How are Aunt Pearl and the boys?"

"Everyone is doing fine. The boys are working and going to school, and your aunt is taking care of the house and me."

"How about the lawsuit. Anything new?"

"Nothing yet—still waiting for the case to be heard. The lawyers feel strongly about things going in our favor. You don't worry about that—just focus on your education. We will be fine."

"I always think about you guys. I miss you all."

"We miss you too, Nick. We'll see you this summer, right?"

"Of course. I can't wait!"

"Okay. I gotta get going. My rehab starts in twenty minutes."

"I'll call you again soon. Tell everyone I said hello."

During his second year at school, Nick was consumed by schoolwork, basketball, and martial arts training. He had no time for socializing.

Isiah said, "Would you like to go to the women's basketball game tonight?"

"I don't know if I have time, Isiah. Maybe."

"Why don't you socialize, Nick? You never go out and have fun with anyone."

"You know how my schedule is. I'm too busy for a social life."

"You have to see this point guard on the women's team. Margherita Cortese is an awesome player—and she practices with the guys sometimes too!"

"She can run with the guys?" Nick asked.

"Oh, yeah. She is a beast with the rock."

"Okay. I guess I could use a break from studying."

Nick watched Margherita run the point and could not take his eyes off of her. "She is unbelievable!"

"I told you so, man!"

"She handles the ball like a pro."

"She has a killer shot too."

After the game was over, Isiah said, "You want to stop at a friend's house for a small get-together?"

"Sure, but I don't want to stay too late. Let's go."

While Nick was enjoying the party, Margherita walked in with her teammates. His eyes lit up.

Isiah said, "What a coincidence! Margherita is here."

Isiah's girlfriend Laura was best friends with Margherita and told Isiah that she wanted to meet Nick.

"Nick, this is Margherita Cortese. Margherita, this is Nick Leader."

The couple shook hands.

"My friends call me Maggie."

"Can I call you Maggie?"

"Sure, why not?" she replied with a smile.

"So how do you like it here at UCLA?"

"My parents taught me to be very respectful, but I am not crazy about all the rules around here."

"Yeah, I feel you," Nick replied.

"So what is your major?" Maggie asked.

"I'm majoring in business management with a minor in economics. How about you, Maggie?"

"My major is computer science with a minor in computer forensics."

"I would have never guessed that one. You're a jock and a nerd?" Nick said.

"Yeah, I guess that is not a common pairing, but my dad had a clone—and you're looking at her."

"Your dad must be beautiful," Nick said with a grin.

"Aren't you a flirt," she replied with a smile.

"Actually, no. I haven't really made time to socialize since I've been here. I really didn't want to leave Michigan for school. My father insisted."

"Why did he make you go away to college?"

"I was getting too close to my mom's side of the family, which my dad did not approve of. He decided to send me away so I couldn't spend any more time with them."

"What's so bad about your uncle's family?"

"Nothing, but they are blue-collar workers. My dad owns a huge corporation. He was afraid that I would end up like them instead of him."

"That sounds like a bad situation. I'm sorry he pushed you away but, at the same time, I'm glad that he pushed you away. How else would have we met?" Maggie smiled.

"I guess you're right. I can't argue with that."

"I have seen you play every game since you started college. I'm impressed, Nick."

"Thank you, but why didn't you introduce yourself sooner?"

"My mother taught me never to ask a boy out."

"I respect that. I agree with your mother's philosophy, but I wish we had met sooner!"

Nick and Maggie spent the whole night talking and getting to know each other.

The following week, Maggie walked up to him after practice. "Hey, Nick, how was practice?" she asked.

"Great, Maggie! How was your practice today?

"Great! I have to get my small forward to run the floor faster. She needs to get in better shape."

"I had that problem once with one of my teammates. I asked him to start working out with me. Within a couple of weeks, I had him in condition," Nick said.

"Man, I should have thought of that," Maggie replied. "Maybe we should hang out more often."

"Yeah, I could be your personal advisor." Nick moved in for a kiss. "How would you like that?"

Maggie kissed him back. "I think I may need you to start right away."

Nick and Maggie went out for Mexican food.

"So, what do you think?" Maggie asked.

"I love this place! My favorite food is Middle Eastern, but I've always liked Mexican too."

"I like Middle Eastern too," Maggie said. "Have you found a place near school yet?"

"No, not yet. Maybe we'll have to find one together." Nick reached for her hand. "I really like you, Maggie."

"Yeah, I really like you, Nick."

Maggie and Nick made their way back to Nick's dorm room. No one was there. Nick decided to kiss Maggie again, and she was very receptive. They went on for a while before Maggie had to excuse herself.

"I really should be getting back to my place," she said. "I barely know you, and I think it's too soon for this."

"I get it. I can wait—if you can," Nick replied. *You're the girl of my dreams. I better be willing to wait!*

"Thank you for understanding, Nick. I need to get out of here before I change my mind." Maggie kissed him again. "Oh my God. I gotta go!" Maggie rose to her feet, straightened her hair and clothes, and headed for the door.

"I'll walk you to your dorm," Nick said.

"Okay, thanks."

On the walk over, Maggie and Nick barely said a word. Once they reached her building, Nick gave Maggie a kiss. She looked into his eyes and said. "Good night, Nick."

"Good night, Maggie." Finally, he pulled himself away from her. Nick really felt something strong for Maggie, and he could tell that she felt the same.

The next night, Maggie had a game. Nick and Isiah decided to attend. Maggie was brilliant once again and led her team to victory.

After the game, Maggie invited Nick to her dorm for a victory celebration with her teammates.

"So how did you enjoy the game, Nick?" asked Maggie.

"You were great! I love the way you control the tempo and call most of the plays."

"Thanks. My coach is awesome. She lets me do my thing," Maggie said.

"You guys definitely will be going to the Sweet Sixteen this year," Nick said.

"You think? I hope you're right. That would be amazing!" Maggie kissed Nick.

"I think you're very special, Maggie!" said Nick.

"Yeah, ditto," she replied. "Follow me." Maggie led Nick to her bedroom.

After locking the door, Maggie threw Nick onto her bed.

Nick was nervous—and aroused—as Maggie began to take off her top.

Maggie straddled him while looking deep into his eyes. She didn't say a word. She waited for him to make the next move.

Nick took his cue, flipped her onto her back, and kissed her. They would spend their first night together, and it was the beginning of a great romance.

The couple was inseparable for the remainder of the school year. When summer vacation arrived, they decided to spend it together. Before going home, Maggie asked Nick to meet her for lunch at a Middle Eastern restaurant. Maggie decided to surprise Nick with some of his favorite cuisine. "So how do you like this place, Nick? My friend told me they have the best Lebanese food here."

"Thanks for remembering. Looks and smells authentic to me," Nick replied.

After they ordered their lunch, Maggie said, "We need to have a conversation before I take you home with me."

"Is everything okay?" Nick asked.

"Yeah—we're good, it's not about us. This is about my father. He is a computer forensics specialist for the FBI."

"So what exactly does a computer forensics specialist do for the FBI?" Nick asked.

"Well, for instance, when there is a murder case on a federal level, my father visits the crime scene. He takes all the evidence into account to recreate the scene of the crime with a sophisticated system. This allows him to project what is the most probable scientific answer to the events that took place."

"Wow, that sounds like a very interesting job."

"He really isn't supposed to talk about work with anyone besides federal officers."

"Why are you telling me this?" Nick asked.

"You need to know some things about my family and me before I introduce you to them," Maggie said.

"What? Is he a big deal or something?"

"No, but I was always by my father's side as a child. When he would bring his work home, I would watch him like a hawk. One day, when I was ten years old, he left his computer on while grabbing some lunch. I went on his computer and figured out his password. I saw some things I wasn't supposed to see—and he caught me."

"Did you get in trouble?" Nick asked.

"No, but my father asked me how I was able to find his password and get into his files. I told him that I didn't know. I just did. He wasn't mad at me. Instead, he was impressed by what I had done at such a young age. From that day on, my father would work with me. He taught me how to problem solve, program, design, and pretty much everything there was to learn about computers until I left for college. As I got older, I began to use my skills to do some things that my father would not approve of."

"Were you stealing from people or just hacking?" Nick asked.

"No, I wasn't stealing," Maggie replied. "I was hacking into certain corporations' websites. Some unethical corporations were cheating some of my friends with online charges."

"What were you doing to their sites, Maggie?"

"I would plant a virus on their website so they wouldn't be able to cheat people out of their money anymore," she replied.

"Do your parents know about this?"

"No! They would never approve!" she replied.

"I think that's great, Maggie! I'm really turned on right now!" Nick grabbed her hand with a smile.

Maggie laughed and replied, "I really like you, and I want you to know everything about me before I commit to a relationship with you."

"We've been spending every day together for months. What took you so long to tell me this?" Nick asked.

"Because if you're going to meet my family, you have to know everything—and now you do." Maggie kissed him.

"There's nothing you could tell me that would scare me away," said Nick as he embraced her. "I really want to meet your family!"

PHASE 6

Summer Vacation

September 2009, California

Nick eased his GTO into the driveway of a well-kept, two-story home in an upper-middle-class neighborhood. "Very nice."

"Thanks," she said. "You ready to meet the parents?"

Nick laughed. "Come on. It can't be that bad, can it?"

She smiled, leaned over, and gave him a kiss. "You'll see. Come on. Let's go in."

Maggie said, "Mom, Dad, this is my boyfriend, Nick Leader."

"Hello, Nick. My name is Tom, and this is Teresa. I feel like I already know you. We watch you on television when the Bruins play. We are huge fans of the team and you."

"Thank you, sir. It's great to meet the both of you. Maggie talks about you all the time."

"I hope she's not teaching you any of my post moves," Tom said.

Everyone laughed.

"Dad, please quit bragging about your basketball skills," said Maggie.

"I taught you everything you know, young lady," Tom said.

"Maggie definitely has benefitted from your tutoring, Mr. Cortese," Nick said.

"Yes, Father. You were a great mentor," Maggie said.

Mr. Cortese and Nick began to talk about how the basketball season had played out, the upcoming season, and what changes needed to be made to improve the team.

Mr. Cortese asked Nick to join him in the backyard. "How well do you know my daughter, Nick?"

"We just met at one of her basketball games at the end of the season, but we have been spending a lot of time together since."

"My daughter is a very strong-willed person. She is very respectful, but she can be a bit of a rebel at times."

"She is a very confident woman on the basketball court—and with her computer skills. I'm very impressed with her," Nick said.

"I know exactly what you're talking about, Nick."

Nick said, "I grew up in a wealthy family, but I don't exactly get along with wealthy people. I find them to be very pretentious. With me, it's more of what you see is what you get. I don't need my father's lifestyle to be happy."

"That's good to hear, Nick. I would not be comfortable with some spoiled rich kid courting my daughter."

"I've never met anyone like her, and I can't imagine being without her."

Maggie's little sister walked into the living room. "Hi, Nick. My name is Jessica. It's great to finally meet you," she said as she shook his hand.

"Hello, Jessica. Nice to finally meet you," replied Nick.

"I watch you play basketball on TV. You're really good," Jessica said with a smile.

"Thank you. I'm happy to be here with all of you. Maggie is always talking about you, Jessica."

"I love my sister. I want to play basketball next year. I'm gonna be as good as she is one day."

"We'll practice with you this summer, and when we're done with you, you'll be the best player on that team," said Nick.

"Can we go outside and practice now?" Jessica asked.

Mrs. Cortese said, "We have to get ready for dinner first, young lady. You may practice with Nick and Maggie after dinner."

"Okay, Mom." Jessica rushed to the kitchen to set the table.

While Nick and Maggie were visiting with her family, Jessica would follow them everywhere they went. She soaked up every minute with her sister and Nick.

The three of them were practicing basketball in the driveway. Jessica asked, "Can I please go to Michigan with you and my sister? I would love to meet your family."

Nick said, "You may go with us as long as it's all right with your parents and sister."

"Okay." She smiled. "I'm gonna go ask them." Jessica ran into the house.

Later that night, Maggie and Nick were watching TV in the living room. "Are you sure about bringing my sister to Michigan?"

"If it makes her happy, it will make you happy—and that's all I want."

"You're earning big points right now. You know that?" Maggie replied with a kiss.

"I've really enjoyed teaching your sister over the past couple weeks. She's a great kid."

Mr. and Mrs. Cortese gave permission for Jessica to go to Michigan.

The next day, Mr. Cortese approached Nick. "Nick, can we please speak privately for a moment before you leave?"

"Sure, sir." Nick followed him out to the garage.

"I will be blunt, Nick. I must remind you that I would not trust my daughters to fly off to another state with just anyone." Tom smiled.

Nick hugged him and said, "I assure you, sir, that I will protect them with my life."

"You'd better," Tom replied.

Nick and the Cortese sisters exited Metro Airport, and a limousine pulled up in front of them.

Maggie looked at Nick and asked, "What's with the limo, big shot?"

"It's for your sister, Maggie."

"Oh, okay," Maggie replied.

The limo drove them to Nick's house.

"You didn't tell me you lived in a mansion, Nick," Maggie said.

"Well, it's technically not a mansion. It's five thousand square feet."

"Looks like a mansion to me," said Jessica.

"Come on, you guys. Let's go meet my parents." Nick laughed.

Lena greeted them at the door. "Hello. My name is Lena. Please come in. It's great to meet you both."

"Great to meet you as well, Mrs. Leader," Maggie replied with a hug.

"What is your name, young lady?" Lena asked.

"Jessica," she replied.

"You are beautiful—just like your sister," Lena said.

"Where is Mr. Leader?" asked Jessica.

Nick replied, "Let me guess—Working late as usual?"

"Please excuse my husband for being late. He usually works past dinnertime. We will start without him. I hope you ladies like grilled chicken stir-fry."

"Oh, that will be fine, Mrs. Leader. We're not picky eaters," Maggie said.

They were about thirty minutes into dinner when Nick heard a noise in the kitchen.

Michael entered from the rear door, opened the refrigerator door, and grabbed a beer. He took his time before entering the dining room. "Sorry, everyone. I had to work late again."

Nick said, "Dad, this is my girlfriend, Maggie, and her sister, Jessica."

"Nice to meet you, ladies," replied Michael. He picked up his beer and took a swig.

When the night was over, Lena showed the girls to the guest room. "I hope this bed will be good for the both of you. We have another guest room if you would like your own rooms."

"No, thank you, Mrs. Leader. That's okay," said Maggie. "Jessica would like to sleep in the same room with me."

"I understand, Maggie. Sleep well, ladies. Good night."

"Good night, Mrs. Leader."

"Oh my god, Maggie. This place is huge!" Jessica said.

"Yeah, I know," Maggie replied.

"How many rooms do think there are?" asked Jessica.

"Well, I counted six bedrooms up here, that huge living room, the formal dining room, and that beautiful kitchen. Probably three bathrooms up here, and a couple downstairs. That's about fifteen rooms, I would say."

"Unbelievable! Nick is rich!" Jessica said.

"It doesn't matter what his parents own. That is not who he is. He is different. Believe me, I know him well enough to realize that he is not some materialistic rich kid."

"Oh, no. I don't think so either," Jessica said.

"Besides, it's not like they have the place draped in gold. Mrs. Leader has a very contemporary style, and I like it."

"I agree, Maggie. She is cool," Jessica said.

There was a knock on the door.

"Come in," Maggie said.

Nick opened the door and asked, "Are you guys dressed?"

"Yeah, Nick. Come on in." Maggie laughed.

"I just wanted to say good night." He walked up to Maggie for a hug.

"Of course, Mr. Leader." She wrapped her arms around him for a kiss.

"Oh, I don't know about you replying to me as Mr. Leader in my father's home!"

"Good thought," Maggie replied. "That is kind of weird, I guess."

"Yes, it is. You ladies get some sleep. We have a long day ahead of us tomorrow."

Nick went to say good night to his parents.

The next morning, Nick brought the girls to meet Uncle Tony and Aunt Pearl. "Hey, Uncle Tony! How are you?"

"Feeling good, Nick," Tony replied.

"Aunt Pearl, how are you doing?" Nick asked.

"Very well, Nick. How are you?"

"Great! I would like to introduce you to my new friends." He smiled as he reached for Maggie's hand. "This is my girlfriend, Maggie."

"Hello, Maggie," Tony replied. "Great to finally meet you."

Pearl walked up to Maggie to give her a hug. "Hello, Maggie. I am happy to meet you, dear."

"Thank you both for having us over. I feel like I already know the both of you. Nick is always talking about his relationship with you. I respect you both so very much."

Tony and Pearl thanked Maggie warmly.

Pearl turned to Jessica and asked, "What is your name, young lady?"

"I am Jessica. Maggie is my big sister," she replied with a smile.

"Very nice to meet you as well, Jessica," Pearl said.

"You too," Jessica replied, smiling back.

Nick asked, "Where are the boys?"

"They are all at work," Pearl replied.

"What time will they be home?"

"They should be home any minute now," his uncle said.

"I can't wait for them to meet Maggie and Jessica," Nick replied.

When the boys returned from work, Nick introduced them. "Can we have dinner tonight at my favorite Mediterranean restaurant?"

Everyone agreed to meet at the restaurant.

Tony said, "Everything is just fine with my health, and our financial situation is stable. Everyone is pitching in to keep us afloat."

"So the lawsuit has not paid out yet?" asked Nick.

"No. It hasn't been resolved yet, but Mr. Grimaldi's lawyers are working on it."

Nick stared down at his plate for a minute.

Pearl said, "Please don't worry about this, Nick. You need to focus on your education."

"We will be just, fine, Nick. Listen to your aunt," Tony said.

Mr. Grimaldi showed up at the restaurant in time for dessert.

"Hi, Mr. Grimaldi," said Nick as he stood up to give Grimaldi a hug. "This is my girlfriend, Maggie, and her sister, Jessica."

"It's a pleasure to meet you both. Nick has told me so much about you, Maggie."

"Thank you, Mr. Grimaldi, I am happy to finally meet you as well." Maggie and Jessica stood up to shake his hand.

"Maggie, I have known Nick since he was ten years old. He is one of the most exceptional people I have ever known. You're very lucky to be with him."

Maggie smiled. "I agree with you, Mr. Grimaldi!"

Paul said, “We should take Maggie to the gun range while she is here.”

Maggie replied, “Yes! I would love to learn how to fire weapons!”

“I would like her to learn, and we would love to go,” Nick replied. “Mom, could you watch Jessica for a few hours while we go to the range tomorrow?”

“Sure, we will go clothes shopping, Jessica,” Lena said.

“Yes!” I would love that!” Jessica’s eyes lit up.

Maggie looked at Nick and said, “I don’t know if that is such a great idea.”

“I promise that my mom will not spend too much money on Jessica.”

“No, I won’t. I promise. I just always wanted to have a daughter and would love the experience.”

Maggie said, “As long as you do not spend too much money, Mrs. Leader!”

Nick said, “Hey, Mr. Grimaldi, I was talking with my uncle before you showed up. He told me that his lawsuit is still not settled.”

“Yes, G. A. Automotive is a very powerful corporation, and they can pay off certain entities to continue postponing the case. This may go on for years, Nick.”

“Can you do anything about this?” Nick asked.

“I am sorry, Nick. The lawyers are doing their best. We have to remain patient. Eventually G. A. Automotive will pay.”

“I understand, but I’m worried about their future,” Nick said.

“You need to listen to your uncle and focus on your education,” Grimaldi said.

“How do you know he told me that? You weren’t even here when he said that to me.”

“Your uncle and I have had this conversation in the past. We both know how hotheaded you can be!” Grimaldi said with the hint of a smile.

“Yeah, yeah. I know. I can’t help it, Mr. Grimaldi. I care about them so much.”

“If you really want to help your family, then graduate from college and become a leader. Even your last name points you in that direction. You will be able to help your relatives—and so many others.”

"Thank you, sir. As always, you're right," Nick replied as the men hugged and parted ways.

Nick, Maggie, and his cousins were putting all of the weapons away in Uncle Tony's basement.

Nick asked, "How did you like the range, Maggie?"

"I had a great time. I think I'm a natural." She smiled.

"You did great, Maggie," Paul said.

"Yes. You were very impressive, Maggie," Nick said.

"You're quite the marksman, Nick," Maggie said as she pointed at Nick.

"Thanks for noticing, Maggie." He smiled.

"We should do this again," Rob said.

"Yeah, sure, Rob. I would love to," Maggie replied.

While they were driving back to his house, Nick said, "How would you feel about going to the gym with me to train?"

"I am a little nervous about doing that," Maggie replied.

"You have nothing to worry about. These people are not mean or angry. They are learning an art form. It might be a misunderstood art form, but it's still an art form." Nick reached for her hand.

Maggie took a deep breath and replied, "I have always wanted to learn. I think I'm ready." She made a fist while striking her other open palm.

Nick looked at her and said, "I need you to remember that no one gets into the ring at first. No one is forced into the ring, and we will just be training for a few weeks before you decide if you want to spar."

Maggie nodded.

Maggie was hitting the heavy bag at the gym.

"You look like you're becoming more comfortable with the training," Nick said.

Maggie paused. "The past three weeks of training have been very helpful. My skill level and conditioning are awesome."

Nick asked, "Do you think you're ready to spar?"

"I think I'm ready!" she replied.

As they geared up, Nick asked, "How many rounds do you think you can last?"

"More than you!" she joked.

Nick laughed and said, "Oh … it's go time!"

The bell rang, and Maggie came out swinging for the fences. Nick quickly went on the defensive, slipping, dipping, and not allowing her to catch him with any shots. Nick showed her what expert footwork should be. By the end of the first round, she fell to the canvas.

Nick said, "I remember my first week in the gym. I was sparring with Ducky, and he allowed me to throw a ton of strikes, just waiting for me to tire. Then, at the end of the round, he hit me with a body shot. I fell to the canvas and couldn't breathe for a minute."

When Maggie caught her breath, she said, "Why am I so tired? You didn't even hit me!"

"It takes more energy out of you when you miss than when you land strikes. When you start out in the ring or the cage, it's best to feel your opponent out in the first round. Figure their timing out, work the jabs and straight strikes while warming up."

Maggie said, "Why didn't you tell me this before?"

"It's best to let someone do what comes natural at first. Like it says on the wall. 'Champions are made—not born."

On their last night of vacation Nick brought Maggie out to dinner at a Mexican restaurant. The waiter walked up to the table and placed a desert in front of her. As she looked down at the plate, she noticed a jewelry box next to her pie.

She looked at Nick and asked, "What's in the box?"

"It's nothing too expensive. It's just a small token of our love!"

Maggie opened the box. "I love it! It's so beautiful. Thank you, Nick." She got up from her chair to give him a kiss.

"You're welcome, Maggie." He kissed and hugged her.

"If I ever get married, it will have to be to you!"

"I love you more than anything in this world, and I feel the same way!"

"I promise to never let anything come between us, Nick," said Maggie as she began to tear up.

"I promise the same to you, sweetheart. I love you."

PHASE 7

Graduation

September 2012, California

Nick Knocked on Maggie's door. Maggie opened the door and jumped into his arms. "How are you, my love?"

"I'm great, sweetheart. Are you ready to hit the books again?"

"Yeah. I'm ready. How do you feel about senior year?"

"I have even more incentive this year. I just spoke with Uncle Tony. G. A. Automotive is still holding up my uncle's case."

"Don't let it get you down, Nick." Maggie brushed his cheek with her hand.

"I'm very upset by the corruption these corporations have been demonstrating for the past several years. They're taking advantage of the employees through a crooked system."

"You should use this to inspire yourself."

"Oh, I definitely will. I promise to put myself in a position to help my uncle and others who are oppressed by this heinous activity."

"Did you hear about the Democratic campaign rally tonight."

"Yeah. It's at the Staples Center."

"Yeah, I heard about it in class the other day. You wanna go?"

"Of course. We haven't missed one since we've been together."

"Great! I'll get ready," Maggie said.

The crowd was pumped up for the event. Maggie said "Look, there's our guy. Jackson looks ready to rock this thing!"

"Oh, yeah. I see him." Nick replied as he looked toward the stage.

One of Berry Jackson's main campaign issues was the future of young students. The students were very impressed by his speech.

Once Jackson left the stage, Maggie said, "Over there. Let's get in line to donate, Nick."

"Yeah, I wanna get a T-shirt too."

"I'm going to give Jackson's campaign all of my spending money for the month," Maggie said.

"Me too, Maggie." Nick smiled as he pulled out his credit card. The couple would champion political causes as often as possible.

Nick was venting some of his frustrations on the heavy bag at the gym.

Conor walked up to Nick and said, "I got you an amateur fight in two weeks."

"Are you sure that I'm ready for a bout, Conor?" Nick replied.

"You've been ready for over a year, man. I cannot believe that someone of your skill level is not going pro!"

"Thank you, Conor. I respect your opinion, and I owe it to you to at least have one fight before I head home." Nick had always wanted to fight in a UFC cage.

Conor had a thick Irish accent, a crazy beard, and a cocky attitude.

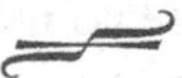

Conor held the focus pads up as Nick warmed up by throwing combinations on them. The locker room at the arena was packed with fighters.

"How do you feel, kid?" Conor asked.

"Confident and excited." Nick smacked the pads ferociously.

"Great. That's what I'm talkin' about."

Once Nick was warmed up, Maggie asked. "Are you ready for tonight, Nick?"

"I can't wait to get into that cage!" he replied with sweat dripping from his brow.

"Please don't let anyone mangle this beautiful face," Maggie said while touching Nick's cheek.

"Not a chance. I'm ready for anything," Nick said.

While the men made their way to the cage, the people in the arena were quiet. The Staples Center seated more than eighteen thousand people and was a state-of-the-art venue, but it was only halfway full.

Conor said, "Your opponent is an amateur with only two fights under his belt. This guy is a great wrestler, so stay on your feet and use your superior striking ability."

"I wouldn't let any of these fighters get me down to the canvas. I'm gonna show everyone my striking skills tonight!"

Nick entered the cage with Conor and a couple of his sparring partners. Maggie sat directly behind Nick's corner.

Nick began to circle the cage, running very quickly from side to side. He would drop-kick the top of the cage with both feet over and over, showing his excellent footwork and skill.

His opponent had tattoos all over his body.

Nick only had one tattoo, a yin yang on his chest, which was black and red. Nick was not fazed. He had five amateur fights in the past, and he had been training with Conor for four years.

The announcer made his way to the center of the octagon. "In the red corner, standing six feet tall, weighing 195 pounds, with an amateur boxing record of five wins and no losses, fighting in his first mixed martial arts contest … Nick Leader. In the blue corner, standing five feet ten inches tall, weighing 194 pounds, with an amateur record in mixed martial arts of six wins and four losses, Mad Max Barns."

Nick looked at Conor and said, "I thought you said that he only had two fights?"

"I couldn't find anyone to fight you with less than nine fights, kid. After all, I am your trainer."

The bell finally rang. Mad Max rushed at Nick, shooting for the takedown. Max attempted to take Nick to the canvas early, but Nick jumped on his opponent's back. The wrestler fell to the canvas, and Nick invited him to try again. The wrestler pounded the floor and tried the same move again.

Nick struck him with a knee to the head and an uppercut to the chin. Max fell to the canvas, and the crowd screamed for Nick to finish him off. Nick wanted him to get back up before he struck again. Max shook his head and got back up. Nick peppered him with jabs, and the crowd cheered.

Max couldn't get past Nick's offense, so he threw combinations of punches and kicks. Nick decided to finish him off and threw a one-two to the head.

Max raised his arms to cover his face.

Nick saw the opening to the liver, threw a left-hook kick, and knocked the wrestler down with two minutes remaining in the first round. Max gasped for breath and could not regain it in time to continue.

The official called the match, and the crowd cheered. *Now this is what I expected my match to feel like.*

Nick, Conor, and Maggie went back to the locker room to celebrate.

Conor said, "Are you sure about going to work for your father, man?"

"If it doesn't work out, I know where to find you," Nick replied.

Maggie said, "I think you could be a champion if you wanted!"

Nick thanked them all before heading to the showers.

PHASE 8

The Journey Begins

July 2013, Michigan

Nick walked on air after winning the fight and graduating from college.

Nick and Maggie walked into the Leader home.

Michael said, "Congratulations, Nickolas."

"Thank you, Dad." Nick gave his father a half-hearted handshake.

Michael handed Nick a set of keys. "This is what you get when you achieve, son." Michael pointed to a new Corvette in the driveway.

Lena came to the door, smiling broadly.

"Thank you, Mom and Dad," Nick said. *Finally, I get the car I asked for seven years ago.*

"I am very proud of you," Michael said. "I want you to join me at Leader Industries."

Nick said, "I will think about it, Dad. Maggie and I need to spend some time deciding what we want to do as a couple first."

"I will pay you more than any other company in the world, being fresh out of college and all!"

"Dad, it's not about the money. It's about the right fit for both of us."

"I know that this is where you belong, son. Where else do think you will have the opportunities that I will afford you?"

"Dad, I get it. I'll take some time to research my options and get back to you."

"You will eventually run the family business, Nickolas."

"Thanks for the offer, Dad. Excuse us while we freshen up before dinner."

Nick went to the Leader Industries banquet hall for his graduation party.

"What should I do, Uncle Tony? My dad wants me to join him at Leader Industries, but Maggie is not sure about living in Michigan."

"What do you want to do, Nick?" asked Tony.

"I want to help people in the workforce—like yourself—who are being underpaid and mistreated."

"Follow your heart and use your powers to the best of your abilities. Maggie will wait for you to establish yourself. Once you achieve your goals, you can move on to the next phase of your life."

"I'm still not sure how I can affect these changes in the corporate world on my own."

"Throughout history, whenever there has ever been any kind of change or a revolutionary movement, it was always supported by the wealthy," Tony said.

"If I take over the family business one day, it won't change the way other corporations run their businesses," Nick said.

"If a huge corporation like Leader Industries can change, affecting thousands of lives, then word will get around—and people will want to work for you. I believe in you, Nick!"

"Thanks for the advice, Uncle Tony. I have always respected your opinion, and I value your experience. I love you!" He hugged his uncle.

Grimaldi walked up to Nick and handed him an envelope. "Congratulations, Nick! I am very proud of you, son. You are going to be a great addition to the business world!" He reached for a drink from one of the servers.

"Thank you, Mr. Grimaldi. I'm happy to see you here. I was just speaking with Uncle Tony about that. I am torn between living in California with Maggie and taking a position with a company near her or letting her go for now and working with my father."

"If you really want to make a difference in the world, you will have to work somewhere that you will be respected as well as having influence with ownership," Grimaldi said.

"I understand. I will do what is best for everyone—even though I do not want to risk losing Maggie."

"Maggie will never find another man like you, Nick. Trust me when I say that she will wait for you," Grimaldi said.

"There you are," Michael said, "Giovanni, please speak with my son. He needs reassurance about his place in this world."

Nick glanced at his father in disapproval.

"Michael, how are you tonight?" Grimaldi replied.

"I'm very well, but my son is confused. He could use your guidance, Giovanni."

"I'm not going to get in the middle, Michael. Nick is a very intelligent man. I'm sure he will make the right decision." Grimaldi smiled at Nick.

"Thank you again, Mr. Grimaldi. I respect your input."

Nick joined Maggie at the head table. "I just had two very deep conversations with my uncle and Mr. Grimaldi. They both seem to think I should take the position with my father."

"Are you all right?

"Yeah. I'm fine," Nick said.

"I could hear your father from across the hall."

"I'm used to his behavior by now. Don't worry about me, Maggie. I'm fine." Nick took a sip of champagne.

"I really don't want to be apart, Nick. I also want you to be the man you were always meant to be. I want to go home, spend some time with my family, and begin my career in California."

"I want to be with you, Maggie—no matter what it takes—but I don't know if working for any other company will allow me to make a difference in this world," Nick said.

Maggie asked, "Do you really believe that you can make a difference?"

"If I work for my father and take over the company one day, I will actually be able to affect thousands of lives within the company and possibly change the culture of corporate America as well."

"Once you establish what you need to, call me. We will figure out a way to be together again. For now, we are going to be extremely busy with our new careers. It's probably better this way."

Nick hugged her and said, "We will be together soon. I wouldn't have it any other way, sweetheart."

"We probably should take a little time apart since we have spent every day together for the past two and a half years," Maggie said, holding his hand.

"Do you need any help packing—maybe a ride to the airport?" he asked.

She chuckled and said, "Are you sure you wouldn't rather have a limo take me, big shot?"

They both laughed.

Nick joined his father in the family business as his assistant. He wanted Nick to experience the intricacies firsthand and be involved in the day-to-day operations of a successful corporation. Nick would work many hours with his father and learn how to run the business like no one else. Michael introduced Nick to each his division leaders. There were five divisions of Leader Industries: the military division, the financial division, the benefits and retirement division, the IT division, and the marketing division.

Nick arrived home late, but it was still early enough to call Maggie in California. "Hey, Maggie, how are you and the family doing? Is everything going okay with your new job?"

"We are all just fine, but the new job fell through. I've been applying every day though."

"Are you kidding me?" Nick said. "You're overqualified for any IT position!"

"Yeah, that's what they keep telling me. They tell me that they cannot pay me enough. I've been asking for the going rate, but they are not willing to pay that much in this economy."

"What are you going to do?" Nick asked.

"I can make more money working for the Federal Reserve with my father, but I'm worried about working for the government. My father is warning me of the risk involved. Finding certain information could be dangerous to federal employees. He has seen coworkers disappear suddenly without explanation. He would retire sooner, but he needs to wait for my sister to graduate from college."

"I'm sorry to hear that, Maggie. Why don't you come work for me at Leader Industries?"

"Thank you for the offer, but I don't think that's a good idea, Nick. We are lovers, and that may be a conflict of interest. You're just starting your career there, so that could be a problem down the road."

"Okay, if that's how you feel, but the offer stands as long as you like. As far as you working for the Fed, I'm not in love with that idea, but you do what you must. I will support any decision you make."

"Thank you, Nick. That's one of the reasons I love you so much," Maggie said. "How are things going for you?

"I'm appreciative of the position, but my father has me chasing after him with all five divisions on a daily basis. This is so much harder than college."

"All five at once? Is he crazy?" Maggie asked.

"I'm not exaggerating. He is putting me through the wringer. He has me working at least ten hours a day, six days a week. I barely have time to sleep."

"What are you going to do?" Maggie asked.

"I'm going to learn everything I need to. I have no other choice if I want to make a difference one day. Besides, if I quit, I would most likely be in the same position that you are."

"True," Maggie said. "You can do it. Stay strong, Nick."

"Thank you. I'll be fine, Maggie. Call me when you decide what you're going to do about the job."

"I will, Nick. Please don't worry about me. Just focus on your objective," she replied.

"I love you, Maggie."

"I love you, Nick."

The following day, Michael called Nick into his office. "How are you feeling, Nickolas?"

"I'll be fine, Dad. I am adjusting to the influx of information."

"Yes. It is a lot to consume all at once. Let me know if you're feeling overwhelmed. Maybe you need a break."

"Not a chance!" Nick said. "I will be just fine. I'm willing to work and sleep without any distractions."

"Very good answer, Nickolas. Welcome to my world," Michael replied. "We have another meeting in ten minutes with our financial division." Michael rushed for the door.

Nick grabbed his briefcase. *He sure moves fast for a big fella.* Nick did not agree with all of his father's business philosophies. Michael was harsh with his demands of board members and his subordinates. The employees seemed intimidated. Michael ruled with an iron fist.

Nick's mother walked into the kitchen, "Are you all right, Nick?"

He said, "I just opened my first check. I can't believe how much these people earn."

"Nick, please stop worrying so much. You are working so many hours and giving so much of yourself. You earned that money."

"Should I accept this kind of money when others are struggling so much?"

"If you feel so badly, why not give to charity."

He thought about Mr. Grimaldi and how unselfish he was with his wealth. "I will use this money to support charities, political candidates, and activist groups that are attempting to level the playing field between the wealthy and those who are less fortunate."

"There you go, Nick." Lena smiled. "Use the money to make a difference."

"Thanks, Mom." Nick kissed her and ran up to his room.

Nick pulled up to Pearl's house and waved.

"Hello, Nick. How are you today?"

"I'm great, Aunt Pearl! How are you feeling?"

"Very good. Thanks for asking, son."

"How are you, Nick?" Tony said.

"I'm great, Uncle Tony." Nick replied. "I really need to thank the two of you for everything you have ever done for me. You taught me the importance of what it means to be a part of a real family—a family that loves sharing the important moments in life. You treated me like your own son, and I will never forget how you helped mold me into the man I have become. I love you both with all of my heart."

"We love you too, Nick. No matter what happens, we will always be here for you!" Tony said.

Pearl said, "We are family. Even though your father really never accepted us, we always wanted to have a relationship with you and your mother. We love you very much, Nick."

"You both know I feel the same way. As a token of my appreciation, I want to buy you a new home. I will be putting a down payment on a new house for you with my first paycheck."

"No way, Nick! That's crazy. We can't accept this," Tony said.

"I work so many hours a day that I don't need a home of my own right now. I feel that I owe you so much for practically raising me. Please accept this offer as a token of my appreciation."

Tony said, "I have no idea how to respond to such a generous gift. Thank you, Nick."

"Great. I will open a savings and checking account in our names and deposit money in the account every month to pay the bills for your new home. You won't have to worry about the expenses."

Nick went to visit his cousins at the restaurant. Nick said, "Hey, cuz. How are you doing?"

Paul replied, "Just breaking my butt for peanuts!"

"Do you have five minutes to talk?" Nick asked.

"Sure, what's up?" asked Paul as they stepped outside.

"How much do you guys need to open your own restaurant?" Nick asked.

"I don't know—probably half a million to start a decent-sized place."

"I can have that for you in a couple of months. Start looking for a place to lease," Nick said.

"Wow, cuz, Thank, you! Let me go get Rob and Frank."

"I am doing very well with Leader Industries. I set up some showings for your parents to look at some new homes. I will be buying them a house in the suburbs, and I want to invest in the three of you. I will be a silent partner. You will have complete control of the operation. I want you to be financially independent and eventually use this restaurant as a springboard that will allow you to have at least two more locations."

"Are you sure that you can deliver on this deal?" asked Frank.

"You will never have to worry about money again!" Nick said.

"Why are you doing this Nick?" asked Rob.

"Like I explained to your parents, I owe you guys for being one of the main influences in my life. You all helped me to become the man I am today. I love you guys!"

The boys thanked Nick profusely and walked over to Nick's car.

"How do you like that new Corvette?" Frank asked.

"I'm trading it in for a Tesla Roadster," replied Nick with a smile.

"What kind of car is that?" Frank asked.

"An electric car." Nick showed them a picture of the Tesla on his phone.

The boys were impressed with the design and style of the Tesla.

Nick said, "I want to change this world for the better. An electric car is better for the environment."

His cousins wished him the best and returned to work.

Nick's father called him into his office. "What position do you see yourself in with the company, Nickolas?"

"Well, it's been a trying six months, but I have been thinking about that recently. I would like to take on an executive position in the human resources department. I want full control over all future hiring decisions," Nick replied.

"Why human resources?" Michael replied.

"I think I can help improve the versatility of our workforce and create a more productive environment," Nick said.

"I am not sure how you are going to do that, but I will give you the benefit of the doubt. I still want us to have daily meetings though," Michael said.

"Sure, Dad. No problem," Nick said.

Nick became the director of human resources. In a meeting with his team, Nick said, "We need to hire a more diverse workforce. People who come from different backgrounds. People who are outgoing and interested in learning about one another as well as growing our business. We need to step away from individuals who are so focused on their own growth. We need people who are interested in working with others to build an environment that is more family oriented. Any questions?"

"I have a question, Mr. Leader," his assistant said. "Even if we have an applicant who is more experienced than another, we should give more consideration to those who fit your guidelines?"

"Yes, Bella, exactly. We are building an environment that will demand a specific group of personalities," Nick said.

Nick and his team swept through the divisions, reviewing each employee. They searched for employees who were high-energy, positive influences on each other and who were willing to work as a team. He sat down with the employees and asked them about their contributions to the company and their strengths and weaknesses. Nick would weed out the self-centered individuals while clarifying how much work they had in store. Once they figured which employees needed to be replaced, the team would post the positions on the human resources website. Finally, interviews would be given with the desired candidates. They replaced a significant portion of the workforce.

One of the board members approached Nick in his office. "Excuse me, Nickolas." Mr. Bush ran the military division. Bush had been in the military. He was a very large man with a shaved head and a deep voice. "I have been made aware of some changes you have implemented over the past six months. Many of my colleagues and I are very concerned with these moves that you're making, Nickolas."

"I don't want you all losing any sleep on my account, but I am in charge of the human resources department now. Have you not read the recent quarterly reports, sir? We just set a new record in growth. There are websites that rate corporations for their employee satisfaction. We have been recently named third in the nation."

"Well, I have not seen the reports yet, but I will look into them. I don't mean to step on your toes, Nickolas, but you are shaking things up quite a bit. How many more changes do you have in mind?"

"I believe that we have made enough adjustments thus far to achieve our immediate goals. That is not to guarantee any one position for the future though. Day to day, Mr. Bush." Nick smiled.

Bella knocked on the door.

"Yes, Bella. How may I help you?"

"You have that thing in five minutes, sir," Bella whispered.

"Thank you, Bella. If you'll excuse me, Mr. Bush?"

"Sure, Nickolas. We will speak later. Good day." Bush rushed out of the room.

"Thank you, Bella. I thought he'd never shut up," Nick said.

"You're welcome, Nick. I thought you could use a reprieve." Bella laughed.

"Mr. Bush is not happy that we replaced nearly 25 percent of the workforce.

"The employees respect the changes and your philosophies, Nick. They work harder as a result."

"Bush doesn't care about the employees. He is worried about his own position. He and his colleagues are similar to those we replaced. They must feel threatened by us."

"Keep up the good work, boss." Bella's phone rang, and she rushed to pick it up. "Nick Leader's office. Yes. I will have him join his father right away. Your father would like you to see him in his office right away."

"Okay, Bella. I'm on my way."

"How may I help you, Dad?"

"I just read the quarterly report. I also noticed that productivity has increased throughout the entire workforce. Nickolas, what are you doing to get all of the departments working so well together?" Michael asked.

"Our new employees are a different type of people. The previous director had been hiring the most self-driven individuals. Our new employees come from diverse backgrounds and are interested in learning about each other's cultures. I am recruiting people from all over the country."

"Hmm … I guess I can't argue with the numbers," Michael said.

"No, you can't, can you?" said Nick.

"That brings us to our next topic. I have decided to promote you to vice president of Leader Industries." Michael stood up and extended his hand.

Nick reached out to accept it. "Thank you, Dad. I have learned so much from you over the past year. I believe that I am ready to take on whatever you need me to!"

Maggie's phone rang. "Hello, Nick. How are you, babe?"

"I'm great, sweetheart. I have great news. My father just offered me a vice president position."

"Oh, man. That's awesome, Nick. Congratulations. When do you start?"

"Thank you, Maggie. Next Monday. I can't believe I've come so close to my objective in so little time."

"This is better than you imagined, Nick. I'm so happy for you."

"Maybe my father is not as bad as I thought."

"I wouldn't go that far, Nick."

"How's everything going for you, Maggie?"

"The same. No changes here. I'm just trying to be patient."

"Hang in there, sweetheart."

"I have to go. I have an interview in an hour."

"Okay, Maggie. Good luck."

"Thank you, babe."

Michael was on an important conference call with an overseas facility. "What do you mean you can't cut the costs any lower? We had an agreement with the supplier. How many times do I have to make these calls before I get it right with you people." He stood up and screamed at the top of his lungs. Suddenly, he began to feel a pain in his arm. He clutched his chest, dropped the phone, and crashed to the floor.

A woman on the cleaning crew screamed, "Help … help." She called 911 immediately, and Michael was rushed to the hospital.

Nick and his mother rushed to the hospital.

The nurse said, "He is in surgery right now. Once the surgeon has completed the procedure, he will be out to speak with you."

Nick held his mother's hand and said, "Mom, do you have any idea what's going on with dad?"

"All I know is that your father has been complaining about indigestion for the past couple years. He takes medication for that and his cholesterol."

"I've been working closely with him for over a year now, and I didn't have a clue."

Nick and Lena waited for hours. When the surgery was finally complete, the surgeon said, "I am Dr. Vincent. Your husband had a major heart attack tonight. We did everything humanly possible. Just as we thought he was going to pull through, he seized. I am sorry to have to tell you this, but Michael didn't make it."

Lena broke down in tears.

Dr. Vincent said, "I am so sorry we couldn't save him, Mrs. Leader. We tried our best."

"Thanks for all of your efforts, Dr. Vincent," Nick said.

Nick called Maggie, "I have some bad news. My father just suffered a major heart attack."

"Oh, my. Is he okay?"

"I'm afraid not. He dead, Maggie."

"What? Dead? No way."

"Yeah. I can't believe it either."

"I am so sorry, Nick. I'll take the next flight out."

"Thanks, Maggie. I love you."

"I love you, baby."

Maggie pulled up to the funeral home and Nick was waiting on the front steps. "Are you gonna be all right, Nick?"

"Yes. I'm fine." Nick clutched her tight.

"How is your mother?"

"She is still in shock. I knew my father wasn't the picture of health. He smoked, he never worked out, and he was overweight. He always had great energy though. I thought that he was stronger than this."

"I guess he was the perfect example of what not to be," Maggie said.

"Yeah. We better join my mom inside."

Nick sat with his mother and Maggie.

Uncle Tony walked up and said, "Lena, how are you holding up?"

"I don't know, Tony." She put her head on his chest. "I feel lost."

"It's gonna be okay, dear. We're here for you."

Pearl put her arm around Nick. "Are you okay, son?"

Nick hugged her. "I'm fine, Aunt Pearl. Just surprised is all."

Rob, Frank, and Paul walked up to them.

"I'm so sorry for your loss, Aunt Lena," Rob said.

Paul said, "How are you holdin' up, cuz?"

"I'm good, Paul. I just have a lot on my mind."

"You know what you have to do, Nick. This is your time."

"Yeah, cuz. I know."

Grimaldi and Nick walked to the back of the room.

"I knew this day would come, but I never thought it would be so soon," Nick said.

"Well, here we are. You have to be ready—like it or not. This is your opportunity to change the game, Nick. This is what you sacrificed for during the past year, and now the time has come. You know what you have to do. Just keep on doing what you have been doing since you joined Leader Industries. Continue to create the culture you envisioned as a young man."

"Yeah, I get that, but it's one thing to chip away at the plan as the director of human resources and another to oversee all the divisions while trying to do the same. I'm not sure that I'm ready."

"Are you kidding me? You were born for this moment!"

"You're right. I have been preparing for this day for years now. I will do this!" Nick stood up. "Thanks for that. I guess I just needed a little encouragement."

"You're welcome, Nick. Now focus on the task at hand."

The room emptied, and Maggie said, "Well, it's time to deliver on your promise to your uncle. I feel like we will be together soon."

"Me too, Maggie. I think we just got one step closer today. So, what about your career?"

"I decided to interview for the job with the Federal Reserve. My dad helped me get an interview last week. I'll have a couple more interviews before they make their choice."

Nick said, "Do what you must, Maggie. I think it is important to gain more experience as soon as possible. Once you have that under your belt, you will be able to find something better."

"Yeah, I feel the same way. I miss you so much though. Are we ever going to be together again?"

"Of course, babe. Do what you have to do, and we will be together again soon. I promise."

"I know. It just seems like we've been apart for so long. I trust that we will be fine."

"For sure, Maggie—sooner than later."

PHASE 9

Taking the Mantle

September 2014, Michigan

After the funeral, Nick returned to Leader Industries to take over as the new owner and CEO. Nick called a meeting with the board of directors. "I want to thank all of you for your support of my family over the past week. I realize you were very close to my father—maybe even closer to him than his own family. I also realize that many of you are unhappy with the changes I have been implementing since I started with the corporation. I suggest that you become accustomed to these changes because they have just begun. If any of you are not comfortable with my philosophies, I suggest you find another corporation in which to invest!"

Bush cleared his throat and said, "Nickolas, we all realize that you and your mother hold majority shares of Leader Industries, but your father built this team. We have invested much work and many years in this corporation. You cannot expect us to change a successful formula. This system has made us one of the most successful businesses in the country."

"I respect each and every one of you," Nick replied. "I also appreciate all of your hard work and dedication for my family's company. But this is a new era for Leader Industries. I'm going to take us back to the business model of the fifties and sixties—while using innovative minds to propel us into a prosperous future. Okay, then. If no one else has any objections, we will call an end to this meeting."

"Be careful what you wish for, Nickolas," Bush said as he walked out of the conference room.

Michelle, the new office manager, said, "Nick, I don't know how to tell you this, but your idea for the new employee nap room has created a problem."

"I was not aware of a problem," Nick replied.

"It appears that some of the employees are taking advantage of the new benefit. They are taking more than the allotted thirty-minute break."

"I'm sorry to hear this. Remove the benefit temporarily. I will issue a statement to each division, making them aware of the problem. We will return this benefit next week. If anyone abuses the benefit again, we will permanently remove it. Bella, can you please make arrangements for me to attend the next Fortune 500 conference. It takes place in a few weeks at the MGM Grand in Las Vegas. If possible, I would like you to book me a speaking engagement at the conference."

"You got it, Nick," Bella replied.

In Las Vegas, another speaker had dropped, allowing Nick to take her spot. There were nearly one thousand professionals in the convention room. The place was filled with executives from nearly every corporation in America. Nick could barely stand their arrogance and elitism.

Nick took his place on the stage. "Hello, my name is Nick Leader of Leader Industries. I am here to speak on behalf of the minority owners in this group. We share a philosophy unlike most others. I am very concerned about the future of America. My father's policies have proven to be less successful than our current model. I encourage all of you to use my system and implement these changes. If not, there could be extreme consequences. The American workforce is very disgruntled. We are on the verge of a revolution—a class war—and if that happens, we will all be in a losing situation."

Nick couldn't help but notice that the crowd had begun to shrink, but he continued to deliver his message.

When he finished, only a small group was left in the room. They expressed their support for what Nick was implementing with Leader Industries and exchanged contact information.

Grimaldi said, "I am very proud of you, Nick. It takes a lot of guts to get up in front of all those corporate leaders and go against their beliefs. You get it!"

"Thank you very much, sir. I just wish that I could have gotten through to more of them."

"I want you to remember something, Nick. Every great movement starts with an idea. In time, it can become a reality. Be patient and persistent and you can achieve anything!"

"I understand, sir. I look forward to learning from your experiences."

Nick visited his uncle after the conference.

"I like where you are going with this, Nick," said Tony. "I think it's great that you have found others with similar beliefs. I suggest that you team up with Mr. Grimaldi."

"I wanted to ask him if he would join me and assist in revamping the board of directors. Do you think he would be interested?"

"Mr. Grimaldi is a great man. We've had conversations in the past about the culture of corporate America. I think Mr. Grimaldi would be very interested in joining you at Leader Industries. You may be interested in what he has to offer."

"You seem to know that he would be willing to help me."

"He helped me financially in my time of need, and I believe he will help you, Nick."

"I had a feeling that it all didn't add up—between the mortgage and feeding five people. The boys weren't earning enough to cover all the bills. Why didn't you tell me that Mr. Grimaldi helped you out?"

"Neither of us believed you should have been concerned about what was going on with me. You needed to focus on your future. We must have made the right decision because everything has worked out just fine."

"Yeah. I get it, Uncle Tony. I guess I shouldn't take it personally. You did what was best for me, and I will return the favor now."

"Just be the man you were always meant to be, Nick. Change corporate America for the better."

"I will, Uncle Tony. I promise. I will go visit Mr. Grimaldi."

Nick visited Grimaldi later that week. "Uncle Tony told me that you helped him financially when he had his accident."

"I like your Uncle Tony and believe that he was unfairly treated. I did what any caring person in my position should do. You are a very special person, Nick. I have always respected you and your family."

"Thank you, sir, for everything. I have always wondered why there isn't a Mrs. Grimaldi."

"Well, about a year before I had met you, I was actually engaged. I have had a girlfriend since high school, but I could never find the right one. Gemma Bello was the most beautiful person I had ever met. We were inseparable and fell in love immediately. As we were about to tie the knot, Gemma was killed in an automobile accident. Since then, I haven't been able to bring myself to find another."

"I'm so sorry to hear that. I had no idea," Nick said.

"Thank you, Nick. We have to focus on the future and do our best to create a positive environment. Between my father and Gemma, I cannot rest until I make things better."

"Speaking of creating a positive environment, would you be interested in investing in Leader Industries?"

"I am not sure why you would need me," Grimaldi replied. "I have been following your progress since you joined the company and am very impressed with what you have achieved in such a short period. You have made Leader Industries more successful while managing and compensating the workforce much better than your father had. You increased profits and production. The shareholders will not accept anything less than 100 percent—and you're giving it to them. What else can I bring to the table that you have not already implemented yourself?"

"Thank you for recognizing my achievements. As you know, I want to change the culture of corporate America as well. I need to completely recreate Leader Industries into my own vision first. I could use your wisdom and experience in dealing with powerful board members. I need to replace the dictators my father picked."

"For many years, I have had the same qualms that you have about the ever-decreasing corporate culture. I don't have a family of my own, so I have always thought of you as the son I never had. I would be very interested in working with you one day—and in passing on the knowledge I have acquired—but I am not sure you understand exactly what you're up against." Grimaldi frowned. "I think you need to do a little more research on what is really going on in the corporate world. Once you have the total perspective and you feel that you are capable of taking on the powers that be, then come to me and we will talk some more." Grimaldi shook Nick's hand and wished him a good night.

Nick felt a strange sense of confusion as he walked to his car. He had felt so confident that Grimaldi would accept his offer. He could not stop replaying the conversation in his head. Nick decided to take Grimaldi's advice and researched his next move.

The following day, Nick decided to redouble his efforts from his college days when he had attended rallies and made small donations to several activist groups. He wanted to find groups that were gaining ground in the class war and the climate change war. Nick also was a supporter of a senator who was running for president. Nick was ready to assist Senator Eli Landers with his presidential campaign. With more than thirty-five years of experience, Landers had sincerity in his message, which concentrated on many of the same issues and concerns that Nick had for the country. Senator Landers also wanted to return the country to its former greatness, and Nick believed that he was exactly what it needed to turn things around.

Nick discovered that Eli was having a campaign rally in Michigan the following week. Nick sent e-mail to the senator's campaign manager and asked to have a one-on-one meeting after the rally. A few days later, Eli's campaign manager confirmed the meeting.

Thousands of people gathered in Flint, Michigan, for the rally. Everyone was pumped up for the senator's appearance. The rally was exciting, and Eli was so very inspirational. After the rally, Nick met with Senator Landers. Landers was nearly seventy-four years old, about six feet tall, and had a bit of a hunch. He had receding white hair, but his energy was contagious.

"Hello, Mr. Leader," Landers said as they shook hands. "I have been made aware of your passion in regard to changing the corporate culture by stopping the greed and helping empower the middle class."

"It is a pleasure to meet you, Senator Landers. Please call me Nick. I am very excited to join your initiative. I—and several corporate leaders—agree with you and your philosophies. We will support you and your efforts to increase a tariff, which will not allow American corporations to remain profitable if they continue to manufacture in other countries. Based on recent history, we know this will result in an increase of American jobs."

"Thank you for being so informed, Nick. How do you feel about alternative energy?" the senator asked.

"Very strongly. I believe we must fight climate change—first and foremost. We must save our planet and create more new jobs as well."

"Are you personally involved in any alternative resources with Leader Industries?"

"I have had conversations with some of my division leaders, addressing these options. We are going to be investing in these operations very soon. I have just recently taken over the company."

"Very good to hear. We need young corporate leaders like yourself to step up and advocate for change."

After an hour, the senator's campaign manager said, "Senator, we need to get to the airport for the next rally."

"All right. I'll be right there. Sorry Nick, I must cut our conversation short."

"No problem, Senator. Thank you very much for your time. Good night.

Over the next couple of weeks, Nick would contact the activist groups and meet with them to find out how the battle was playing out. Nick offered financial assistance, but he soon realized that—no matter how much money he donated to the cause—there was no quick fix. Corporate America was even more powerful than he had thought.

Nick returned to Michigan to meet with Grimaldi.

Grimaldi said, "I also support the senator. He is the real deal, and we need him in the White House!"

"I visited with several activist groups who are fighting against climate change and income inequality. I'm going to be supporting them as well."

"That's inspiring, Nick. You have a better understanding of what you are up against now, don't you?"

"Definitely. I feel great about the number of people who are willing to stand up for what's right. I realize it is not going to be an overnight fix, but I'm in it for the long haul!"

Grimaldi said, "You never fail to impress me, Nick. I will invest in you and in Leader Industries. I will consult with you about how to implement the changes to bring your vision to a reality!"

"Thank you very much, sir. I promise that you will not regret your decision!"

The next day, Grimaldi said, "There are some obstacles you must be prepared for now that you are the owner and CEO of Leader Industries. I must warn you that, if we do this, you will be in for a war with the board of directors!"

"What can they do to me? I own this company!" Nick replied.

"Leader Industries has many investors. I have seen large corporations go through changes like this, and it can get dangerous for people who want to do the right thing."

"Are you suggesting that they may try to have me killed or something? You are exaggerating, right."

"No. I have seen it happen. We must carefully and strategically replace the men or women in these positions. I have a plan. I will buy a huge number of shares to reduce the market share before any of them can. This will prevent them from attempting a hostile takeover."

"Sounds like you know what you're doing, sir. I trust you."

"We must also search for leaders to replace them. We need individuals who have similar values and beliefs to us. We must find people who are not afraid to go against the status quo."

"We need to come up with a plan to replace them."

"I have already begun to work on that!" Grimaldi said.

Nick called a board meeting and said, "Most of you know who this man is." Nick pointed to Grimaldi. "Mr. Bush is familiar with Giovanni Grimaldi through dealing with our military division. Mr. Grimaldi is the owner and CEO of Grimaldi Industries. He has accepted my offer to join us as an executive advisor for all divisions of Leader Industries. I'm sure that Mr. Bush can testify about Mr. Grimaldi's accomplishments in the world of military weapons manufacturing."

After a few moments of nervous silence, Bush said, "Yes, we have had several business collaborations over the years. He has assisted us in developing our military division with your father's support."

Nick said, "I have brought you all here today to explain what it I have been observing with Leader Industries over the past year and a half. I am very happy to have been able to make the necessary changes and create the type of environment that resembles a great era in American history—a time when employers worked with employees to grow and prosper as one united entity. This current model—the us-against-them mentality—was created by corporate leaders in this country in the 1970s."

Richard Bundy said, "I am not sure that your father would agree with the changes you have implemented, Nickolas. It is my understanding that you are taking less of a salary than your father to overcompensate the employees. This could be a slippery slope. Next thing you know—you'll be asking all of us to decrease our salaries."

"You must be clairvoyant, Mr. Bundy. That is exactly what I have called all of you here for today."

"You must be joking, right?" Bundy said.

"Not at all, sir. I have taken 20 percent less of a salary than my father did, and I will be asking all of you to do the same. We must show the industry how to create a successful corporation through teamwork and unselfish leadership."

The board members looked at each other and grumbled.

Bush said, "Young man, you have no idea what you are up against. We have been working in this industry since before you were born. We have earned our positions, and I believe that I speak for the entire board when I refuse to accept any less than what I am currently earning."

Nick said, "So, in an economy that is nowhere near as successful as it was fifteen years ago, where wages have gone down for the average employee, where benefits have been all but removed, you are not willing to accept less for the betterment of the corporation?"

Bundy said, "We are all highly educated individuals. We have earned our salaries. If the masses choose to improve upon their lives, then they may do the same."

Nick said, "We all know that what you claim is impossible. There will never be enough white-collar positions for more than two hundred million workers in this country. We must increase the average salaries of the lower-class incomes to create a strong middle class. That starts with lowering the salaries of corporate leaders who are overcompensated."

Bush said, "We all have contracts. Good luck with your endeavor!"

The board members filed out of the boardroom.

Grimaldi said, "Predictable. I expected this reaction, Nick."

"Yes. Me too, sir. I'm not concerned with their feelings. We will replace each and every one of them. Let's go to my office and begin to contact some of our projected replacements."

"I'm ready, Nick," Grimaldi said.

Nick said, "What do think about bringing Maggie in to work for us?"

"In what capacity?" Grimaldi asked.

"We need to dig up some dirt on these men, right? Why not have Maggie use her hacking genius to help."

"I love that idea. Call her right away."

Nick picked up the phone. "Mr. Grimaldi and I were just speaking about filling a position over here."

"What does that have to do with me?" Maggie asked.

"We want you for the spot."

"What's the job?"

"We need a highly skilled computer operator."

"All right. Sounds like a fit. When do you need me?"

"Tomorrow."

"I'll be there," Maggie said.

Maggie arrived the next day, and Grimaldi greeted her with a hug.

"I'm so happy to have you working with us," Nick said.

"What's so important that you had to have me fly here in less than twenty-four hours?"

"We have a bit of a dilemma," Nick said.

"Let me get this straight. You want me to hack your board of directors to find as much dirt as possible so that you can replace them all?"

"You got it, Maggie," Grimaldi said.

"Okay. Where's my office?" she asked.

Nick walked Maggie a few doors down the hall to her new workspace. She was afforded the highest-quality equipment and a nice view.

"I like it, boss, especially the proximity to your office."

"You should. I had my IT department spare no expense on your tech."

"Let's do this then," Maggie replied.

Maggie spent hours researching every computer, cell phone, laptop, and answering device that the board members used. With Nick taking notes by her side, they uncovered everything they needed to oust them.

"We have dirt on each and every one of the board members," Maggie said.

Grimaldi grinned. "Great work, Maggie. That was quick. You're even better than Nick bragged."

The wheels were put into motion. Nick and Grimaldi began to go on the attack and used the most damaging information against Bundy first. He was served with a notice from the district attorney. Once he was made vulnerable, Nick was forced to replace him. A few weeks later, Bush suffered the same fate. Rumors began to swarm the building. The remaining board members became nervous.

Nick called another meeting. "Thank you all for attending. I am happy to say that we have been fortunate enough to bring in Mr. Museveni of Uganda to lead our financial division. Mrs. Burgess of Australia will lead our military division. These fine people are the best of the best in their respective fields."

The remaining members said nothing.

Grimaldi placed an envelope in front of each of the men. "I will ask the three remaining members of the board to meet with me today, individually, at the times indicated in your letters."

Grimaldi and Nick did not have legal reason to terminate the men, but they were able to find some minor infractions that would make their careers difficult.

Business News reported that there had been a very large shakeup at Leader Industries over the past several months. Some of the board members were being investigated for unethical business activities. Richard Bundy was accused of embezzlement and was set to face trial. Reginald Bush was found guilty of sexually harassing one of his assistants. He refused to acknowledge his guilt, even though the evidence was clearly corroborated by two witnesses at the company. When Bush lost his case, the remaining board members resigned.

After dinner, Grimaldi and Nick sat down for drinks.

"Nick, I feel like I can trust you with anything. Do you feel the same about me?"

"Of course, sir. I wouldn't be the man I am today—and I couldn't have achieved my goals with Leader Industries—without you."

"I have been developing a radical plan for more than ten years now. I also have been searching for a man who can lead a revolution."

"What do you mean by a revolution? Like Thomas Jefferson or Abraham Lincoln?"

"Not quite, Nick. I was testing a stealth fighter for the air force that my company was working on to improve its performance—"

"I didn't know that you were a pilot?"

"I was a test pilot for the air force before I went into weapons manufacturing. I was able to test prototype fighters on my own. I came across something in the Nevada desert that I think will change all of our lives. I was testing a top-secret cloaking device on a stealth fighter."

"Wait a minute. Did you say cloaking device?"

"Yes, you heard right. While on the test flight, the fighter stopped responding to my inputs. I thought I had lost control, but the fighter was still in controlled flight and took me off of my predetermined course. I lost communications and radar and had no idea where I was going. The fighter landed on its own in the middle of nowhere. I was concerned, but I was drawn to something in the distance. I carefully exited the fighter and looked over my shoulder at a shiny object in a dry lakebed. The sunlight drew me toward it. It seemed like some kind of shiny precious metal or jewel. I began to feel some type of presence in me. I realized the object was not a treasure, but I had to find out what exactly it was."

Grimaldi dug with his bare hands and a survival knife. The object got bigger as he dug. He finally unearthed a human-sized suit made of a material he had never seen before. He picked up the suit and returned to his fighter.

Nick asked, "What was so special about the suit."

"I returned to my test facility and studied the suit on my own. I attempted to put the suit on a fight mannequin, but I couldn't find any zippers or buttons. I secured the suit on the mannequin by tying its arms and legs around the back of the dummy. I'd never felt anything like it before. The material was strong and lightweight. I tried to tear it, but it was too sturdy. I pulled out a hunting knife and attempted to stab through the material, but it was impenetrable. I decided to fire on the suit with a forty-caliber handgun, but the suit absorbed the bullets. I loaded an AK-47 and emptied the magazine into the suit with the same result. I tried a clip of fifty-caliber armor-piercing rounds, but they would not even scratch the suit. I stepped it up by using an antitank rocket, again, but it could not penetrate the suit either."

Nick asked, "Are you kidding me?"

"No. I couldn't believe it myself. I noticed that any debris or explosive force that was deflected from the suit would not spread more than one meter away. There seemed to be some type of force field containing the blasts from any collateral damage outside its range. Seeing all of this gave me enough confidence to test the suit while wearing it myself. I removed the suit from the dummy and held it up against my chest. Suddenly, it morphed to my body. I couldn't believe what I was witnessing!"

"No way! It morphed to your body?"

"Yes. For the next test, I took my knife and attempted to stab through the suit. I raised the knife over my head and stabbed at my leg. The knife bent like plastic. I then aimed the forty-caliber gun at my foot and pulled the trigger. The suit protected me. I set a Claymore explosive just an inch farther than a meter from myself. I also set up three test dummies. All three were positioned a meter and a half to the left, right, and behind me. I set the Claymore to explode with my back facing it. When the Claymore exploded, the suit covered my entire body. I felt nothing from the explosion. From inside the suit, I could see a containment bubble that absorbed the energy from the blast. The test dummies did not move or have a scratch on them. When the suit absorbed the energy from the blast, it seemed to give me a natural adrenaline boost that made me feel super-alert and energized. The suit transferred the energy from the blast to my body. It scared me at first, but it made me feel like an Olympic athlete. When I took off the suit, there wasn't a scratch on my body or on the suit. I contemplated the consequences of such a powerful entity, and I came to the realization that I should lock this technology away from the world. It could be too dangerous in the wrong hands. I put the suit in a safe place and never told anyone about what I had found—until now."

Nick said, "This is unbelievable! Where is the suit? You're telling me that you haven't used it for anything after all these years?"

"I have never taken the suit out of my vault since the initial testing. I know it sounds unbelievable, but I felt it needed to be saved for the right time—and the right person. I believe that this is the time and that you are the person."

Nick asked "What do you mean?"

"Remember when I mentioned how the changes in the past forty-five years have been for the worse?"

"Yes."

"Well, I want to reverse this. I want to realize the dreams of our forefathers and every selfless great leader throughout history who wanted to help the downtrodden and unfortunate. In our revolution, we will concentrate on our country first. We will fight to change our nation's current energy usage by demanding that they shift to alternative energy sources. In addition, we will create jobs. When we are successful, the change should spread throughout the world."

"Like in the 1950s, 1960s, and 1990s?" asked Nick.

"Yes, exactly. In the past, the rest of the world looked up to the United States—even our so-called enemies. All of that changed in the past fifteen years. My plan—like the changes we implemented with Leader Industries—is a small example of what could be."

"How does the suit play into the revolution?" Nick asked.

"We are going to be going up against some very powerful forces. This will not be a peaceful revolution—even though I would like it to be. It will not be enough just to have state-of-the art weapons because we're just a small team. We're not an army. These corporations are not just going to agree to change for the better. They will attempt to kill you and your loved ones. They have been known to use Special Forces like the Black Ops, privatized mercenaries. We will not be able to force change on our enemies or project force without consequence, especially without the powers and the anonymity of the suit."

"I see what you mean. This will be dangerous and nearly impossible without the suit."

"Without the suit, we would need an army. Instead, we will have five stealth fighters with remote function, cloaking capability, and an unparalleled armor plating that will be able to withstand missile attacks and have underwater capabilities. We will also have an armor-plated military transport armed with state-of-the-art weaponry. Finally, we will have state-of-the-art weapons designed to stop our attackers—not kill them—as well as East Coast and West Coast bases."

"I guess you weren't kidding when you said you had been planning this for over a decade."

"No, I wasn't. Our revolution will begin by negotiating with the current power corporations. Eventually we'll move to the gas, automotive, and oil corporations. You will visit with them and explain that they will either invest in alternative energy or be replaced. If they do not agree with our demands, we will destroy the current infrastructure, replace it with alternative technologies, and reinvest in the American workforce."

"Wow!" Nick said. "This seems nearly impossible. Are you sure we can pull this off?"

"I was not sure until I met you, Nick. I watched your development as a child and between you and the suit I motivated me to research this opportunity. The alternatives are in many countries and are very efficient. I have been in contact with the best alternative energy scientists in the world. They have informed me how to proceed in order to bring our plan to reality. I have everything in place to convert the utilities. I just need a very special someone to be the hero!" Grimaldi stared into Nick's eyes.

"I trust you with my life, Mr. Grimaldi. I want to thank you for seeing something in me at such a young age and for trusting in my ability. I have always thought about changing the system in this country—even as a boy. I want to take advantage of my power and influence. I'm in!" Nick extended his hand to Grimaldi.

The next day, Nick had a meeting with the board of directors. "I will be appointing a new CEO of Leader Industries. I have decided to focus on investing in other markets."

Edward Ellis, the director of human resources, asked, "Why are you making these changes? What business will you be looking to invest in?"

"I'll be starting a new division on the West Coast that involves alternative-energy resources," Nick replied. "I'll be promoting someone from within to be the new CEO of Leader Industries.

By week's end, Nick had made his decision. "Bella, please ask Mr. Ellis to join me in my office."

"Yes, sir," Bella replied.

Nick asked Edward to have a seat. At UCLA, they had bonded over politics. Edward was a tall, slender fellow with long, fair hair. He dressed like a hipster in college and was a passionate political activist.

"I have been thinking about who I can trust with this very important position, Edward."

"We have known each other for years, and I know that you will make the right decision."

"I think I have. You are the new CEO of Leader Industries, my friend."

"Are you serious, Nick?"

"Absolutely, Mr. CEO. You understand what we are trying to build, and you are the right person for the job." Nick stood up and extended his hand.

"I am so thankful, Nick. I promise to make you proud."

Nick realized that leaving his family's business was a risky proposition, but he felt committed to the revolution.

PHASE 10

A Revolutionary Idea

April 2015, Michigan

Nick and Grimaldi visited an old warehouse in a remote location. It had not been occupied for decades.

"What do think, Nick?"

"It's a mess, but it definitely has potential."

"We'll have it modified. You won't recognize this place when it's completed."

"I like the size of the building. We should have no problem housing the vehicles, weapons, and systems for the revolution."

"Without a doubt. This building was used to manufacture military vehicles and weapons during World War II. I remember learning about this facility when I had first started Grimaldi Industries. There are no neighbors for miles. This will be perfect for our base of operation."

Grimaldi asked Nick to meet at his home, "How do you feel about taking on some military training with a former Special Ops commander?"

"What kind of training are you talking about?" Nick asked.

"Military—weapons, vehicles, aircraft, combat, parachuting—the basics."

"Where would I be training?"

"You will be training in climates with extreme temperature differences—you also will be tested in high-altitude drops."

Nick had only experienced these types of training in simulation, but he would not let Grimaldi down. "I can do this. I think that's a great idea!"

"I understand your apprehension, Nick," Grimaldi said. "You will be completely safe. I will have my best man train you."

"When you say your best man, who are you talking about?" Nick asked.

"I have known Commander Adams since my military days. We became very good friends, and he eventually came to work for me at Grimaldi Industries. Because of him, I created my own military-contracting division. Commander Adams is the head of that division. He is one of my most trusted advisors. His full name is Ulysses S. Adams, but you will address him as Commander Adams."

"After all these years, you're just now telling me that you have a Special Ops team of your own?"

"Well, I really don't want this kind of information circulating all over town. You must understand that I am a man who is perceived in different lights from different worlds. There are those who know me from a military perspective, and there are those who know me as a philanthropist through my many charitable endeavors."

"You are able to reach a broader scope of people, places, and business. Amazing, Mr. Grimaldi."

"You must trust me when I say there is no angle that I haven't thought out. I will not allow you to go into our revolution unprepared."

"I am willing to do whatever it takes to succeed in changing the culture of corporate America and saving the planet."

"I will have Commander Adams work with you in the following weeks. He will prepare you for a Black Ops mission that one of my crews will be taking on in the near future. Also, I have made you an appointment with my physician. You need a full physical before you begin training and wearing the suit."

Nick completed his physical with Dr. McKenzie and prepared to meet with Commander Adams the following day.

Maggie was staying at Nick's house until they found a place together.

"Maggie, I am sorry, but I have to leave for a month or two."

"I just moved here, Nick. Are you kidding me?"

"I'm sorry, sweetheart, but it's very important that I take care of this new business with Mr. Grimaldi."

"Where will you be traveling?'

"Not completely sure. Overseas, Nevada, maybe California? Depends on how things go."

"I'm not happy with it, but I understand how important this is for the environment and your goals."

"Thank you so much, Maggie." Nick hugged her tight. "You're the best. I love you so much, baby."

They spent the rest of the night together, but Nick was not ready to tell her about the revolution just yet.

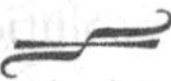

The men met at Grimaldi's training facility. The facility, like the warehouse, was in a remote area. It had indoor and outdoor training posts. Commander Adams was a tall man with broad shoulders and white hair. He said, "All right, Leader. I hope you're ready because this is going to be very intense. We will be fitting six months of Special Ops Training into a four-week program. I hope you're up to the task!"

"I am as ready as I'll ever be, sir!" Nick replied.

For hours, Commander Adams trained Nick in the basic intricacies of handguns and assault rifles. The commander had Nick take apart the weapons and reassemble them until he could do it blindfolded.

They spent the next few days at a firing range, training Nick in military armaments—from small arms all the way up to a heavy arms—including handheld rocket launchers and armor-piercing .50 caliber rifles. Nick finished off with vehicle-mounted antitank missiles. Nick scored at the top of the curve in all the testing.

The next phase in the training was to head out to the desert and the mountains for testing on survival and climate assimilation. The men boarded a C-130 transport and were airdropped in the middle of the desert at dawn.

The commander said, “Leader, if you’re going to survive a mission, you will have to train for the severe climate changes that will occur from very cold nights to the harsh heat of daytime. There are not too many places in the world where these weather changes could kill a person, but the desert is one of them. We will be spending a week here—so get comfortable.”

“I am ready to do this, sir!” Nick jumped to his feet.

The men began to unload their gear.

The commander said, “We will be going on a hike, Leader.”

A couple of hours later, the commander stopped and mixed a powdery substance with warm water from his canteen. The commander told Nick to do the same with his rations.

After Nick drank the nutrient solution, the commander laughed and said, “The only time anyone would be satisfied by this slop would be in these conditions!”

The men traveled for a few more hours and stopped for lunch.

“How are you doing, Leader?”

“I’m good, sir.” Nick prepared another drink for himself.

“How are you enjoying that refreshing warm water, Leader?”

“I have had worse, sir.” Nick replied.

The commander laughed. “It is time to set up camp.”

“Why are we setting up camp so soon, Commander?”

“The sun is beginning to reach its peak, and we cannot travel in the heat. We would not survive if we attempted to do so. We will seek shelter during the night and the daytime. It’s time to take a nap.”

As the men woke from their rest, the commander said, “We will be heading out again, Leader. You see that that peak to the northwest?”

“Yes.”

“We have three days to make it to that point and another three days to make it to the other side of the mountain.”

"That seems like a lot of terrain to cover in such a small time frame, sir."

"It is, but I have done it before—and you will complete it now. We will be tested by unforeseen elements on our journey. The possible peril I'm referring to could kill us, and I don't just mean poisonous snakes or scorpions!"

Nick gulped, but he hid his fear from the commander and marched on.

The following day, the commander said, "It's time for dinner, Leader." He pulled out an MRE of beans and rice, and Nick did the same. "Have you ever been so fortunate, Leader?"

"I'm sure there are people in the world who have it much worse than this," Nick replied.

After dinner, the commander picked up the pace. A sandstorm suddenly came upon them. Nick and the commander raced into a nearby cave, just barely avoiding the storm.

"That was almost too close for comfort, Leader. You did a good job of reacting without me having to give an order. You have very good reactionary skills. That is what it takes to survive a mission under extreme conditions."

"Thank you, Commander. I enjoy training very much—whether it is in the gym or in military drills."

"Good to know, Leader!"

They rested four a few hours.

When they reached the mountains, the commander said, "Be careful on this terrain, Leader. The rocks and sand may give out under your boots."

"Yes, sir. I'll be aware."

Five hundred feet away, a large animal rushed at Nick, but he jumped out of its path.

The commander pulled out his pistol and fired a warning shot. The animal scurried up the side of the mountain.

"Are you all right, Leader?"

"I'm okay, sir." Nick's heart was pounding. "What was that thing, Commander?"

"That was a ram! It could have easily thrown you five hundred yards."

Nick said, "I'm ready to continue, sir."

The last major obstacle of Nick's survival training would be camping overnight on the highest peak of the mountain.

The commander said, "We must prepare for the cold, Leader. We will set up camp here."

The men peeled off their backpacks.

"May I ask you a question, Commander Adams?"

"What is it, Leader?"

"What do these extreme conditions have to do with what I am preparing for?"

"That is the most frequently asked question, Leader. Whenever I train soldiers for combat, there is one common denominator. It is not enough to challenge one's physical limitations. It is more important to prepare the mind to withstand unbearable conditions."

"Makes sense, sir. I have been tested in many different aspects of combat and sports, but this has been the most dangerous so far."

"I will prepare you for the worst. If you survive, you will be all the better for it. Let's get some shut-eye."

Nick and the commander were awakened when their shelter lifted off its surface, throwing them in the air.

The commander yelled, "We need to secure our tent, Leader." He attached himself to Nick with a second safety line that was fastened to the mountain. The severe winds pulled out one of the ice anchors from the mountainside. The mountain shelter became unstable, and the men had to rush to secure the shelter to save themselves. The commander searched one side as Nick approached the opposite side.

Nick found the loose anchor swinging in the wind. "Over here, sir."

The commander quickly reattached the anchor, and they went back into the shelter.

"Good work, Leader," the commander barked.

"Thank you, sir. That was crazy." Nick rubbed his arms and legs for warmth.

"We should be fine for now. Get back to sleep, Leader."

Nick was too amped to fall back asleep, but he kept quiet.

After another night of unrest, the two men headed for their final destination at the base of the mountain. A helicopter arrived to pick them up. Nick dozed off on the ride back to base.

The commander yelled, "We're under attack! Put this on, Leader!" He threw a parachute to Nick. "Gear up, Leader!"

Nick's senses were assaulted by the sound of gunfire and explosions. He put on the parachute and secured it.

The commander yelled, "You're on your own, Leader." He pushed Nick out of the helicopter. "Watch your altitude, Leader!"

Nick was disoriented as he went into a quick head-over-heels flip. Instinctively, he regained control. Nick checked his altimeter, readying himself to pull the cord. He did so just in time and landed just outside of the base.

He looked up as the chopper descended slowly and realized there was no threat. He picked up his gear up and headed to the base.

The commander said, "Glad you could make it, Leader. Ready for a shit, shave, and shower?"

Nick said, "Attack?"

The commander chuckled. "That was just fireworks and a few gunshots for your benefit, Leader. There was no attack. It was just a test—and you passed!"

Nick turned and headed to the barracks. "For my benefit? What the hell?"

For the final phase of training, the commander took Nick on his first HALO jump (high-altitude, low-opening jump). The C-17 soared to its maximum altitude. They were wearing oxygen masks and full military gear. As the rear cargo door opened up to reveal the clouds and sky, Nick's breathing began to increase.

The commander said, "Don't forget, Nick, we are not opening our parachutes until we reach two thousand feet!"

Nick yelled, "I understand, sir!" He closed his eyes and took a deep breath.

Nick looked up and saw a red light. The green light was the signal to jump. The commander led the way, and Nick found himself in an out-of-control spin, which made him even more nervous.

The commander grabbed him by the arm to stabilize him. Nick felt like he had been falling forever and reached for the cord.

The commander yelled at Nick to look at his altimeter, and Nick realized that he was only at 35,000 feet. He began to go into controlled maneuvers with the commander.

They were getting closer to the release of their parachutes: 15,000 feet … 14,000 feet … 13,000 feet … 12,000 feet. Nick felt another adrenaline rush as the ground became clearer. "This parachute better not fail me!"

The commander signaled to Nick to get ready to activate his chute. Nick checked his altimeter again: 5,000 feet … 4,000 feet … 3,000 feet … 2,000 feet. Nick closed his eyes and pulled the cord. The chute emerged, relieving his anxiety.

When they landed safely, the commander asked, "Nick, are you okay?"

"I'm good, Commander Adams," Nick replied.

The men returned to the training facility.

"So what did you think of that drill, Leader?"

"That was one of the most intense experiences of my life, Commander!"

"That is what most people say, Leader."

"Has anyone ever died in the HALO jump, Commander?"

"No, but a few have passed out."

Nick thought, *I would like to do that again!*

The commander decided to call it a day, and they headed back to the barracks.

The next day, Nick woke to find that the commander had already returned to the base in California. Nick was flown by helicopter to meet the commander at the test facility. As he approached the compound, he looked down at his destination. It looked like a movie set.

A huge wall surrounded the complex. There were several buildings with small signs that described their functions. Men and women were training in different areas. Some had weapons, and others were doing cross-country obstacles, climbing ropes, jumping over tall walls, and sprinting through finish lines.

Commander Adams approached Nick and asked, "What are you doing here, Leader?"

"What do mean, Commander?" Nick asked.

"What are you doing all of this specialized training for, Leader?"

"Let's just say that I need this training for future endeavors. Mr. Grimaldi explained to me that you are a man of integrity and that we could trust you to be discrete about this operation. We may need your expertise in the future to assist us in some restructuring missions. These teachings may be a very important piece in that puzzle."

"Of course you can trust me to be discrete, Leader. I have made a living at this."

Grimaldi entered the complex via chopper. "Good morning, gentlemen. We will be bringing in a team of Black Ops contractors to work with you for a mission in the Middle East. You will have fake identification from a deceased Black Ops contractor to memorize." He handed Nick an envelope. "We will disguise your fingerprints as well. The identity of the man you will be taking on is David Jones. You must not let anyone from the team know your true identity. We will finalize your military training with Commander Adams and the contractors before you leave for the mission. By the end of this training, you will be prepared to function as a soldier with the team."

Nick said, "So once we're done here, I will be going into the mission with these men?"

"Yes, Nick. These are the men you will be counting on to protect each other in the field."

"Sounds like a great plan, Mr. Grimaldi!"

The next morning, the mercenaries arrived for preparation. Grimaldi introduced everyone to each other. The commander would take over immediately to prepare the men for the mission. They would start with hand-to-hand combat.

"Okay, men, which of you—besides David—has the most hand-to-hand combat training?"

Nick climbed in to the cage while the other mercs held their positions.

"I got this one, fellas." Jimmy Jenkins stepped up to the cage. He was a demolitions expert. Jimmy had a southern accent and was loud and obnoxious. Jimmy had served in just about every tour of duty for the past ten years. He could rig any type of explosive from just about any distance. Jimmy said "He don't look like much to me!"

"Very good, Jenkins," the commander said. "Gear up."

The men slipped on their headgear and gloves.

Nick said, "Full contact, punching, kicking, and grappling—no low blows, no striking to the back of the body from the waste up. Do you understand these rules?"

"Yeah, I got it, son," Jenkins said.

"Someone start the bell," Adams yelled.

Jenkins led with a right-hand strike. Nick slipped the attack and went on the defensive, waiting for Jenkins to throw his right hand again.

"Come on, man. Are you scared to hit me?" Jenkins yelled, laughing derisively. He threw a lead right hand again.

Nick timed it perfectly, slipping the strike, and Jenkins landed on his backside. He rushed again, but Nick struck with a lead jab, a right hand, and a kick, knocking Jenkins to the canvas.

The other mercs jumped out of their seats.

Nick asked, "Are you okay to continue, Jenkins?"

"Okay, Jenkins. That's enough for you today. Anyone else want to go?" the commander barked.

The rest of the team would not respond.

"That's what I though. Let's hit the firing range next."

The men looked at each other as though they wanted no part of Nick.

Nick would continue to prove his worth on the range as well—as would everyone on the team. Throughout the remainder of his training, Nick only made a few small mistakes. However, he was able to adapt quickly enough, with the covert assistance of the commander. Nick was able to convince the mercs that he would be more than a competent teammate.

The commander said, "You have done very well, Leader. I'm happy with your progress."

"Thank you, Commander Adams, for everything. I couldn't have done it without you. I promise I'll make you proud."

"My father once explained to me that being unprepared is like being prepared to fail. Just remember your training—and everything will be fine. You are fully prepared, Jones."

The team traveled to the Middle East. At Grimaldi's direction, Nick had packed the alien suit.

The team was assigned to secure a location from the Taliban in a small village in Pakistan. The team was adjusting to the new environment when fifteen Taliban soldiers attacked in the middle of the night. Everyone was asleep except for Gerardo Sanchez—the overnight guard. Sanchez was the team transportation specialist. He was always covered in automotive oil and was capable of dismantling and reassembling an engine as quickly as anyone. Fortunately, he had been drinking so much coffee that he could have heard a tick move.

When Sanchez heard a noise in the brush, he radioed Team Leader Peter Vataj. Vataj was from the Bronx. He was one of the top weapons experts. Pete was a tall, skinny man with dark hair.

They all took their places quickly. The team was calm, collected, and organized. The villagers were hidden in the barracks. Vataj ordered Jenkins and Ming to stay with them while he and Nick joined Sanchez to engage their attackers. Pao Ming was the tech specialist and one of the leading hackers in his field. Pao was short and had an upbeat attitude.

Nick's suit fit like a second skin, but he was nervous about his first gun battle. He kept sharp and followed every command from Vataj. Slowly, the pair made their way to the west side of the village.

After Vataj signaled for Sanchez to throw a rock into the brush, he picked up a heavy rock and waited for the command. Vataj signaled to Nick to be ready to fire when Sanchez launched the object into the brush.

The enemy heard the crash as they turned in the direction of the distraction, firing their weapons at the decoy.

Vataj gave the command, and Sanchez and Nick fired. After a few minutes, there was silence.

Sanchez shook Nick's arm. "Jones, are you okay?"

"Yeah. Sorry. I zoned out for a minute," Nick said.

"We need to advance. Check the area for more threats," Sanchez whispered.

"I'm ready," Nick said.

Vataj radioed back to the barracks to be sure that the enemy had not penetrated their defenses. Once he was satisfied that the threat was kept at bay, he signaled for Sanchez and Nick to advance into the wooded area with him. Slowly, they scanned the area for enemy casualties. They found ten dead bodies.

Despite the number of casualties, Vataj felt that a threat was still imminent. He signaled for the men to take cover. Once they were secured behind a solid wall, Vataj took out a grenade and signaled his intentions. The men readied themselves for the blast. Vataj threw the projectile fifteen yards forward.

Nick had readied himself with a grenade and scanned the area. He pulled the pin and heaved the explosive at the enemy.

Vataj and Sanchez fired on the area as well. Within moments, the fire ceased. Vataj surveyed the area while waiting for the smoke to clear. He signaled for the men to advance once again. Vataj found five more bodies and gave the order to return to the village.

The following day, Nick asked, "How long have you been doing this, Vataj?"

"Ten years now," he replied.

"I had never killed before last night," Nick said.

"Yeah, I could tell, kid."

"Do you ever get used to it?" Nick asked.

"Well, some of us do—and some of us die," Vataj said.

"You mean either do or die, right?" Nick said.

"Exactly, Jones. This business isn't for most people—no shame in that," Vataj said.

Grimaldi received the details of their first mission and decided to contact Nick, "Nick, are you okay?"

"I'm fine, Mr. Grimaldi, but I'm not sure I can continue."

"Talk to me, Nick. What are you feeling?" Grimaldi asked.

"I have never killed before. I'm not sure if this is worth it."

"I understand what you are feeling, Nick. I have been in your shoes before."

"You have killed too?" Nick asked.

"Yes, Nick. I have been in combat situations. At first, I felt shock. I had to remind myself what the objective was all about. In combat and in life, we must fight for what is right and against what is wrong. You will have to accept death if you want to conquer evil."

"I don't know. I guess I just never realized how difficult it would be to take a life."

"I understand completely," Grimaldi said. "This will be the most difficult part of the revolution. If you are not willing to accept it, there is no hope for the planet or workers like Uncle Tony."

"I understand. I want to help people. I want to be the man who all of you believe I am."

"Then you'll continue?" Grimaldi asked.

"Yes. You're right. This is the time—and I will be the one!" Nick felt energized again.

The team was assigned a mission in a larger village. Alex McCoy, the medical specialist, sat with Nick. Alex was scrawny, sarcastic, and witty. Alex had served in Afghanistan, saving hundreds of lives while on duty. "Are you okay, Jones?"

"Yeah, I'm fine. It's scary, but I think I'm starting to get used to this place."

"That is scary, man. You seem to have taken to this group," Alex said. "Well, don't get too comfortable. That's when it bites you in the ass, man."

A truck pulled into the village, and six more Black Ops contractors joined them. There was no conflict in the second village, and Nick felt more at ease. Over the next couple months, Nick's team went on a few more missions—some with casualties and some without. His team was successful in every mission, and Nick learned what it took to be a part of a military team.

In another village, they settled in for the night. Twenty-five Taliban soldiers surrounded the village and attacked in the middle of the night. There was a large explosion near one of the lookout posts. The team scrambled from building to building, killing off each threat. Unfortunately, some of the villagers were harmed.

When the smoke cleared, the mercs realized Jenkins had been killed in the explosion. Nick was upset and confused. Throughout his training, he had not felt the pain of losing a fellow soldier. The pain cut through him like a knife. He felt partially responsible. Nick understood the true purpose of his training. He knew he must be able to accept the reality of death.

Later that evening Vataj was standing over the corpse of Jenkins.

Nick asked, "Did he have any family?"

"No," Vataj replied. "He was a loner. We will send his body back to Washington to be buried."

"I thought it was bad enough to take a life. Losing one is even worse."

"Let it go, Jones. No shame in a good cry." Vataj placed his hand on Nick's shoulder. "You need to accept the wins along with the losses. You have done a great job here, Jones. Time for you to move on." Vataj handed Nick his orders to return to California.

PHASE 11

Team Rebel Is Born

July 2015, California

While Nick was overseas, Grimaldi had been working on the construction of their location on the West Coast. He was having the finishing touches finalized. Grimaldi also was developing a new division between Leader and Grimaldi Industries. This division would become the alternative-manufacturing entity and would work with companies in the area. Their plan to reside on the West Coast in the winters was coming to fruition.

As the plane touched down, Nick couldn't help but reflect on the time spent with Black Ops. It felt so surreal to him.

Grimaldi picked him up at a private airstrip. "Are you all right, Nick?"

"I'm fine, sir. I just never imagined that it would be so intense," Nick said.

"Are you mentally prepared for the possibility of what a revolution may result in?"

Nick said, "I understand why you kept me with the Black Ops team for so long. I thought you would have pulled me sooner, but I realized why after one of my teammates was killed. Now I understand the risk and am fully prepared for the revolution!"

"These men understand the risks of their profession, Nick.

Unfortunately, from time to time, we lose men to these missions. I pay these men more than any other contractor in the industry. I also insure these men so that if one of them dies in combat, the families are taken care of. I refuse to send my teams to oil refineries and manufacturing plants to protect corporate profits. We focus on humanitarian missions, securing villages, and helping people who cannot defend themselves. I had you wear the suit because our future depends on you. Did you have to use the powers of the suit?"

"No, I was focused on surviving, but I did notice that I was able to move much more quickly and athletically than usual!"

"Very good. I feel strongly about continuing," Grimaldi replied.

"I feel focused and ready to begin the revolution."

"Okay then, we will have to assemble a small team."

"I'm worried that we won't be able to find people who can be trusted!" Nick said.

"I understand your skepticism, but we must fill these positions in order to be successful. We will need a computer specialist for hacking top-of-the-line security systems and a versatile mechanic for all the vehicles we will be using. Last but not least, we need someone to be the go-between of Leader Industries and the revolution."

"I will recruit Uncle Tony to be my liaison and right-hand man. There is only one person we can trust with the hacker position. Maggie is trustworthy and as anticorporate as they come!"

"Obviously Maggie is qualified, but are you sure you want to involve her in the revolution?"

"Do we have any other options?" Nick asked.

"Of course, but no one I would trust as much as Maggie."

"Then I will recruit her."

Grimaldi said, "Our mechanic position will be filled by my younger brother. Joey was an engineer in the air force for twenty years."

"How long has Joey been retired from the military?" asked Nick.

"A couple of years now. He's only forty years old and is bored with his new job. Joey is just like us when it comes to his political views."

Nick and Grimaldi agreed to start recruiting their team instantly.

Nick called Maggie and asked her to join him in California. She gave him the okay and flew out immediately. Nick picked her up at the airport, and they went straight to her apartment for some intimate time. Maggie had been sharing an apartment with Laura, Isiah's girlfriend from college.

After a couple of days together, Nick said, "I have been learning so much more about the state of the union in the past couple of years. We, as a planet and a country, are in big trouble. Politically and fiscally, we are at a crossroads. Change is necessary and vital."

"I get that, but haven't you already begun to address these problems with Leader Industries?"

"Yes, I have—with great success—but I have learned that it will not be enough. Mr. Grimaldi has opened my eyes to other options since I've begun working with him. He has taught me so much over recent months, and I believe that everything has finally come into place for us."

"What do you mean?" she replied.

"Do you remember how I felt about my uncle being hurt and my father not helping him?"

"Yeah, I remember."

"I decided to work for my father to get the power and influence to invoke real change in this country."

"What does this have to do with me meeting you in California, Nick?"

"I'm here to finally ask you to join me—along with Mr. Grimaldi, Uncle Tony, and Mr. Grimaldi's brother Joey—in a plan to change the culture of corporate America and reverse climate change."

"How are we going to do this?" Maggie asked.

"Mr. Grimaldi has been laying the groundwork for a revolution over the past ten years. He has been searching for a man like me to lead the revolution. I believe in this revolution, and I know you can help us fight the corruption and unfair treatment of hardworking Americans like my uncle. I haven't been completely honest with you about what I was doing for the past few months."

"Excuse me? What exactly do you mean?"

"I was training with a military commander. Grimaldi had me join a Black Ops team."

"You what? How could you do something like this without asking me how I would feel?" Maggie pulled away from Nick. "You told me you were working on alternatives! You lied to me!"

"I understand why you're upset, Maggie. I'm sorry I lied. Please allow me to finish before you reply so that you are fully aware of the circumstances. I prepared for battle with a military commander. I trained with him for a month. I went to the Middle East for several missions with the Black Ops team. Mr. Grimaldi is a contractor with many teams of soldiers who protect innocent people from terrorist groups."

"Are you crazy? Why would you do this—and what does this have to do with corporate America?"

"This training was essential for preparing me for the revolution," Nick said.

"You could have been killed! How could you put yourself in such a position?"

"Well, that's the crazy part. I really was in no real danger. Mr. Grimaldi found an alien suit ten years ago. This suit is amazing, Maggie. It has unimaginable powers."

"Have you ever lied to me before?" asked Maggie.

"Never—I wouldn't dare. I love you too much. You must believe me when I tell you that I was never in danger."

"Okay. If I believe in this magical suit, how are we supposed to take on corporate America?"

"Mr. Grimaldi has supplied us with all of the weapons and equipment to fight for our country. We need you because you are the best computer specialist I know. Mr. Grimaldi has done the research on your background and is confident in your abilities as well. More importantly, we cannot trust just anyone. We need you, Maggie!"

"You should have told me about this sooner!" Maggie punched him in the arm.

"I wasn't sure I could actually do this until I went through the training. I wanted to be sure I was capable before committing and asking you to commit!"

"Please never keep me in the dark again. I tell you everything. You need to do the same!"

Nick said, "I'm sorry. I promise!"

"Are you sure about taking on corporate America?"

"Someone has to do this. No one else is willing to step up or is even able to!"

"All right, then. Count me in." Maggie hugged and kissed Nick.

"Great!" Nick squeezed her tightly. "I knew you couldn't turn me down."

"But I would like to spend a week with my family before we begin the revolution."

"Sure. We can do that. I'll let Mr. Grimaldi know that we'll be in Michigan by Monday."

Nick drove out to the renovated warehouse to meet Grimaldi. After getting lost, he pulled up to the driveway.

"Mr. Grimaldi, where is the warehouse?"

"Under your new home." Grimaldi pointed to the house.

"What are you talking about?" Nick asked.

"I had the foundation built up around the warehouse—with the exception of the rear bay doors. They were left exposed for the stealth fighters to enter and exit."

"Thank you. How did you pay for all of this?"

"I used investment funds from Grimaldi and Leader Industries. I couldn't have you and Maggie living in a warehouse! You need to have immediate access to the base. I had this home built for the two of you."

"Wow, that was a genius idea, Mr. Grimaldi!" Nick said as they entered the home.

"I understand that you and Maggie are not interested in anything fancy, so I had the smallest possible floor plan designed—with four extra bedrooms. We must be able to accommodate the entire team in case of emergencies."

"Of course. That makes sense."

"Have you spoken with your uncle yet?" Grimaldi asked.

"Yes. He is ready for duty," Nick said.

"Great. Everything is coming together."

Grimaldi said, "The suit can be modified to whatever design you want. Just imagine a pair of thermals when you put the suit on. You will be able to disguise yourself in the future. Just imagine the identity that you need to portray, and the suit will morph immediately."

"Amazing! If I see a person and imagine being that person, the suit will reflect my thoughts?"

"Absolutely. I have tested it myself," Grimaldi said.

Grimaldi led Nick to the vault and showed Nick the procedure for entry. "This is how you will access the suit."

There was a bio scanner for their hands and a retinal scanner. Grimaldi placed his head into the scanner, opening the vault. Nick was impressed by the number of weapons on the walls. Grimaldi walked up to a hidden door and put his hand on a glass plate. It made a digital sound and exposed the door. In the hidden room, Nick saw a shoulder holster with two guns, a pair of grappling devices, a pair of nunchucks, and a backpack.

"Please place your fingers in the slots of this lockbox."

The box lit up, made a sound, and opened.

Nick picked up the suit and said, "I'm ready to get started, Mr. Grimaldi."

"Okay, put it on."

Nick placed the suit against his chest, and it consumed his frame.

"Take the afternoon to experiment with the different abilities of this alien technology."

Mr. Grimaldi left Nick alone to examine the suit.

Nick noticed how strange the suit appeared. It was like nothing he had ever seen. It had the appearance of a medieval dragon skin or an exotic sea creature and had scales that would change color according to the surrounding light sources. The suit did not feel as it looked—it was not rough or jagged like a dragon's skin or scaly like a sea creature. Instead, the suit had the smoothness of the finest silk or the skin of a young woman. It was strange, playing with Nick's senses.

Later that evening, Nick explained to Grimaldi what he had discovered about the suit.

Grimaldi replied, "I think we should just allow the suit to take on whatever image it will naturally. This will allow you to be camouflaged in the shadows and be unnoticeable to your adversaries."

"Yes. The suit would change color—according to my emotional state. What type of weapons should I use for the revolution?"

"You will have a military harness, adding two perfectly balanced handguns attached to each side. You also will have grappling devices attached to each arm. You will have two pairs of nunchucks, C-4 explosive packs with timers, flash grenades, smoke bombs, a backpack with a parachute, retractable wings, and jet boots. You will also have other weapons at your disposal for specific missions."

"It looks like we have all our bases covered!" Nick replied.

"What do you want to name our hero?" Grimaldi asked.

Nick replied, "Rebel!"

Grimaldi smiled and raised his fist in the air. "Perfect!"

The team assembled at the Michigan base, and Nick showed the house to Maggie.

"So what do think?" Nick asked.

"I like it, but I thought we were visiting the base."

"Well, we are—it's underneath the house. We had this house built over the warehouse to hide and give us quick access to our base."

"Brilliant! I love that idea! Can we check it out?" she asked.

"Let's wait for the rest of the team. They'll be here in a minute,"

There was a knock, and Grimaldi opened the door. "This is my brother, Joey."

Joey was a clean-cut man who was about six feet tall. He had fair hair and wore a leather air force jacket with blue jeans.

Nick walked up to Joey to shake his hand.

Grimaldi said, "Joey, this is Nick Leader."

"Great to finally meet you, Joey. This is my girlfriend, Maggie."

"Hello, Maggie. Happy to meet you all," Joey said.

Just then, there was another knock on the door.

"Come in, Uncle Tony," Nick said. "How are you doing?"

"Feeling good. Ready to begin my new job." Tony laughed. "I haven't worked for a while, and I'm ready to get back into the flow."

Grimaldi shook Tony's hand and said, "Well, you better be, Tony. We have a lot of work to do." He showed everyone around the main floor and the assigned rooms in case of emergency. "I have known each and every one of you, with the exception of Maggie, for most of my life. I have done my due diligence in regard to her qualifications. I believe we have assembled the best possible team to achieve our goals. We will confront corporate America, emphasizing the severity of climate change and the importance of acting immediately in order to save our planet. We will also persuade them to put an end to manufacturing in other countries. Preaching this global economy has destroyed the middle class. These corporate leaders act as though they are helping other countries, but in reality, they move manufacturing jobs from one place to another, paying pennies on the dollar. They are not helping people in other countries. They are only increasing their own hidden bank accounts." Everyone was 100 percent committed. They felt that there must be change if the planet was to be saved and if the American dream were to be realized again.

Team Rebel would begin training with the equipment and systems. They had unlimited access to Grimaldi's complete military arsenal, which included specially modified stealth aircraft with remote function. Artificial intelligence would be at the command of the team.

Grimaldi led the team to the control room. "We have a state-of-the-art computer system with three eighty-inch monitors. We will use these monitors to display maps of the locations that we will be infiltrating as well as studying blueprints and following the stealth fighters via remote feeds. We will be able to take control of any security system in the world. This allows us to penetrate and eliminate any obstacles or threats."

"That's music to my ears," Maggie said.

"If you make your way to the two-way window, you will see the entire training facility. A series of monitors shows the entire structure, including the rooms in the house and the grounds. A set of monitors in the master bedroom is hidden in the wall in front of the bed."

Grimaldi led them to the next room. "This room will be for medical examinations. I have a surgeon on staff with Grimaldi Industries. Dr. McKenzie is one of the leading medical experts in the world. He has been my family doctor since I was a boy. Dr. Mckenzie has several PhDs. We will have a MRI and an ultrasound machine delivered next week."

The next room was Grimaldi's office. "I didn't want to crowd you, Maggie. When you are working in the control room, I can get some work of my own done in here."

"Makes sense. We all need our own space at times," Maggie said.

"Are there any other rooms?" Nick asked.

"Yes, a few, but I haven't really decided what we will use them for. We can brainstorm and decide later." Grimaldi led the team to a hidden elevator. "We are in the training area." Grimaldi unveiled a large warehouse full of military toys.

"This is huge!" Joey's eyes lit up.

Tony said, "Where did you find this place?"

"This is an old military manufacturing plant. They used this building in World War II to build vehicles and aircraft," Grimaldi said.

"Mostly women worked in these operations, right?" Maggie said.

"Yes, they did—and we were all very proud of their accomplishments. They would be proud of what we are about to do as well," Grimaldi said.

"This place is unbelievable!" Tony said.

"Yes, it is. To the left, we have the explosives booth and firing range. To the right, we have the physical training area with heavy bags, workout equipment, a lap pool, and a basketball court."

"Thank you, Mr. Grimaldi," Maggie said.

"Yes, sir. Thank you very much for that," Nick said.

"You are both welcome. There is also a court outside."

The next area contained a launchpad. It was the largest area of the warehouse, and it was capable of housing five stealth fighters at once.

Grimaldi put his hand on a glass plate next to a keyboard and Grimaldi gained access to the computer. He typed in codes to slide open doors that were built into the floor. Once the doors were completely open, he pressed another key, lifting five stealth fighters from the belly of the base.

"Oh, man. They are beautiful!" Joey began to inspect one of the planes.

"You can say that again!" Nick said. "I can't wait to learn how to fly one of those."

Grimaldi walked up to Nick and put a hand on his shoulder, "You will, my friend. You will."

"What else is down there?" Tony asked.

"I'm glad you asked, Tony. That is our next stop." Grimaldi led them to a door, put his hand on a glass plate, and used the bio scanner. The door revealed another hidden elevator, and the team descended into a vault. Grimaldi used the retinal scanner to open the door. The door was ten feet tall, ten feet wide, and a foot thick.

"Very impressive, Mr. Grimaldi. No one will be able to get past this system," Maggie said.

"I hope you could," Grimaldi said.

"I'm sure I could if I had to," she replied.

"That's what I want to hear," Grimaldi said. "Let's go inside. This is where we house the weapons and explosives." The four walls were filled with handguns, machine guns, rifles, and martial arts weapons.

Nick pulled a pair of nunchucks from off of the wall. "Look what Mr. Grimaldi got for me. You definitely know my style, sir."

"Yes, I do, Nick."

There was an island in the center of the vault. Grimaldi opened the drawers, exposing ammunition, explosives, and surveillance equipment. He led the team to a secret door at the back of the vault and placed his hand on the bio scanner. Inside, the team saw a holster with two guns, stainless-steel nunchucks, a set of grappling devices, and a backpack.

"Very nice layout, Mr. Grimaldi," said Maggie.

"Thank you. We will have all the necessary weapons to win this revolution."

"What's in the lockbox?" Tony asked.

"That's the suit," Nick said.

"What suit?" Tony asked.

"Can we see this suit?" Maggie asked.

"Not at this time," Grimaldi replied. "Let's head back to the control room for now."

Once the tour was complete, Grimaldi said, "Over the past fifteen years, I have spent time in Germany exploring their infrastructure. I am very impressed with the alternatives that have been implemented over the past couple decades. Solar, wind, and other alternatives have been put into effect throughout most of Germany. I was driving along the autobahn and noticed solar panels along the areas in which we have lawn or shrubs on our expressways. They are so much more advanced than we are. Thanks to the corporate leaders who are lining their pockets with fossil fuel profits, we are behind. They won't stop until the world melts and they drown in their own greed; 98 percent of scientists agree that climate change is at an irreversible tipping point and we must act immediately to minimize this drastic change."

"I cannot believe that we are not taking advantage of these technologies," Tony said.

Grimaldi said, "The future of the planet is being threatened every day, and we must fight for change. I have developed relations with many alternative companies, and we have established our own manufacturing base in California with Leader and Grimaldi Industries. We will be manufacturing windmills, solar panels, and batteries. Also, some of these companies have been constructing windmill farms on properties in states that house the current infrastructure of power. If power and gas corporations do not agree to conform, we will create the jobs that will replace the utilities across the country. Employees of the utility corporations will not have to worry about losing their livelihoods because we will offer them positions at our new manufacturing plants before anyone else can fill them. I have been assured by these alternative companies that we can count on their participation in the conversion of the utilities if necessary."

"I am not sure that Grimaldi and Leader Industries investing in these alternatives is such a good idea," Maggie replied.

"Are you suggesting that if anyone was to discover the true identity of Nick or me that they would accuse us of conspiring to destroy the current infrastructure for our own interests?" Grimaldi asked.

"Well, yes. Whether it was true or not, that is exactly what they would accuse you of."

Nick said, "If we stand by these alternative companies and trust them to step up and produce more facilities, will they supply the necessary power?"

"That is where the problem lies. Several political leaders have asked these companies to increase operations in the past, but they are primarily gaining business in residential areas. There is very little commercial business growth. There is not enough corporate interest in alternative sources for them to be profitable enough. If we ask them to shoulder the responsibility, we will fail," Grimaldi said.

"We have no other choice but to invest in the alternatives?" Joey asked.

"Absolutely. If there was another way, I would implement it. I have considered all the possible scenarios. We must be aggressive with the alternatives."

The team agreed with his plan.

Nick said, "You have definitely put us in a position to take on these tyrants."

Maggie said, "Nick, we need to visit Germany when we have a chance. I want to see this for myself!"

PHASE 12

Training Completed

The team made its way to the vault.

Grimaldi said, "Nick, please place your hand on the scanner." A light shined, and the system recorded his fingerprints. "Now place your head in the optical receiver." The system repeated the sequence.

"That was easy enough," Nick said.

"Your iris has been accepted by the system. You now have complete access to the vault." Grimaldi led Nick through the door. "Open the box." Nick could barely contain himself. He opened the box to a glimmering reflection of the suit. Nick held the suit against his body, and it consumed his frame. "Where are the holsters for the guns, nunchucks, and grappling devices?"

"There will be no need for holsters. The suit will absorb the weapons for storage," Grimaldi said.

"What do you mean?" Nick replied.

Grimaldi handed Nick the handguns. "Where would you normally holster your weapons?"

Nick picked up the guns and went to holster them, crossing from right to left and left to right as though he had on a shoulder holster. The suit pulled the guns from his hands, automatically holstering them.

Nick asked, "Did you see that?"

Grimaldi handed him the backpack. Nick tossed it over his shoulders.

The suit camouflaged the backpack. Nick put the two sets of titanium nunchucks over his shoulders, and they morphed to the suit.

Grimaldi handed Nick one of the grappling devices.

Nick latched it onto his arm, and it disappeared from sight. Nick picked up two C-4 explosives, inserting them into the sides of the backpack. He inserted the smoke bombs and concussion grenades into the suit and placed several magazines along the side of each leg. All of the weapons disappeared into the suit.

"This is unreal!" Nick said. "I feel as though there is nothing weighing me down."

"As far as I know, this suit will give you ten times your own strength—plus your adrenaline will boost you to greater lengths," Grimaldi said. "I only tested the suit for a few weeks, so more than likely, you will discover many more abilities than I had."

Once Nick was fully geared up, Grimaldi led him out to the training area. They began with some exercises, Nick wanted to see what it felt like to be fired on by an assault rifle. He said, "What if I am shot in the face?"

"I know you did not wear the mask in the Middle East, but you will be wearing a mask as Rebel. It will cover your face completely to protect you and your identity."

"Where is the mask?" Nick searched the suit.

"The mask is in your thoughts. You have to imagine the mask. The suit will create the mask from your thoughts."

Nick imagined a clear helmet, and suddenly he was wearing it. "Whoa! This is crazy!"

Grimaldi held up a mirror, showing Nick his image. "It gives you a human likeness without revealing your identity."

"Yes, it does look good," said Nick.

"I like your choice," Grimaldi said. "Walk over to that wall and unmask yourself."

Nick imagined himself without the mask.

Grimaldi picked up a rifle and began to fire at Nick, starting at Nick's feet and working his way up to the head. As he got closer to Nick's skull, the suit automatically masked him again.

Grimaldi said, "This technology is like nothing I have ever tested in thirty years."

"That was unbelievable!" Nick said. "A little too close for comfort, though. It felt like I was being poked by the ammunition. I had no problem breathing with my face covered, and it seemed as though I didn't even have a mask on!"

"Walk over to the pool," Grimaldi asked.

Nick stood by the water, and Grimaldi pushed him into the pool. Nick dropped to the bottom of the pool and sat on the floor for nearly five minutes.

Maggie watched from the control room and ran down to the pool. "Is he okay? What are you going to do?"

Nick sprang out of the water from the bottom of the pool, flipped over Grimaldi and Maggie, and landed like a gymnast.

Nick screamed, "Oh yeah!"

"Are you crazy?" Maggie said.

"No, I am invincible!" he replied.

Maggie looked at Nick and asked, "How the hell did you hold your breath for so long?"

"I wasn't holding my breath. The suit fed me oxygen somehow. I was breathing normally. The suit has some type of gill system."

"I thought you were drowning!" Maggie said.

"Calm down, Maggie. I'm fine!"

"Please settle down. There is so much more training to be done." Grimaldi brought Nick and Maggie to the basketball court. "Do you think you can make a basket?" He handed a ball to Nick.

Nick laughed, picked up the ball, and shot it. The ball hit the ceiling. "What the hell just happened?"

"You have to learn to control your emotions, Nick. You must remember that the suit will give you at least ten times more strength and athleticism. As well as your adrenaline. The higher your heart rate and emotions, the stronger you will become."

"What if I strike someone in hand-to-hand combat?"

"You could possibly kill the average person, but a trained soldier or a professional fighter may be able to take more force from the suit."

"You want to play some one-on-one?" Maggie asked.

"You should spend at least a half an hour a day training one-on-one with Maggie for control purposes. Just remember to take it easy with the rough stuff."

Maggie laughed and stared at Nick. "You're going down!"

Maggie beat Nick 12–3.

Nick said, "I was getting pumped up to play, but it was working against me."

Maggie laughed and said, "Maybe you'll have better luck tomorrow, Rebel!"

"I'm going to take this suit off and beat you right now!"

The next test was practicing with the guns and nunchucks on the targets and the heavy bags.

Grimaldi said, "You will have access to a large array of weapons on the base as well as in each fighter and vehicle. You will carry these primary guns at all times. These are smart handguns with advanced computer technology. They were designed to be multifaceted with a few capabilities and can fire any standard round. The barrel conforms to whatever round has been placed in the magazine. This button at the end of the slide, where the hammer usually would be on a revolver, is the settings key. The first setting is for tranquilizer darts. One tranquilizer dart will render the average person unconscious for about an hour, but a trained soldier of a larger size may not go down at all. You may have to fire a second dart in that case. The second setting is for concussion bullets, which are similar to mini-concussion grenades. They are the size of a nine-millimeter casing. These should be used for larger opponents. The effects will cause dizziness and then unconsciousness. This ammunitions was created to avoid death—unless you fire too many tranquilizer darts or concussion bullets at an attacker."

Nick asked, "Does anyone else have these weapons?"

"Not to my knowledge, Nick, but you never know what you'll run into in the field. The third setting is for standard shells, and the fourth setting is for mini-rockets that are electronically linked to the targeting system on your weapon. You will attach a rocket to the muzzle, aim at a specific target, and pull the trigger to set the tracking. Once you let go of the trigger, the rocket will launch. Whether the target moves or not, the weapon will track it and destroy it."

"Impressive! I've never seen anything like this," Nick said.

"Let's start with the heavy bags and nunchucks."

They went over to the 150-pound heavy bags, and Nick asked, "Why are the bags hanging like this?"

"You should mix up your attacks on each of the bags. If you focus on one bag at a time, you will tear it to shreds," Grimaldi said.

Grimaldi set a timer for three minutes, and Nick began to throw punches, kicks, elbows, and knees at the bags.

The team watched in amazement as the timer went off.

Grimaldi asked, "Do you understand what I mean now?"

"Yes, I do," Nick said. "I almost knocked a few of the bags off their mounts!"

"Remind me not to piss you off, Nick," Joey said.

"Try the nunchucks on one of the bags," Grimaldi said.

Nick pulled out the nunchucks and warmed up with several strikes. He focused his attack on one of the bags, unleashing several combinations. By the eighth combination, the nunchucks were beginning to tear off parts of the bag. The bottom half of the bag went flying across the room, and Nick screamed, "These chucks are amazing!"

Grimaldi said, "Do not use them against an opponent who is not wearing armor. These nunchucks are made of titanium and could kill a man with one blow. You do not want to kill anyone!"

"Agreed. I will be very cautious in my attacks," Nick said. "I understand that this is to be approached as a diplomatic operation—and that force only should be used if necessary."

"Yes," said Grimaldi. "Only if they leave you no other alternative. Are you ready to test your handguns?"

"Yes, sir. I feel good about my timing with the heavy bags and nunchucks."

The men walked over to the firing range.

"Hand me one of your guns please," Grimaldi said. "These weapons have scanning capabilities, and they will only fire to specific handprints. You'll see that this is like no other weapon." Grimaldi released one of the magazines from the handgun, "The left side has tranquilizer darts. The other half has concussion bullets. The tranq darts are designed to knock an average-sized person unconscious for approximately one hour. The concussion bullets will be used for larger threats, causing the same outcome."

Grimaldi returned the magazine into the gun and handed it to Nick. He took aim on one of the targets and set the weapon on tranq. Nick emptied the magazine on the silhouette, placing a perfect group in the center. "I like it," Nick said. "Very smooth trigger pressure and very accurate." He switched the weapon to concussion and stepped over to the next booth. He fired twice, tearing the silhouette to pieces. "Very powerful!"

"Use this artillery in moderation."

"I understand. One dart for the average size-person—and one bullet for the larger ones."

Working with the weapons was much easier than the basketball court. He had this one under control within the day.

Grimaldi showed up the next morning, knocking on the door.

Maggie said, "Good morning, Mr. G. How are you today?"

"I am fine. How are you guys?"

"Nick is just getting out of the shower. He said he feels great today. I'm doing well too."

Nick walked out of the bathroom and said, "Hey, Mr. Grimaldi. How are you today?"

"I am fine, Nick. Maggie just gave me a nickname—Mr. G. I like the sound of that."

"I like it too!" Nick said.

"Are you ready to begin training today?" Mr. Grimaldi asked.

"Yes, sir!" Nick suited up and met Grimaldi in the training area.

Grimaldi handed Nick a C-4 pack explosive. "Go into the explosives booth, press the ignition button once, plant it on the wall, and turn your back to it."

Nick entered the room and set the timer for ten seconds. The room filled with smoke and flames, but Nick exited the room—unharmed.

"Are you okay?" Grimaldi asked.

"That was unbelievable!" Nick replied. "The suit tightened up like a cocoon. The powers of the suit changed my vision. It was like I was wearing military optics. I saw the explosive burst into a thousand pieces. I saw you watching me. I could see everything clearly."

"You are beginning to realize powers I never had," Grimaldi said. "Also, if you were to face the blast, it would make no difference. The suit will protect you either way, Nick."

Nick inspected himself for injuries. "Not a scratch."

As he held another C-4 pack, Grimaldi said, "If you press the button on the C-4 pack once, you will have ten seconds until detonation. Twice, twenty seconds. Three times, thirty seconds. If you hold the button down, the timer will run quickly—up to as many hours as you need. You must wear a proximity ring at all times to stop the detonator from exploding. If anyone else tampers with the timer, the explosive will detonate immediately."

"I got it, sir."

The next obstacle would be to head out to the woods for a night operation.

Grimaldi showed Nick a map of the terrain. "Nick, I set up a test course for you, starting here at the black dot and ending at this red X. We are going to see how effectively you can navigate the targets and terrain in the dark. Choose one of the weapons on the table."

Nick studied the map and decided to use an assault rifle. There was only a partial moon. He masked himself and began to maneuver into the tree line. A fifty-caliber gun fired at him, striking him in the chest.

In the earpiece, Grimaldi said, "You're dead. Continue on!"

Nick was frustrated by his lack of awareness as well as by being taken out so easily in his first attempt. On the positive side, he had received an adrenaline rush from the attack. He immediately noticed that his senses were enhanced. He was able to see clearly in the dark after being fired upon. The suit used the energy from the gunfire to heighten his emotions. Using his newly acquired senses, he suddenly heard things in the brush. Through the night-vision lenses on the mask, he saw a rabbit running through the woods. He saw the rabbit go into its den and watched it settle into the earth.

As he moved on the path, Nick could hear a large weapon behind a tree. He scanned the area and avoided the attack. Nick decided to dismantle the weapon from above. He leaped into the air, climbed the tree like a monkey, and looked down at an M-60 assault rifle on a tripod. He dropped a pair of his nunchucks, and the weapon began to fire. Nick descended on the weapon, tearing the ammunition belt from its feed. The weapon was rendered useless.

Grimaldi replied, "Very impressive, Nick."

Nick became faster and was able to sense every little movement. He could sense everything in the dark like it was daylight.

As he climbed a steep incline, Nick did not notice a thin nylon filament across his path. He tripped the line, unexpectedly setting off a trap. He could feel the line and hear the pin begin to release from a Claymore explosive. Nick reacted with a burst of energy and quickly traversed the steep incline. He was able to avoid the explosion and the shrapnel.

Nick reached high ground and saw a wide ditch filled with bubbling tar. The moat was sixty feet wide, and Nick could not see an end on either side. He didn't remember seeing it on the map. He wasn't sure if he could go around the moat because it had a sheer rock face to his right and a heavy hedgerow leading around the bend. Nick thought about turning back and finding another way around. He headed back down the hill and saw a series of explosions. An artillery barrage was progressing up the hill. As the explosions came closer, Nick ran to the top of the hill, taking a life-or-death leap across the moat without getting a drop of tar on his suit.

He landed on the other side of the moat and heard the next trap. He scanned the area and was able to see through the boulders as though he had X-ray vision. He could see two Gatling guns on tracks. If he cleared each boulder, the guns would spray the clearing with lead. Before the weapons could fire on him, Nick threw two C-4 packs at them. With a spectacular explosion, he eliminated the threat.

As he headed down the path, he could see the finish line.

Grimaldi said, "Very good. You can return to base now."

"You have a hell of an imagination, Mr. G. Where did you get the hot tar from?"

"We set these courses for our Black Operations testing. We have never quite set a course so extreme though. I had to get creative because the suit is like no other technology we have come across. We will push this suit to the limit!"

"This suit is spectacular, Mr. G."

"I was stunned by that jump," Grimaldi said.

"I can't wait to see what you have planned for me next!" Nick said.

Nick entered the vault and thought, *I wonder if I can fit the weapons and the suit in the box to transfer everything to and from future destinations.* He tried to fit the whole arrangement in the lockbox. The weapons and ammunition fit in the box. Grimaldi had the lockbox customized to fit all the equipment. The lockbox was encased in a super-lightweight titanium alloy. After Nick secured the suit, he met Maggie and Grimaldi in the control room.

Nick said, "I can't believe how tremendous this technology is! I feel like we have a great chance of succeeding in our revolution!"

"I was watching you on the training course," Maggie said. "This technology is like nothing I have ever seen. I was monitoring your vitals through the biometric system we put in the suit. They showed next to no acceleration in your heart rate. It was as if you were going for a jog. Some of the other readings showed enjoyment instead of fear."

"I was having fun!" Nick replied.

"I think Nick has this under control," Maggie said.

The next day, Nick started his training with the grappling devices.

Grimaldi asked Nick to release one of them from his arm. "When you put them on, the suit will absorb them to protect them from damage."

"How much weight can they hold?" Nick asked.

Grimaldi took out a thin line and said, "This one thin line, similar to a fishing line, has a ten-thousand-pound failure rating. Once it is woven to full size, it will have a similar width to a USB cable—with more than twenty times that strength.

"Awesome." Nick tested the weight of the device. "They are so light."

"These devices are very versatile. You will be able to fire these lines with multiple attachments and ranges. They will have their own built-in laser-range finder and material analyzer so that each device can find its range and know what it needs to penetrate or grab on to easily. To operate these lines, we have implemented a low-frequency voice-command signal that is synced to your com system. Once you activate the lines, you have to develop certain hand and wrist actions to release the lines. The tips can change shape into any configuration, and the materials analyzer can determine which end will be needed, whether it be a grappling hook, a piton, a flat magnet, or a super-advanced head with the properties of a gecko's foot that will stick to any surface. This will allow you to be very aggressive without breaking certain surfaces. We have been working on this device for years. We developed the prototype a few years ago. You will be the first in the field to have this technology.

"No one has used it in the field before?" Nick said. "Extraordinary! I can't wait to test it out myself!"

Nick reattached the device to his arm and made his way to the far end of the warehouse. He looked up to the ceiling, raised his arm straight up, tapped on his palm, and fired a line at a steel beam. He gripped the line and tested its strength. Once he felt confident in the security of the line, Nick opened his palm, triggering the device to recede. He was quickly propelled to the top of the ceiling. Nick hung there for a couple of seconds, looking down at the platform. He was suspended in the air. Nick took a deep breath, reached his other arm toward the next beam, and fired another line. He began to advance from beam to beam. As he gained confidence in the grappling devices, Nick began to alternate lines between each device, traveling back and forth throughout the training facility. After an hour, Nick stopped for a break.

Grimaldi asked, "What do think, Nick?"

"The ceiling is much higher than it looks from the surface, but I'm getting the hang of it."

"The hooks can penetrate rock and release easily with specific muscle movements that you will learn."

"This is amazing! With a couple of weeks of practice, I should have this down pat."

The next test would be facing Maggie in basketball. Nick said, "I have a game plan for you today!" He began to post her up, low to the basket. He spun off of her and dunked the ball. Using this move, Nick scored three baskets in a row.

Grimaldi said, "This plan is not going to help you with your control of the suit, Nick."

Maggie said, "Finesse, Nick. We're looking for finesse. No dunking—and no easy layups. Just pure shooting. Get on the perimeter and try to make a shot, Rebel!"

Nick went to the top of the key, squared up, and shot one in her face. Brick!

She rebounded the ball, chuckled, and took control of the contest, beating Nick by seven points. As they left the court, Maggie said, "Don't worry, Rebel. You'll get the hang of it soon enough!"

Grimaldi delivered a military-grade ATV that resembled Nick's GTO. The ATV was painted in dark-cherry red with black accents, and it had a black interior.

"The armor on this vehicle is nearly explosive-proof as well as being fully loaded with weapons. It's like an advanced military vehicle."

"You have outdone yourself with this one, Mr. G! I'm very impressed with the design." He took the ATV out for a spin, testing it on one of the courses for about an hour. "This is the most incredible vehicle I have ever driven. I can't wait to use it."

Grimaldi said, "I'm not sure that we will need this vehicle, but you never know what will happen in a revolution. I had it built just in case."

"I understand that we will be using the stealth fighters for the majority of the revolution, but I would love to use the ATV sometime. Do you think we could get a customized license plate?"

"Sure. What do you want it to say? Grimaldi asked.

"The Judge."

Grimaldi grinned. "Are you ready to test the jet boots?"

Nick nodded, and they walked over to the launchpad. A flat metal ski-like object was on the platform.

"That is the retracted position of the boot. Once you insert your foot, the boot will conform to your foot."

Nick put his left foot into one of the boots. It quickly adjusted to his foot, securing its way up to his lower calf area and locking onto his foot. Nick had the boots locked within seconds.

Grimaldi said, "I have designed this slim backpack that will propel your wings so that you can paraglide and free-fall. You will have voice command for this option. The backpack will also carry a parachute, which you will need for safety purposes until you perfect your flying skills with the jet boots."

"I feel like a spy with this gear," Nick said.

"Are you ready?" Grimaldi asked.

"Yes, sir."

Nick began to test the limits of the jet boots. At first he ascended awkwardly, nearly crashing into several trees. Eventually, though, he improved.

Grimaldi said, "Do not fly too high, Nick!"

"Okay, sir."

Nick flew around the city for an hour, looking down at the beautiful view. He maneuvered through buildings and leaped from rooftop to rooftop. Once he began to feel more confident, he pushed the limits of the jet boots, ignoring Grimaldi's order. Nick reached an altitude of thirty thousand feet. Unfortunately, he had also reached the limit of his fuel supply. The boots began to sputter, and the engines died. Nick began to free-fall, but he did not panic because he had the parachute.

Maggie shouted, "Grimaldi, his boots are out of fuel."

"What's going on up there, Nick?" Grimaldi asked.

"I'm guessing that I ran the fuel out," Nick replied.

"How high did you go?" Grimaldi asked.

"Probably a little too high," Nick replied.

As he began to reach terminal velocity, Nick relaxed. His descent began to slow, and webbing extended from his wrists to his ankles. The suit transformed into an advanced wing-suit. Nick began to take control of his descent, releasing his parachute with perfect timing. He navigated successfully with his newfound capabilities.

After a few days of training, Nick was land without the parachute.

"It's time to take Phantom-1 out for a spin, Nick," said Grimaldi. "If we are going to take on these powerful corporations, you must be prepared to travel from one end of the country to the other. You will be visiting many different states as we take on our enemies. You must be prepared to fight against other aircraft in case the corporate leaders have an arsenal to match us."

"Understood. I'll prepare for any possibility," Nick replied.

Grimaldi said, "You will use the autopilot for a couple of days. The fighters are set up by remote from the base as well as your voice commands."

"Great. I'll fly out to Lake Superior. There's little chance that anyone will see me out in the middle of the largest lake in the world."

"Our stealth fighters are the quickest jets in the world. They are modified to be more effective than the current model that is used by the military. Three designers assisted me in the creation of this advanced technology. They were curious about why we hadn't sold the fighters to the military. I had them sign a confidentiality clause, restricting them from making this technology public. I have foreseen a day when we could use these fighters to gain the advantage we need against certain powers that be."

"Do you believe the government may get involved?" Nick asked.

"That is exactly why. We cannot trust anyone."

"I understand. What other features are on these fighters?"

"They are also loaded with thirty-millimeter cannons, state-of-the-art missiles, upgraded armor, and cloaking technology. The fighters also include vertical short takeoff and landing capabilities—V/STOL—which will allow you to ascend and descend vertically like a helicopter. Also, they are capable of underwater functions."

"No way. Like a submarine?" Nick said.

"Yes, like a sub. They can open up from the underbelly to pick you up and drop you off on the fly with a specially advanced vacuum system. You will be as safe as possible with this technology."

"I'm a bit nervous, but I'm ready to go," Nick said.

"Can you go to the rooftop and wait for a minute, Nick?" Grimaldi asked.

Nick walked over to the elevator, making his way to the rooftop. As he looked up, Phantom-1 quickly descended upon him and swallowed him into the cockpit. "This is what it feels like to be vacuumed."

Grimaldi said, "Would you like some company?"

"No, sir. I got this one," Nick commanded Phantom-1 to fly out to Lake Superior.

Grimaldi joined Maggie in the control room. "Maggie, we need to refer to Nick as Rebel while in the suit, especially when we're communicating with him via radio."

Maggie said, "Control to Rebel."

"Go for Rebel."

"Can you read me?"

"Loud and clear, Control." Rebel began his departure under the cover of darkness. Heading north over Lake Michigan, Rebel felt comfortable enough to take over the controls, slowly maneuvering over the dark waters.

Maggie noticed that Rebel had disengaged the autopilot. "He has already taken control of the Phantom, Mr. G."

Grimaldi said, "Control-1 to Rebel."

"Go for Rebel."

"Are you positive that you are ready to take the controls so soon?"

"Rebel to Control-1, I think I can do this." He practiced basic flight for an hour. He began to move faster with every circuit, gaining confidence, and ascended to the clouds.

Grimaldi said, "Control-1 to Rebel."

"Go for Rebel."

"Careful—not too high," Grimaldi said.

Rebel replied, "What is my flight envelope?"

Grimaldi said, "The limit is fifty-thousand feet or eight miles. Keep an eye on your instrument panel for the warning signs."

Within minutes, Rebel was at the peak of the flight envelope. The instrument panel lit up, and the siren warned Rebel that he needed to pull back. He lowered his throttle and leveled out, ending up in Canadian territory.

Grimaldi said, "Descend below radar level so that you are not detected by the military."

Unfortunately, a couple of freighters had seen Rebel's safety beacons and reported the sighting to the Coast Guard, which relayed the message to NORAD.

"Too late!" Rebel said. Two F-16 fighters were approaching on radar.

"Do not let them see you! Cloak now!" Grimaldi said.

Rebel wanted to have some fun with the fighters and decided not to cloak.

The lead fighter said, "This is Lieutenant Lombardo of the United States Air Force. Unidentified aircraft, please identify yourself. You are approaching US airspace!"

Rebel began to accelerate toward the fighters, diving quickly below them and barely missing one of them.

Lieutenant Lombardo called to his wingman, "Fire!"

The Phantom was much too quick.

"Pursue with caution, North-Star-2." The F-16s did a 180, keeping their distance.

Rebel headed toward the western tip of Lake Superior, two hundred feet above the water. "It appears that the UFO has no intent to harm. Move in closer to confirm what type of aircraft we're dealing with." The F-16s proceeded with caution.

"North-Star-1 to base, unmarked, unidentified aircraft is attempting to flee. Not sure of its intentions. We are in pursuit. Permission to fire?"

"Take the threat out if necessary, North-Star-1."

The fighters were able to bridge the gap and continued in hot pursuit.

Rebel pulled a 180, headed east, and took the fighters by surprise. He accelerated, full throttle, and blasted through the sky.

The F-16s had trouble keeping up with the Phantom. Rebel was enjoying the chase while testing the Phantom's capabilities.

"This is Lieutenant Lombardo of the United States Air force. Identify yourself—or we will be forced to fire on you!"

Rebel would not reply, attempting to avoid their attacks.

Lombardo said, "I have a shot! Missile away!"

Phantom's defensive system alarm and lights began to go off in the cockpit, warning Rebel of the attack. Rebel fired his flares and shifted hard left, evading the attack as the flares destroyed the missile.

North Star-2 fired its cannons at Rebel, hitting its target.

The Phantom was not damaged by the attack. Rebel pulled up, excelling full throttle and outran the F-16s. He flew to Hudson Bay, blasting into full supersonic power and leaving the F-16s as a distant memory.

The lead fighter said, "North-Star-1 to Command."

"Go for Command."

"We lost him … cannot pursue … aircraft too quick!"

"Return to base, Lieutenant."

When Rebel returned to base, Grimaldi met him on the landing pad. "Nick, why did you allow the fighters to see you?"

Nick jumped down from the Phantom. "Even if they reported what they had seen, no one would believe them. They would sound crazy!"

"I was more concerned with them shooting you down! You are a rookie pilot!"

"I realize that I violated their airspace, but if worse came to worst, I would have let Phantom-1 take over the controls."

"We needed to test the cloaking device in actual formations. I realize the Phantom jets are stealthy and—for the most part—undetectable to radar, but you cost us precious time!"

"When the radar attempts to detect the aircraft, the stealth technology can deflect and absorb some of the radar, but how does the cloaking device function?"

"First of all, it has a special radiation-absorbing ability so that any stray radar that would have been deflected will be completely absorbed into the device. It uses that to help power itself, and it can project a false radar image like a decoy up to several hundred miles from your location. It also controls the special skin on the Phantom—like with your suit. We replicated, as close as we could, the cephalopod function of the suit. The miniaturized super-computer in the fighters is designed to use several cameras that mimic the surrounding area to disguise the fighters from any onlookers."

"I'm sorry to have worried you, Mr. G. I promise to test the cloaking device tomorrow."

The next day, Nick joined Maggie for another game of one-on-one. He was getting better with his shot, and she only beat him by four points.

Nick said, "Get ready to lose tomorrow!"

"Talk is cheap, baby!" Maggie laughed and headed to the control room to work on the computer system.

Nick moved to his training on the grappling line. He swung from beam to beam for about an hour.

Grimaldi yelled, "Looking great!"

Nick looked down to acknowledge him, lost control, and fell to the ground.

Maggie hurried over to him. "Are you hurt?"

"Just my pride."

"You have to stay focused!" Grimaldi said.

Nick said "Sorry," as he got up and went back to training.

Grimaldi asked, "Are you ready to take Phantom-1 back up north?"

"Yes, sir."

Grimaldi said, "This time, we want you to fly at a lower altitude to be detected visually by the ships and civilians. They will undoubtedly contact the military. Then you will use the cloaking device instead of running from them!"

Nick headed out, and Maggie and Grimaldi went to the control room to establish radio contact.

"Control to Rebel, can you read me?"

"Loud and clear, Control!" Rebel flew his patterns for an hour.

"Control-1 to Rebel."

"Go for Rebel."

"We need you to fly over some highly populated areas. Head toward Chicago—you will definitely be seen by the time you reach it."

"Yes, sir!" Nick said.

Just before Rebel reached Chicago, he detected four fighters on his radar. They were heading toward him. Rebel monitored their communications.

"Windy-1 to Command, we are approaching the reported location of the unidentified aircraft."

"Confirm a visual sighting before taking action, Windy-1."

"Copy that, Command."

Rebel headed downtown to practice his stealth-cloaking modes.

"Control-1 to Rebel. We have four fighters on approach to your location. You only have one minute before visual contact. Ready yourself to cloak."

"I'm going to test Phantom-1's maneuverability and camera technology between the buildings. When the fighters get too close for comfort, I'll cloak."

Grimaldi said, "I like your plan. I don't think they will fire on you due to the civilian traffic. Just remember to use the autopilot if they start firing at you."

Rebel circled over downtown and waited for the fighters.

"Windy-1 to Command. We have nothing on radar, but we do have a visual on an unidentified object."

"Attempt to make contact and request identification."

Rebel kept visual contact with the fighters as they approached. He began to take evasive action through the steel-and-glass canyon of the Windy City.

"This is United States Air Force Central Defense. Unmarked aircraft flying over the city of Chicago, you have no markings. You must identify yourself immediately—or we will force you to land!"

Rebel began evasive maneuvers, dodging the fighters for a few minutes, and headed out to Lake Michigan.

Maggie said, "Control to Rebel."

"Go for Rebel."

"Why are deviating from the plan again?"

"Need to test the submarine capabilities before I finish with the full cloak test."

"You wanna let us in on these plans next time?" Maggie said.

"Sorry about that. Gotta go."

"We have the unidentified aircraft over Lake Michigan. It will not respond to radio contact and is fleeing. Request permission to fire!"

"Take that bastard down, Windy-1!"

Windy-1 fired on Rebel, but the Phantom's defense system warned of the incoming missile and automatically fired decoy flares. Rebel plunged in to the lake for cover. As the Phantom submerged, the missile followed the flare and exploded. While submerged, Rebel turned back toward the city.

"Command, we are twenty miles out from shore. Send the Coast Guard out for recovery. The unmarked aircraft crashed into the lake. There is no debris on the surface. It appears that that the pilot blacked out and lost control."

The fighters circled the area and headed back to the base.

Rebel blasted out of the water a couple of miles inland on his way back to the city.

"Windy-3 to Command, you are not going to believe this—unmarked aircraft has emerged from the lake and is heading toward the city!"

"Command to Windy-3, do not let that UFO out of your sight!"

The fighters accelerated as Rebel advanced toward his objective. He maneuvered through the building as the fighters scrambled to catch up with him.

Windy-1 ordered the fighters to split up and flank Phantom-1.

Windy-2 reported, "I have him in the northeast quadrant!"

The other fighters converged on his position, but Rebel began to retreat.

"Windy-1 to Windy-2. Follow me to the east of that brown building. Windy-3 and 4, flank to the west. We have him this time!"

Rebel cloaked at his next turn.

"Command to Windy-1, Do you have visual or not?"

"Negative, Command … we lost the aircraft."

Rebel used the Phantom's V/STOL capabilities to hover a couple of hundred meters above the fighters.

Rebel said, "They're heading back to base. That was great! I played with them. They thought they had me at that last turn. Mission accomplished!"

A few weeks later, Nick finally beat Maggie on the court. After all of the intense work, he was ready to begin the revolution.

PHASE 13

The Arrival

Nick called for a team meeting. Everyone was confident about the results of the training and felt prepared for the revolution.

Grimaldi said, "I have ordered the MRI and ultrasound machines in case of an injury during battle. Dr. McKenzie will be able to check everything in case of an emergency."

"You really think we'll need that?" Nick asked.

"I think that's a good idea," Maggie replied.

Grimaldi said, "Better safe than sorry. I feel ready to begin the revolution!"

Joey stood up and said, "I have been in a military setting for half of my life. I feel that everyone here is prepared. I'm ready to kick some corporate ass!" He pounded his fist on a table.

"Yeah, me too!" Tony said. "I am sick and tired of these people running our country into the ground! Let's do this!"

Maggie said, "I have been in high-pressure battles on the basketball court, leading my teams throughout the years, and I am very competitive. However, I've never experienced this type of intensity. I learned a great deal with you all. I am ready to take on these oligarchies!"

Nick made his way to the center of the control room. "I want to thank all of you for dedicating yourselves to this revolution. Most people do not have the strength of character that is necessary to even think about attempting such a great feat. I'm proud to call you my family, and I know that we will prevail!"

"Very good," Grimaldi said. "This is the type of energy we need to win this revolution. Does anyone have any questions?"

Nick said, "No, sir. I'm ready!"

"I'm ready too!" Maggie replied.

Tony and Joey nodded.

"Okay. We will begin tomorrow afternoon," Grimaldi said.

The next morning, Grimaldi asked everyone to meet in the control room. "Nick, I feel that it is important to have some type of public introduction before you visit the corporate leaders. We cannot just attack them under the radar and allow the corporations to accuse you of being a terrorist."

Nick said, "Yes, I understand completely. What did you have in mind?"

"I don't know if any of you have been watching the news, but there has been a pattern of bank robberies over the past six months in Chicago. They occur every four to six weeks."

Nick said, "I heard about those animals. They have been killing the security guards before exiting the scene of the crime. It's a shame. The security guards make next to no money. These guys are sick, and we need to stop them now."

"Maggie has already analyzed the projections in our system. They show the patterns that have been used over the past six months."

Maggie said, "I have calculated where the next robbery will take place. The criminals are due to hit again soon. There are three banks within a five-mile radius that are estimated to be the next targets within the up in coming week or so."

Grimaldi said, "We will be able to tap into all the security systems throughout the country with this technology. We will begin to monitor the systems immediately. Nick, you will be orbiting the projected area until the robbers strike again."

Tony said, "Once you take these bank robbers down, it will give the public a positive perception of Rebel before we attack the larger issues."

Maggie said, “You must be very careful during the rescue. Do not to allow any civilians to be injured!”

Grimaldi said, “Yes, Nick. Please be very careful. It could be bad press if you kill one of the bank robbers. It would definitely be fatal for the revolution if a civilian died during a mission!”

Nick replied, “I understand. I promise to be responsible during the missions. I’ll do my best never to put a civilian in danger!”

Nick geared up and said, “I’m ready to head out.”

“Are you nervous?” Maggie moved in for a hug.

“No. I feel prepared, confident, and ready to introduce Rebel to the world.”

“This is it, Nick,” Grimaldi said. “Remember your training—and you’ll be just fine.”

“Thank you. I promise not to let you down.” Nick replied.

As Rebel approached the target zone, he thought about his objective. The economy was in decline, and crime rates had been increasing since 2005. There had been at least one bank robbery attempt a week in each major city.

Rebel had been hovering overhead for a couple of hours without any activity.

Maggie said, “Control to Rebel.”

“Go for Rebel.”

“Rebel, apparently nothing is happening today. If they were going to rob a bank, they most likely would have done so by now. You should bring it in.”

“Copy that, Control. I’m headin’ back.”

When Rebel was halfway back to base, Maggie said, “Control to Rebel.”

“Go for Rebel.”

“An alarm just went off at Commerce Bank at 21352 Grand Boulevard. I programmed the address into Phantom-1. We have a bank robbery in progress!”

“Got it. Phantom-1 has the controls,” Nick said.

Rebel arrived at the scene within ten minutes. The bank was on the first floor of a four-story complex with windows in front and street access.

"Rebel to Control."

"Go for Control."

"Looks like the police beat me."

"Yeah, we have the feeds. I've programed the layout on your monitor." Maggie had hacked into the camera feeds. "Rebel, there are four bank robbers wearing clown makeup. They have ten customers and four employees as hostages."

After viewing the floor plan, Rebel said, "I have a plan."

"What are you thinking?"

"I'm going to land in front of the bank. I'll walk up to the commanding officer and introduce myself. I'll explain that I'm here to assist them—and then I'll storm past the police line, blast open the front door, overtake the robbers, and save the day."

"Sure, no problem!" Maggie replied. "Be careful, Rebel."

When Phantom-1 landed in front of the bank, the barricades had been set up to keep pedestrians clear. Bystanders and the police stared as Rebel exited from the underbelly of the aircraft in his silver suit.

"My name is Rebel, sir. I have been sent to take care of these men once and for all!"

The commanding officer asked, "Who sent you?"

"Someone from above," Rebel reached in his backpack and tossed a disc toward the entrance. It slid across the street and magnetized to the lock on the door, exploding the doors and breaking them open.

The hostages screamed and cried in fear.

Rebel charged through the entrance, pulling out both pistols and firing tranquilizer darts at the criminals. Rebel was able to hit three of them with ease, rendering them unconscious. However, one of the assailants slipped the attack and sprinted for cover.

Rebel pulled out a pair of nunchucks and threw them at the fleeing robber. They hit him in the back of the head, knocking him unconscious.

Rebel turned to check on the hostages and breathed a sigh of relief, confident that he had the scene under control.

Maggie said, "Nick! Behind you!"

He whirled around just in time to see the barrel of a shotgun firing on him.

The hostages screamed in fear.

The suit absorbed the blast, and Rebel felt the power surge as his suit turned dark red. Rebel's adrenaline spiked, and he rushed the robber before he could rack another slug into the chamber. Rebel swept the attacker off of his feet with a forearm to the head, knocking the man unconscious. Rebel cuffed them all with zip ties and asked the hostages and bank employees if they were okay. They were unharmed and began to settle down.

Rebel notified the police that the scene was secure. The media had arrived just after Rebel entered the bank, and they rushed to bombard him with questions. "Who are you? Who sent you? Where are you from? Are you with a secret government agency? How were you able to withstand that shotgun blast? Are you wearing a vest? How come there are no markings on your aircraft? Are you from another planet?"

Rebel asked them to calm down. "I cannot answer all of your questions at this time. My name is Rebel. I am here to rid this country of the corruption and greed that is destroying both the planet and the American dream. I am not here to chase after common criminals such as these bank robbers. These crimes are the concern of local police and FBI. I decided to get involved with this particular case because these bank robbers have been on a six-month killing spree. They were killing innocent security guards. My concern is with the more insidious criminals—the white-collar criminals who have been at the forefront of the middle-class decline and the climate-change issues we've been experiencing for decades. Corporations have been secretly destroying this country for more than forty years. The oligarchy will soon be dealing with me!"

The media started yelling, "What do you mean by white-collar criminals? Which corporations are you talking about? Who is going to be hearing from you?"

Rebel would not answer them. He returned to his fighter, and within seconds, he was out of sight.

Grimaldi turned on the evening news. The reports were mostly positive. Some reporters were speculating that Rebel worked with a secret government agency, and others believed he was an alien.

One of the witnesses from the bank said, "One of the robbers shot Rebel in the face, and he just stood there like it was nothing! I didn't see any bulletproof vest bulging under his suit."

Another witness said, "Rebel is a hero—regardless of where he is from!"

The bank manager said, "Rebel saved our lives. I have been in the banking industry for over three decades and have seen quite a few robberies in my time. I don't care if he is an alien or where he is from. All I know is that this was the most incredible rescue I have ever witnessed!"

Grimaldi said, "I feel that we should wait a few days for the news to travel throughout the world. We can see how the people react to Rebel's actions. We may gain more popularity or receive negative input that will prepare us for future situations."

Nick said, "I suggest mapping out a plan for the East Coast Power Corporation. Maggie, please set up a fake investor meeting with them."

Maggie said, "I'll look up some European billionaire who is involved in an electric corporation in Germany and use him as a front. We'll track the CEO's location so I will know when they are available to negotiate."

PHASE 14

The Revolution Begins

The team gathered in the control room to initiate the operation.

"Okay, everyone, we will be making our first mark in the revolution today. Rebel will visit with the East Coast Power Corporation. Later this week, he'll visit their West Coast leader. He will explain our position and encourage them to join with the alternative energy companies. If they refuse, we will be forced to eliminate the current infrastructure, replacing it with an alternative."

"Sounds pretty extreme," Joey replied with a smile. "I like it!"

Grimaldi said, "I have created a company with an anonymous owner. The CEO of this company is a retired business owner I have known for twenty years. He has been gathering investment funds and donations from the corporate leaders Nick and I met in Las Vegas. They have agreed to invest in the reformation of corporate America. When the time comes, we will have the support of these allies."

Tony said, "What will we be needing the company for?"

Nick said, "If we must destroy the infrastructure, we will need to supply generators to the homes and businesses that do not have backup power. Also, when it's time for alternatives, we will need investors."

Maggie said, "Let's hope it doesn't come to that."

Joey and Nick prepped the Phantom for takeoff, and the team reviewed the plan.

"Okay, is everyone ready?" Nick asked.

"Ready," Maggie said.

"We are thoroughly prepared, Maggie. There's nothing to be concerned about," Grimaldi said.

"He's right, Maggie. Nick is going to be great!" Tony gave Nick a hug. "Just keep your cool. Make it clear what you are negotiating and respond as though you are giving them no choice in the matter."

"Nick, you'll fine," Grimaldi said.

"You got this, Nick," said Joey.

"Thank you all for everything. I'm ready to kick some corporate ass!"

Maggie embraced him and kissed him. "Be careful—no macho stuff."

Nick said, "I promise. You have nothing to worry about."

The fifty-story headquarters had golden archways throughout the entrances, multiple waterfalls, and expensive landscaping.

"Rebel to Control."

"Go for Control."

"How many companies reside in this structure?"

"They are the sole tenant, Rebel," Maggie said.

"This place is mammoth. These corporations should share the wealth with their employees instead of building empires to house their operations." Approaching the rooftop, he landed in cloak mode.

Maggie tapped in to the building's security system and camera feeds. "Ready to proceed?"

"Ready," Rebel said.

Maggie said, "A security guard is about to turn the corner."

Rebel hugged the wall, using the suit's powers to blend in with scenery.

The guard walked by without a clue.

"You're clear, Rebel."

"That went well." Rebel smiled.

"Amazing," Maggie replied.

Rebel made his way to the assistant's desk and said, "Hello. I have a ten o'clock appointment with Mr. Davidson."

"Aren't you the alien who stopped the bank robbers in Chicago? What planet are you from? Can I have your autograph? I am a huge fan!"

"I'm sorry. I don't have time to answer all of your questions. Maybe some other time. Can you please let Mr. Davidson know that I'm here?"

"Of course. I'm sorry, Rebel." The assistant immediately called Mr. Davidson to explain that Rebel was the investor with whom he had the appointment.

Mr. Davidson said, "Have Rebel wait. I need you to come into my office."

"Excuse me, Rebel. Mr. Davidson asked me to see him first."

"Sure, no problem."

Mr. Davidson had been with a dozen corporations over four decades. He had white hair and black eyes. "Please repeat what you said over the phone."

"Rebel is your investor appointment, sir."

"You mean the bank-robbery guy? Go stall him for a few minutes."

The assistant returned to her desk. "Mr. Davidson needs a moment before he can meet with you, Rebel."

"Not a problem," Rebel replied.

Mr. Davidson called his head of security, "Get in my office immediately."

Mr. Nash entered the office from the rear entrance.

Davidson said, "That superhero guy from the Chicago bank robberies is outside my door. I don't know what he wants with me, but I know that it can't be good!"

"I suggest that we have the entire security force surround the office. If he becomes hostile, we can handle the situation."

"Good idea, Nash."

Nash picked up the phone and yelled, "The lines are dead!"

"Where is my cell phone?" Davidson barked.

Nash handed Davidson a cell phone, but there was no reception.

Maggie had jammed all the towers. "You're clear to enter the office, Rebel."

Rebel said, "Please remain at your desk for the next fifteen minutes or so while I negotiate an increase in pay for you."

"Good luck with that!" she replied.

Rebel attempted to enter the office, but the door was locked. "Rebel to Control."

"Go for Control."

"The office is locked. Please find me an alternate entrance!"

"No problem. I'm transmitting a schematic to your display." Within seconds, the display showed Rebel a fully detailed map. The main hallway led to a corridor, which led to the back entrance to the office. Rebel entered the CEO's office and said, "My name is Rebel. Please relax. I'm not here to hurt anyone. I just want to negotiate with you."

"What do you think you're achieving by ambushing us like this?" Davidson asked.

"This is not an ambush. I have an appointment, sir," Rebel said.

"You're not an investor!" the CEO said.

Rebel said, "I have very important issues to discuss with you."

"Okay then … since you're here."

"For decades, you and other corporations in this country have been polluting the environment with inefficient sources of energy production such as fossil fuels. You are destroying the planet. Alternative sources of energy have been established for decades, but you and your fellow corporate leaders have suppressed them for far too long. It is time for change. Also, you are overcharging for the power. Most people are not able to afford your rates. People have their power shut off continuously because of your greed. This has got to stop."

"What exactly are you proposing we do?" Davidson asked.

"The alternative utilities are ready to be implemented. With just a phone call, I could begin the process. If you want to stay in business, the alternative companies can use your current power lines to run power from windmills to residential homes and businesses. For the use of the lines, you will receive 50 percent of the gross revenue."

"What if we refuse? You will not have our lines, and the people will be without power for months while these companies attempt to incorporate the new infrastructure. That will not go over very well, Rebel."

Rebel said, "At this time, I have at least ten of the most influential corporations in this country ready to donate billions of dollars to the restructuring process and supply temporary energy for the homes and businesses that do not currently have the resources. No one will go without power for more than a week or so. If you do not agree to these changes, I will shut down your operations. The alternatives are prepared to restructure without you!"

The men began to laugh.

Mr. Davidson asked, "How do you think you will get away with this?"

"The majority of the citizens in this country are ready for change. We have a small alternative-energy system in America but the European developments are more proven and established. Most Americans are educated on the subject. I will have power in numbers—and you will lose!"

"Do you really think you can take on corporate America and the law?"

"First of all, you really do not need the bad press. Second, involving the law would be a great mistake. The disparity of wealth in this country is getting worse every year. People are fed up with the cost of living and decreasing wages. Men and women like yourselves are living lavish lifestyles while most others are barely surviving. We haven't had this type of wealth disparity since the Great Depression. The alternative infrastructure is proven in countries like Germany, France, and Brazil. The time is now!"

"You call this a negotiation? This is America. Have you not heard of capitalism?" Davidson pounded his fist on his desk.

"Capitalism is great when it's not abused by corporations like yours. If corporate America wasn't so greedy and cared more about the environment instead of profit, we wouldn't be standing here right now. If you are willing to join forces with the alternatives, they will work with you. You will remain wealthy and regain the trust of the people."

Mr. Davidson laughed and said, "If we attempt to make these changes, we will lose thousands of jobs. You will destroy the middle class!"

"You and your fellow corporate leaders have been destroying the middle class for decades! Your fear-mongering propaganda is old and tired. Save it for your constituents. You have managed to scare the workforce with that bullshit for years, but they are not falling for it anymore. We are prepared to make sure that all the displaced workers will be first in line for the jobs created by the new infrastructure companies. This change will happen—with or without you—and there is nothing you can do to stop me!"

"Who do you think you are to ambush us like this? You cannot just come in here and dictate to us! What are you—one of these tree-huggers? Where are you from? Who are you working with? Do you think you are dealing with some petty bank robbers? Do you know who I am and who I know? I am one of the most powerful men in this country! We are not interested in your demands, Rebel. Leave now—or I will have you thrown out!"

"There is no need for threats, Mr. Davidson. I am very disappointed with your initial decision, but I will allow you some time to reconsider. I will visit some of your other corporate cronies this week. I will return soon to see if you have come to your senses."

The CEO laughed and replied, "Do what you will. I will not need any more time to reconsider. I am confident in our operations. We do not need to change for the sake of the people—or for you!"

Rebel calmly walked out of the office and stopped at the assistant's desk.

"Any luck with that raise?"

"I think I have them right where I want them," Rebel said with a grin.

When Rebel returned to base, Grimaldi said, "I see no compromise in Davidson. It will be next to impossible to come to an agreement with him."

Tony said, "I remember the last time the UAW was negotiating a contract for the workers at G. A. Automotive. We had little leverage, but we did have the threat of striking. The corporation could not afford a shutdown, so they agreed to our terms."

Grimaldi said, "Maybe there is a chance. If the people find that Rebel is fighting for their best interests, they may revolt and stop paying their bills."

Maggie said, "If Rebel made this point to the corporations, they would have the fear of rebellion from all angles!"

Nick said, "That is a great idea! Let's get the word out to the public!"

"Leave it to me." Grimaldi called some of his acquaintances in the press and asked them to spread the message about Rebel's meeting with the East Coast Power Corporation. He returned to the control room and said, "Maggie, can you monitor the East Coast Power Corporation and the West Coast Power Corporation for any type of communication? We need to find out if they are willing to negotiate with Rebel."

Maggie began hacking into their systems.

Nick asked, "Can you also find a way to track the audio and video in their vehicles? Let's see if they are going to set up a secret meeting."

"No problem." Maggie began typing on her keyboard. "One down, one to go."

"You're the best, Maggie!" Nick gave her a quick kiss on the cheek.

Rebel landed on the roof of the West Coast Power Corporation headquarters, and Maggie led him to the main office. "Hello, my name is Rebel. I have an appointment with Mr. Chaney."

"Sure." She pretended to reach for the phone—and pointed a handgun at Rebel. A female mercenary was disguised as the receptionist. "Don't move, Rebel!"

Several mercs disguised as employee's charged into the room and pointed weapons at him.

"Easy. I'm here to negotiate—not fight."

"You're not welcome here," one of the soldiers yelled. "Leave now!"

Rebel remained calm as he thought about what to do.

"Control to Rebel. Just walk out of there. No need to hurt anyone."

"Copy that, Control." Rebel walked toward the exit.

The mercs followed him to the rooftop.

Once Rebel was inside the Phantom, he said, "Rebel to Control."

"Go for Control."

"I want to relay a message to the CEO before I leave."

"What are you going to do?" Maggie asked.

"I'm gonna leave a message."

"Great!" Maggie replied.

Phantom-1 ascended to the clouds. When the mercs entered the building, he returned in cloak mode.

"Rebel to Control."

"Go for Control."

"Please show me the way to the executive restroom through the ventilation shaft."

Maggie searched the blueprint and sent Rebel the image.

"Thank you, Control." Rebel made his way through the shaft, entered the restroom, and hid in a stall.

"Are you going to just sit there until the CEO needs to go to the restroom?" Maggie asked.

"Maybe—or maybe I'll just break through this wall, blast a hole through the office window, and dangle him from fifty stories by his leg."

"Wait a minute … Chaney's coming," Maggie said.

Chaney had pale, wrinkled skin and white hair. When he entered a stall, Rebel exited his stall and waited for the CEO to come out.

"Rebel, someone else is on the way in. Hide!"

Rebel closed his eyes and imagined himself as a random gentleman in business attire. His suit accommodated Rebel's thoughts. He walked over to a urinal.

The man walked in and made his way to the urinal next to Rebel,.

The man looked at the disguised Rebel and nodded.

Rebel remained calm as he waited for the man to finish. He hoped that he would not lose the opportunity to confront Chaney. The man finished washing his hands and made his way out of the room.

The toilet flushed, and the CEO walked over to the sink.

Rebel nodded, changed back in to his suit, and said, "Hello, Mr. Chaney."

"What the hell?" The CEO jumped back, nearly falling onto the counter.

"Sorry. I didn't mean to startle you, sir. I tried to do this the right way, but you decided to ambush my efforts."

"I have nothing to say to you. Help!"

Rebel grabbed Chaney and threw him against the wall. "Be quiet, sir, or I'll have to gag you! I'm guessing that you have already been made aware of my demands. You are going to agree to join forces with the alternative energy companies. You will be allowed to remain in business and keep your fortune. If you try to fight me, you will lose everything!" Rebel let him go and waited for a response.

Chaney remained silent.

"What's the matter? You are the leader of a multibillion-dollar organization. You can't even muster a few words?" Rebel asked.

The CEO said, "The shareholders will not accept less. I don't know where you're from, but capitalism rules this country. You cannot destroy future profits of our corporation without consequence.

"I'm not trying to destroy your profits, sir. I'm merely advocating alternative energy so that we will have a safe and functional planet to leave to our children. Do you have children or grandchildren, Chaney?"

"Yes, I do. I love them and will leave them with a legacy to be proud of."

"What good does your legacy do them if they do not have food or water that is consumable and air that is breathable? What if they have to relocate to another state because their home is underwater?"

"Global warming? Ha. What hoax! I do not subscribe to that notion," Chaney said.

"Science is real. You should take these findings more seriously. This planet is in dire straits. You have a responsibility as an energy provider to this nation. You must protect your customers who trust you and your colleagues."

"I am not concerned with these issues because they are unproven. I will continue to run this corporation as I always have—by putting my shareholders first. They are the investors in this corporation, and they will continue to be rewarded for their investments."

"I'll take that as a no," Rebel replied. "I'm sorry to hear that you have no moral conscience. I guess that the bottom line is all you respond to."

"Money is what runs this world. There is nothing that matters more than power. Money is power, and we will not allow anything to come between us and our power."

"I guess I've wasted my time here, sir. Good day." Rebel raised his right arm, fired a grappling hook at the ceiling vent, and threw it in the corner. With his left arm, he fired another line into the shaft. He ascended to the ventilation shaft and made his way to the rooftop.

The CEO rushed to his assistant's desk and called for security. Ten armed guards ran to the east staircase, and ten other guards headed to the west staircase.

Maggie said, "Hurry up, Rebel. They are almost on the roof."

"I'm moving as fast as I can." Rebel fought his way through the shafts. He made it into the Phantom just as the men from the west entrance broke through the rooftop doors. They pointed their weapons at the center of the roof, but the Phantom was in cloak mode. Just as the guards from the east side reached the rooftop, Rebel fired up the jet, blasting them with fumes. He quickly ascended, leaving the security team clueless.

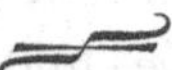

Rebel entered the control room and said, "Well, it looks like we're in for a battle."

"Not a problem," Grimaldi replied. "We will continue to fight for what we believe in."

"I'm ready to go to war!" Nick replied.

Grimaldi said, "Not yet! We will give them a few days. Then we will make our next move."

"These men are unconscionable! It is terrible what greed does to people," Maggie replied.

"Yes they are," Nick said. "But soon, they will be facing Team Rebel!"

The group cheered and clapped.

PHASE 15

This Means War

A week later, Nick said, "Any luck finding out anything about the meeting, Maggie?"

"Not a peep, Nick."

Grimaldi said, "Apparently, they have made their choice. Everything is in order. I have contacted each of the alternative companies to be sure they are ready to implement the transformation."

"What percentage of energy are they responsible for?" Maggie asked.

Nick said, "It depends on which state you're talking about. Overall, in the United States, only 11 percent. Unfortunately, residential homes make up the majority of the customers. Commercial buildings must step up and conform to the alternatives as well."

Joey asked. "What percentage are the alternatives capable of supplying?"

Grimaldi said, "That depends on whether they have the power lines from the current infrastructure. With the lines, 100 percent—without the lines, 75 percent."

Nick said, "Maggie, will you call for a joint meeting with both CEOs at a central location?"

"I'll try, Nick."

Maggie made the call. Once she was done, she said, "They have refused, Nick."

"Then we'll put plan B into effect," Grimaldi said.

"Wait a minute," Nick said. "I will send them another message first."

"What did you have in mind?" Grimaldi asked.

"Joey, let's blow something up.".

"What are you gonna blow up, Nick?" Maggie asked.

"I don't know. Why don't you do some digging for me, Maggie?"

Joey said, "I guess we could take out the generators to each of the headquarters."

"I like that idea," Grimaldi said. "Let's hit them where they live."

Nick said, "Okay, then. Map it out."

Nick flew out in Phantom-1 that night. "Rebel to Control."

"Go for Control."

"Approaching the East Coast target." He hovered over the main generator.

"The target is clear," Maggie said.

"Copy that, Control."

Rebel opened the bay door and dropped down to the surface on the Phantom's towline. He landed in front of the generator, and the cable began to return to the Phantom. He planted three C-4 explosives, stepped away from the generator as the towline returned to his location, and ascended to his fighter.

"Rebel to Control."

"Go for Control."

"First target accomplished. On route to second mark."

"Copy that, Rebel."

Rebel flew to the West Coast headquarters. "Rebel to Control."

"Go for Control."

"Please inspect second generator for clearance."

Maggie checked the cameras. "Clear for attack, Rebel."

"Copy that, Control." He descended upon his prey. "Rebel to Control."

"Go for Control."

"You're clear to detonate."

"Copy that, Rebel."

"What are you waiting for, Maggie?" Grimaldi asked.

"Would you like to do the honors?" she asked.

"No. I would like you to pull the trigger."

Without any further hesitation, Maggie punched the key. "No problem."

The generators were destroyed at once.

"Good work," Rebel said. "Returning to base."

Nick entered the control room and said, "That was easy enough."

"We'll contact them in the morning," Grimaldi said. "Let's see if that changes their perspective."

"I think they'll get the message this time," Maggie said.

"Either way, we will move forward," Nick said.

After an hour of going back and forth with their representatives, Maggie summoned the team to the control room.

Nick asked, "What did you find?"

"The CEOs agreed to meet with Rebel at a conference center in a neutral location."

Grimaldi asked, "What are the details?"

Maggie said, "The conference center is in Oklahoma City. The CEOs want to meet at noon tomorrow. They claim they are willing to negotiate with you, Nick."

"Great! I'll be there," Nick replied.

Grimaldi said, "I believe they will hire mercenaries to kill Rebel."

"Can you hack into the location for the layout?" Nick asked.

"Let me pull it up." Maggie brought up the conference center on the monitor. The building was on the outskirts of the city.

Nick asked, "Tomorrow is Sunday. Will there be any civilians in the building?"

Maggie checked the event schedule. "You'll have the building to yourselves—other than security."

Nick said, "I will have two of the Phantoms on hand to be sure I'm covered. I will show up a little early to survey the area. We'll make sure we have our bases covered before entering the building."

Maggie said, "This may be too dangerous!"

Nick said, "I trained in the Middle East with the Black Ops. The training prepared me to go into battle without the suit, without the Phantoms, and without your eye in the sky. Not to mention, all of these advanced weapons!"

Grimaldi said, "We are fully prepared for this revolution, Maggie. You have nothing to worry about!"

She said, "I'm sorry. I'm just a little nervous about opening this can of worms."

Nick said, "You need to relax and trust us. You must trust the process."

Maggie took a deep breath. "I'm ready. Let's do this!"

"Okay, then," Grimaldi said. "We will resume tomorrow."

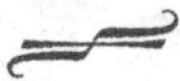

Nick and Joey were preparing Phantom-1 and Phantom-2 for attack.

Maggie wrapped her arms around Nick. "I need you to remember that these men cannot be trusted. You must adopt the attitude that whoever you face off against should not be underestimated!"

"I guess I've been acting a little too cocky lately," Nick said. "I promise not to take anyone lightly."

She kissed him and said, "I love you, Nick."

"I love you too, Maggie."

Grimaldi shook Nick's hand and smiled. "This is it, Rebel!"

Tony and Joey hugged him and smiled.

Rebel approach the conference center half an hour early. "Phantom-2, hold your position a few miles west of the conference center. Land on that mountaintop and stand by."

Rebel circled the conference center, looking for signs of suspicious activity.

Maggie said, "Control to Rebel, can you read me?"

"Copy, Control. What are you picking up inside the conference center?"

"There are about thirty people in that building. I have the two CEOs in a conference room with fifteen mercenaries at the center of the building. I have another fifteen mercs scattered throughout the back entrance area."

"I'll land on the rooftop and make my way around to the back entrance. I need you to keep me informed about where the mercs are positioned."

"Ready when you are, Rebel!" Maggie replied.

Rebel made his way to the back of the loading dock and scanned the area.

Maggie said, "Rebel, there are five men waiting inside the bay entrance to ambush you!"

Rebel found a dirty dock littered with rodents and debris. He passed five smelly dumpsters and jumped on to the dock. He found a window that led to the other side of the wall where the men were waiting. Rebel extended his arms and fired his hooks into the top of the walls, locking in firmly. He stepped back and launched himself into the opening.

The five mercs were waiting to attack him.

Rebel activated his infrared vision and dropped smoke on the men. He descended on them, kicking and punching them. One of the men frantically fired his assault rifle into the smoke and hit one of his peers.

Rebel shot the merc with a concussion bullet, between his eyes, and knocked him out.

Another merc ran down the hall. He slipped in to a storage area and hid behind a drum set.

Rebel used his X-ray vision to find his prey. "Come here often?" he whispered.

The mercenary fell into the drum set, and Rebel fired a couple of tranquilizer darts into the merc's forehead. Once the first group of enemies was eliminated, Rebel said, "Lead me to the next objective, Control."

Maggie replied, "Head to your left, down the hallway. There are five more men hiding in the storage area."

Rebel continued to a large banquet hall with several storage crates and fenced-in enclosures. He climbed to the top of some cargo boxes that were stacked about twenty-five-feet high. He saw one of the men and fired a grappling hook at the man, wrapping the line around his throat with a twist of the wrist. The merc struggled to break free but he could not. Rebel held him in a chokehold while taking out his pistol to fire a tranq dart into the man's leg.

Rebel would have to take on the last two mercs at the same time, and he made his way over to the top of one of the cages. When they were positioned below him, Rebel jumped down on one of the men, knocking him to the ground. The other adversary began to fire at Rebel.

Rebel donkey-kicked the attacker, knocking him into a large storage crate. The merc slowly rose to his feet, and Rebel pulled out both of his pistols and shot both mercenaries.

Maggie led Rebel to the next group and said. "Rebel, these men are just standing out in the open."

"They're not too smart!" Rebel attempted to tranquilize them from a distance, but he missed two of the mercs. They retreated to another room, but Rebel used his X-ray vision to find his targets. He threw smoke grenades at them and grappled to the ceiling.

The men searched for him through the smoke.

Rebel looked down on them and fired concussion bullets at their chests, rendering them unconscious.

"You okay, Rebel?"

"Good to go, Maggie. Which way to Davidson and his cronies?"

Maggie said, "There are fourteen mercenaries remaining. Just to your left, down that last hallway, which appears to be about three hundred feet in length, there are three entrances on each side of the hall. The bosses are in the back hallway with two more bodyguards and Nash. The mercenaries are in two-by-two formation at each entrance of the hallway."

"Are there doors on each side of the conference rooms?" Rebel noticed that the ceiling in the conference hall was about thirty feet tall, which would work to his advantage.

Maggie said, "Yes. You can surprise them from behind and attack two of them at a time if you move quickly."

Rebel entered the rear entrance of one of the conference rooms. Using his thermal vision, he found one of the mercs hiding behind a group of tables. Rebel crawled through the room like a spider and tossed a smoke grenade—without pulling the pin—toward the opposite side of the room.

The merc reacted as predicted, moving out of his secure position.

Rebel took advantage of the opportunity, quickly putting him into a chokehold. The adversary grunted, drawing the attention of his counterpart. Rebel shot the merc as soon as he opened the door. Rebel saw another man at the opposite entrance and shot a dart between the eyes of his target. Rebel zip-tied both men and headed back to the conference room.

Rebel used his thermal vision to find the merc in the corner and made his way to the nearest bar. He picked up a fork and threw it toward the main entrance. The man carefully made his way to the entrance to investigate, and Rebel fired a grappling hook at his mark. As the line wrapped around his throat, Rebel reeled him in like a fish. Just before the man was completely recoiled, Rebel released the line and hit the man in the throat, sweeping him off his feet. Before moving on, Rebel fired a dart in the merc's forehead.

Rebel entered the next conference room, remaining on the left side of the hallway to find the next two mercs. They were bragging about which one was going to kill Rebel.

Rebel laughed out loud to draw their attention and snuck out of the rear entrance to draw them into the hallway.

One of the assassins said, "Should we call for backup?"

"Hell no! We got this!"

Rebel fired a grappling hook to the ceiling, ascending above while waiting for the two men to step out into the hall. The hired guns carefully chased after Rebel as they exited the rear entrance. One of them moved up the hall, and the other moved in the opposite direction.

Rebel swung toward the man and attempted to land on his back.

The man avoided the attack and rolled to the ground. He quickly pulled out his combat knives, which wrapped around his knuckles like a combination of brass knuckles and military knives. Rebel landed and somersaulted back to his feet.

The second merc drew his weapon.

Rebel pulled out his nunchucks, but his enemy attacked. The merc attempted to slice, but Rebel used the nunchucks to defend himself.

The other assassin aimed his submachine gun set on Rebel, but he still could not get a clear shot without sacrificing his partner.

Rebel decided to take out the second merc before he could get off a clear shot. He put away one set of nunchucks, and went into a helicopter spin with the other set. He fended off the knife-wielding foe, pulled out his gun, and fired a concussion bullet at the gunman. Rebel struck the knife-wielding merc in the face with the nunchucks, rendering them both unconscious. "That was cool!"

Maggie said, "No time to admire your handiwork, Rebel. Keep moving."

Rebel decided to approach the room across the hall. He circled around the back to the first set of rooms through the rear entrance. He dropped smoke in the room to get the attention of the nearest mercs.

The men made their way into the conference room, but they could not see anything due to the smoke. As one was about to radio for backup, Rebel knocked him unconscious with a three-punch combination.

The other merc was wearing a gas mask and thermal goggles. He took Rebel by surprise putting him in a chokehold.

Rebel stood up, reached over his head, and grabbed the attacker by the neck. He hurled his attacker across the room and fired two darts at his enemy, knocking him unconscious.

Nash got on the radio and said, "I need all checkpoints to report in now!"

The mercenaries began to check in, but there were only four left. Nash commanded the remaining men to join him. "Let's move to the kitchen. We have this under control! Rig both ends of the service hallway with explosives. Let's blow this bastard to hell!"

Rebel said, "Control, do you have a visual of the CEOs?"

"Yes. They are in the kitchen with Nash and the six remaining mercs. The kitchen is large, and there are plenty of places to hide. They have two escape routes with vehicles ready to retreat. A man is monitoring from the surveillance room—so they will know your every move."

Rebel decided it was time to stop playing. He was ready to confront the CEOs. He walked to the service corridor and tripped a wire. The explosives detonated simultaneously, blasting Rebel into the air. The ceiling and walls collapsed, and Rebel was trapped in the rubble. Smoke and fire filled the area.

Nash said, "Did you see that bastard walk into the Claymores?"

"Yes, sir. He walked right into our trap, but after the explosives went off, I was not able to view the surrounding area. The cameras were destroyed in the blast."

Davidson barked, "I want that bastard's head on a platter! Take care of this, Nash!"

Nash said, "You two heard the man!"

Two of the hired guns headed down the hallway to recover Rebel's body. As they approached the area, Rebel emerged from the ashes. "Look what you did to this beautiful conference center. You guys are terrible hosts."

The mercs fired their machine guns at Rebel, but his suit absorbed the ammunition. The men sprinted toward the kitchen. Nash attempted to grab them by their vests, but he could not slow them down. "What happened? Why were you firing your weapons? Where is the body? Where are you going?"

One of the men yelled, "We blasted him with three Claymores, and it didn't even faze him! Keep your money!" The assassins ran out of the rear entrance.

Nash yelled, "You cowards. Get back here! I will kill you myself!"

Davidson said, "We are paying you and your men a small fortune. You better take care of this now!"

The bosses retreated to their escape vehicles.

Nash ordered his men to hold down the rear entrance so that he and the CEOs could retreat. "I will double your pay for this job. Kill that bastard! Use your grenades and rapid fire!" Nash rushed out the back exit.

Rebel entered the kitchen, and the mercs began to fire on him with their machine guns. One of the men threw a grenade at Rebel, but he caught the grenade and tossed it over his shoulder before it exploded. The men emptied their magazines at Rebel, filling the room with smoke. Once it cleared, the men paused.

Rebel walked through the smoke. "You can give up now. I just want to negotiate."

The mercs retreated toward the exit, but Rebel blasted them with concussion bullets. Rebel said, "Where are the CEOs?"

Maggie said, "The CEOs and Nash exited the conference center and are heading west."

"I'm done with these mercs. Do you have a read on the bosses' exact location?"

"They are en route to the airport. I'll program their location in Phantom-1. Hurry if you want to catch them."

Rebel signaled for Phantom-1, he exited the building rushing toward the Phantom, and was vacuumed up by his fighter. Within five minutes, he caught up to the CEOs. He fired shots at their limousine, forcing them off of the road. As the car screeched to a halt, Phantom-1's bottom hatch opened and dropped Rebel on top of the vehicle.

The chauffeur attempted to restart the vehicle, but Rebel broke the driver's window with his fist and pulled him out of the limo. Rebel told the limo driver to sit on the ground and not move. The back door was locked, but he ripped it off its hinges and heaved it thirty yards. "Do not move! There will be no more fighting. I'm not here to fight. We need to have this out now!"

"We refuse to join with the alternatives and give up control of our business!" Davidson said.

Rebel said, "There will not be any further time allowances. The alternatives are in place. You will either join resources with them—or you will be replaced!"

Chaney said, "Hell no!"

Davidson ordered the limo driver to take them to the airport.

Rebel allowed the driver to get back into the vehicle.

PHASE 16

Walking the Walk

Back at the base, Team Rebel mapped out a plan to destroy the corporate infrastructure.

Grimaldi said, "We should put the drones to good use by sending them out at night with all five of the Phantoms to destroy the infrastructure."

"What are these drones capable of?" Nick asked.

"We have several types of advanced attack drones with many different capabilities. We will use the kamikaze drones for this mission. They are capable of carrying a few pounds of explosives to their targets."

Nick said, "So, they are designed for this type of operation!"

Grimaldi said, "Yes. That's why I call them kamikaze drones. All we have to do is put the type and the amount of explosives that are needed for each operation, and they will sacrifice themselves to carry out their task—either autonomously or by remote command!"

Nick and Joey agreed to take care of the explosives in the morning.

Tony asked, "The targets are the main power grids for the entire country?"

Grimaldi said, "Yes, sir. We are going to eliminate these fossil fuel structures once and for all."

Tony said, "That's a huge undertaking."

Nick said. "A necessary move, though, Uncle Tony."

Grimaldi said, “Trust the process. This is a revolution. We’ll resume in the morning.”

Maggie pulled up a map of the entire infrastructure that showed all the locations that were to be infiltrated. “These generators are on outdoor lots and secured by a building that wraps around them like a wall. The Phantoms will hover overhead in cloak mode and release the drones in the target areas. The explosives will be programmed.”

Joey asked, “Are we sure we have the support of the citizens?”

Maggie said. “I have been keeping my finger on the pulse of the people. Believe me when I say there is a lot of unrest. The working class is sick and tired of the cost of living and poor health conditions that are a result of inferior safety measures related to our utilities.”

“Yes, it’s true, Joey.” Nick added. “I have been researching this for years. As Maggie has found, there is a strong grass-roots effort toward these types of actions. Now is the time to strike.”

Joey said, “I know what you are talking about. I just needed to hear it again. I’m ready.”

Nick and Joey began to set up the explosives in the drones and programmed them to go out into the field.

Grimaldi said, “Are you done packing the drones yet?”

Joey replied, “They’re ready for attack.”

“We followed Maggie’s directions.”

Grimaldi said, “Yeah, other than installing the proper amount of explosive, the drones pretty much do the rest.”

Later that night, the team gathered in the control room with Maggie.

She said, “Everything has been double-checked. We are ready for launch.”

Grimaldi gave the go-ahead, and Maggie launched the Phantoms.

"There are ten states right down the center of the country. Each of them houses the main generators that supply power to the entire country. I have programmed each Phantom to target two states. It should take about two hours to complete this mission."

The Phantoms would arrive at their destinations, cloaking and hovering over the generators as they released the drones onto the facilities. The drones would silently make their way to the main generators and wait their imminent destruction. The power companies did not have a lot of security at the core of their facilities. The majority of the security was set up on the perimeter of the properties. This worked to the advantage of Team Rebel.

A couple of hours went by. The Phantoms and drones completed both phases of the mission without any interference. Once the drones were in place, Maggie had the camera feeds from each of the drones show up on the monitors. The team could be sure they were in their proper places and that no one was tampering with them. In addition, they could be assured that the areas were clear of any personnel who might be in danger from the blast.

Grimaldi said, "This is it. No turning back!"

Nick looked at Maggie and said, "Do it!"

She pressed the computer key and initiated the attack, exploding the drones and destroying the infrastructure of the entire electrical supply of the United States. The team cheered wildly. That moment would define the revolution and send a message to corporate America. An act of that magnitude had never been attempted before.

Grimaldi said, "Now we will see how these corporations respond to our efforts! The electricity will be replaced within a reasonable time frame—and new jobs will be filled soon."

The power was out for most homes in the country. Fortunately, it was May, and people were not relying on their furnaces or air-conditioning.

The press speculated about the cause. "People were calling the authorities and asking whether the event was a terrorist attack. There have been several accidents where traffic lights are not being powered by backup generators. Certain areas where the power hasn't been restored have fallen victim to damage and looting. The National Guard has been deployed to those areas. Fortunately, hospitals, Airports, News outlets, and government building are equipped for such outages—and so are many businesses and some residential homes. Considering the magnitude of this blackout, the situation could be much worse."

Grimaldi said, "Pay close attention to the news reports. We want to see if the power companies will report what they know or if they are afraid the people will realize why they are under attack if they do so."

Nick watched with anticipation to the reports, and he was eager to see the reaction of the people—and if the CEOs would be asked for comment.

Grimaldi called to the delivery companies he had set up to supply the portable generators that would be given to the areas without power. The companies confirmed that the generators were en route.

Maggie said, "I hope they can get those generators out there quickly!"

Grimaldi said, "The assistant to the secretary of energy is a dear friend of mine. I let him know that I have relations with several alternative energy companies that are in place to complete the integration of the windmills into the power grid. They have been under construction for several years now—as have other alternative-energy sources."

The secretary agreed that it could be a turning point in the history of the country. He was apprehensively enthusiastic about the situation. The president agreed.

Grimaldi called the National Guard to make sure the alternative workers were protected against any disturbances that could delay the return of power.

News vans were swarming the headquarters of both power companies and waited for responses from leaders in the disaster areas.

"All air traffic has been grounded, and the military has been put on high alert. Police and fire have been working feverishly to keep order in the streets. So far, there have been no fatalities reported. The country is on edge though, and many continue to speculate about what or who is responsible for this tragic event. We are just receiving information that ten

Fortune 500 corporations have stepped forward to donate a billion dollars to furnish portable generators to the areas without power. Also, four alternative energy companies have recently completed the construction and implementation of alternative energy sources. These windmills are located near the power grids that were destroyed. We can only assume that the sources were built there to use the existing power lines in case of an emergency such as this."

Nick said, "Grimaldi, did you anticipate this type of reaction?"

"Of course, Nick. These are minor issues compared to what we're fighting for. Besides, we will restore order within a couple of weeks. Not to worry."

Tony said, "Can the alternative companies tap into the current power lines?"

"Yes, they can. The president can issue an executive order to declare a state of emergency, which would force the utilities to surrender the use of the power lines to the alternatives in the interest of national security."

Joey said, "Good idea. I hope the president will make that happen. I wouldn't want there to be any backlash toward Rebel."

Grimaldi said, "Not to worry, Joey. If we have the use of the lines or not, the electricity will be restored soon."

Davidson said, "I am not sure if we should call the police or just find Rebel and kill him ourselves."

Chaney replied, "We can't afford the negative publicity. The reality is that we have been robbing the people and polluting the environment for decades. Also, the reconstruction of the grids will take a year—if not longer. We would be politically and publicly crucified. We cannot return the power in a reasonable amount of time. We should just join forces with the alternatives. We hired the best mercenaries in the business, and they were useless against Rebel. We are in a losing situation—any way we look at it."

Davidson agreed.

They contacted the companies that were in charge of the reconstruction of the utilities and set up a meeting to negotiate the terms of a possible contract.

PHASE 17

Not So Tough

The team celebrated its victory. Tony prepared a cart with champagne and chocolate-covered strawberries.

Grimaldi poured each of the team members a drink, and they raised their glasses. "To a successful first mission. Congratulations! I spoke with my associates in the alternative companies. Within a week, the CEOs will meet with them to complete an agreement, which will allow them to use the current power lines. The alternatives have projected that the process should take less than two months."

"Yes!" Nick said. "We will win this revolution! Together, there is nothing we can't do."

"To us!" Maggie toasted. "We make a great team!"

"I want to thank all of you for bringing me in on this," Tony said. "I know that I don't have all the skills that you have."

"We need you, Tony," Grimaldi said. "It's not about your skill. It's about your will and your determination to fight for what is right."

"Yeah, that's what this is all about," Joey said. "We are a team. You bring a certain knowledge and experience to the team that we need."

"Thank you all," Tony said. "Nick, can I speak with you for a moment?"

Nick walked with Tony to the other side of the room.

"I haven't had the chance to let you know that Paul has been accepted to the Air Force Academy."

"What? Are you kidding me?" Nick said. "When did this all happen?"

"He applied three months ago. You've been so busy that he didn't want to bother you."

"Yeah, we have been a little busy. I'll have to call Paul. I'm so happy for him."

"Your aunt and I are very proud."

Maggie snuck up from behind Nick and wrapped her arms around his shoulders.

Tony smiled and walked away.

"You were amazing, Nick. You almost gave me a heart attack a few times, but overall, you were great!"

"You were great as well," Nick said. "I couldn't have done it without you and the team."

"We're a damn good team," Maggie said.

"You just need to remember that Mr. G., Joey, and I have all had military training. We have been in situations that you have not—up until now. You need to trust our judgment. We will be patient with your progress."

"I get that. I'm feeling much more confident as time passes. But no matter how much experience I gain, you're still my man. I will never completely feel at ease with the daredevil stunts."

"I get it." Nick looked her in the eye. "I need to put myself in your shoes sometimes."

"Exactly." Maggie hugged him.

The team celebrated for the remainder of the evening.

The team gathered in the training area.

"I want a meeting with the president of the United States," Nick said. "I think we could convince the president to support the revolution—considering the success we have had so far."

Grimaldi said, "I am skeptical about meeting with the president too soon, Nick. That could backfire. We may need more time to gather public response to the revolution before we know how the president truly feels."

Nick said, "If we gain the president's support now, he may be able to use an executive order to assist us in influencing these companies to stop outsourcing American jobs. If any of our future missions go awry, the president would not be able to support the revolution."

Grimaldi said, "Everything is in place with the alternatives. We should finish restructuring the natural gas corporations and the local water departments. At that point, we may consider a meeting with the president."

Nick said, "That's fine for now, but we must keep a close eye on any statements from the president. There is no way we'll be able to force job creation without the president's influence."

"I agree," Mr. Grimaldi replied. "The next phase in the revolution is to convert the natural gas operations to alternatives. Rebel will meet with the leaders who are responsible for the entire supply of natural gas throughout the country."

"The natural gas infrastructure is virtually controlled by two men?" Tony asked.

Nick said, "The distribution is determined by these two very powerful men, but each state has its own representative who answers to them."

Grimaldi said, "The plan for restructuring is going to be complex. I have been to a facility overseas where an alternative company, led by the research of Professor Stanley P. Miejer Jr., has developed a portable hydrogen creator to supply all the fuel needs for residential and commercial dwellings. This technology will replace the environmentally detrimental sources of fuel so we can operate stoves, hot-water tanks, and dryers that run primarily on natural gas."

"How does this work?" Tony asked.

Grimaldi said, "It works by connecting the system to whatever energy source is available—preferably wind, solar, geothermal, or hydroelectric. This converter may use any source of water. A converter takes the hydrogen, compresses it to a usable pressure, and pumps it out to whatever appliance is being used. The waste gas becomes oxygen. They have mastered conversion kits so that, with minimal effort, all major gas-fueled appliances can be converted."

Maggie asked. "Is this technology ready to be implemented?"

"Absolutely—without a doubt!" Grimaldi said. "American

corporations are subject to the whims of the commodities markets, and the price fluctuations are outrageous due to the changing seasons. With this alternative system, those price fluctuations will be eliminated. Also, natural gas poisons the groundwater supply in areas with fracking. Fracking poisons the water supply. When taken to court and asked for the details of what it is they are pumping into the ground to procure the natural gas, corporations use loopholes in the law to have proprietary protection on the solutions they inject into the wells. So, by law, we are not allowed to know exactly what those chemicals are. Due to the legal patent protection of these dangerous chemicals, we may not discover what these chemicals are until it is too late."

Maggie said, "They waste millions of gallons of fresh water in the process as well. Currently, there are many class-action lawsuits against these corporations from the citizens who live in the fracking zones. These zones are statistically proven to have spiked tremendously with cancer and other mysterious health issues. We can use the lawsuits as another form of attack against them—to discontinue the fracking and eliminate the poisoning of the environment!"

"We must change these methods before it is too late," Tony said.

Maggie said, "This is criminal! I remember doing a term paper on this subject. I learned about the incredible opposition against the transparency of these chemicals that the corporations are using to extract the gas. The chemicals were patented so that we the people cannot have access to the exact ingredients of those chemicals until the patent expires."

"Yeah, well, that's why we're here today!" Nick said.

Grimaldi said, "We will have four major solar corporations handle the transformation of these gas operations. They will tap into our friends in the alternative world, who have agreed to allow us to use the current power grids to run the hydrogen converters until more alternative sources of energy are produced. I have already secured a commitment from Professor Miejer and his company so that the converters can be mass produced with the help of our friends who have invested in our revolution."

"What about the water departments?" Maggie asked.

"I have contracted several private environmental-testing facilities to begin testing each city's water-purification system. We will be sure that these departments are running legitimate testing and purification systems. There has been a lot of fearmongering in the past about tap water being unsafe to drink. Certain corporations want to persuade people to buy bottled water instead of using the water from their own homes, which they already pay for. This is wrong! We must put an end to these practices. We must reestablish confidence in the public water supply and support the system that was put in place to keep the water-supply purifiers at a high standard—as they were meant to be."

The team agreed with Grimaldi, and everyone was excited to continue with the revolution.

At the breakfast table, Nick said, "Can you make a call to the East Coast Gas Corporation to set an appointment?"

"Already done," Maggie said. "I made the appointment for the end of the week.

"Thanks, babe," Nick said, "You're so efficient."

Rebel paid a visit to the headquarters of the East Coast Gas Corporation in Lincoln, Nebraska. Rebel flew around the twenty-story structure and wondered why they needed so much space for just one corporation, which only housed white-collar employees and did no manufacturing.

Rebel landed his fighter on the roof, secured a grappling line to a nearby post, and dropped down to the front entrance. He walked through the front door and made his way to the elevator. Rebel entered Derik Canter's office and approached his assistant.

She asked, "May I please have your autograph Rebel?"

"Sorry, no. I am not a celebrity. I'm just someone who cares a lot."

The assistant called Mr. Canter to announce Rebel.

Canter wore an expensive suit and a gaudy gold watch. "Would you like a drink, Rebel?"

Rebel replied, "No thank you, sir. We need to get straight to business."

"I know why you are here, Rebel. I have a plan to convert a large percentage of the current system over to renewable power and reduce natural gas use."

"How do you feel about terminating the natural gas fracking process all together?" Rebel asked.

"Why would we stop the fracking process completely?"

Rebel said, "Have you forgotten about the multiple class-action lawsuits against your corporation? You are currently dealing with the ramifications of this process, due to the poisoning of the water supplies in the areas where you frack!"

"Ah … we are … getting ready … to settle all of those lawsuits very soon," Canter said.

"Regardless of how many lawsuits you settle, this will not put an end to the poisoning of the water supply. I found an inventor from Turkey who developed a portable hydrogen-converter system that will convert all major appliances to hydrogen operations. I have the financial support of ten Fortune 500 corporations. They are willing to invest in this alternative power source. We will put an end to the need for fracking. You may join in with the conversion process or be eliminated from the picture completely!"

"Your plan has not been proven and is most likely a long shot at best," Canter said. "How long do you project for it to become fully operational?"

"The system already works and is ready for implementation. What is more important, though, is that we bring an end to your process. The citizens of this country are becoming more and more aware of climate change with every passing year. If we are going to save the planet, we must change the infrastructure immediately!"

"What will happen to our workforce? What will happen to the economy if we act too quickly?"

"We both know that you are not concerned about your employees or the state of the union. All you are worried about are your summer home, your European home, your private jets, and your personal yachts that you only use for one month out of each year. How many vehicles must you have in your garages? Your greed is incomprehensible!"

"Wait just a minute. You have no idea the pressure I am under. I have shareholders to answer to. It isn't simple to change the infrastructure. It will take years to implement and millions of dollars."

"Please do not insult my intelligence, Mr. Canter. You and your kind only worry about yourselves. The corporations I mentioned earlier will be opening manufacturing facilities near all of your current businesses so that your people can take over the new jobs we create. As for your fortune, that is up to you. If you would like to join the conversion, you are welcome. You must coordinate with the alternative companies to proceed. This is the only way to move forward with the exchange. Time is of the utmost importance, sir."

"I have no idea what you or these scientists are claiming. Sounds like a bunch of left-wing propaganda to me."

"You may call it what you will, but the facts are the facts. We will reform the infrastructure—with or without you. I have no more time to waste with you, sir."

The CEO sat in silence for a minute. "I will contact my counterpart on the West Coast as well as my board of directors. We will discuss your proposal."

"That is reasonable. Thank you, sir. I will contact you in one week to set up a meeting with you and your counterpart. At that time, we will discuss the terms further." Rebel extended a hand, and Canter accepted.

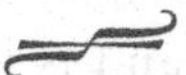

The meeting was set for Jefferson City, Missouri. Canter and Richard Banner were waiting for Rebel in a room at the convention center. Banner wore an expensive three-piece suit and lit up a cigar even though there was no smoking allowed in the building.

Banner said, "I am not convinced that this plan will work. How can we know that Rebel will be able to deliver on his promise of a hydrogen converter?"

"We are also not thoroughly convinced that this process will be sustainable," Canter said. "But did you think he would be able to convert the power corporations the way he did?"

Banner shook his head. "No, I did not. I must admit that Rebel is very resourceful. I also had my people investigate the inventor from Turkey. He is legitimate, and his converter works. He has been perfecting this technology for more than fifteen years."

"Are you sure that it works?" Banner asked.

"My investigator has found that it works perfectly fine … too fine, in fact. I remember him from an energy conference ten years ago. My predecessor had him discredited in the industry. He had him drugged at a party and brought two hookers up to his hotel room while he was unconscious. The women called the police, claiming that Meijer forced himself on them and refused to pay. The cops busted him for solicitation, leaving him with a bad taste in his mouth. He would never return to the States. I thought it was a great idea, but Rebel convinced him to return with his invention. We knew his invention would cut into our personal profits. I am fearful that it will eventually put us out of business. Even if we refuse to join the alternatives, they could replace us and take our share of the market. Realistically, we do not have any other viable options."

Rebel showed up to the meeting with four other men in suits. "Okay, gentlemen. Are we ready to begin the transformation of the utilities?"

The CEOs looked at each other and nodded.

Banner asked, "Who are these men?"

"These are the CEOs of the four companies that will be spearheading the alternative initiative. You will negotiate with them about how the transformation will take place. Please, everyone, do your best to get along. I don't want to waste any more time with this matter."

The alternative leaders did not resemble the typical corporate American type. One of the leaders was Indian, another was Korean, one was African, and the last was Italian. The Korean CEO explained how the PHC would be implemented into the infrastructure. The alternative leaders took turns explaining how they would be able to increase profits and create new jobs.

Canter and Banner listened with interest, but remained skeptical.

Canter asked, "How long until we begin to see profits?"

"We should be fully transformed within twelve months and have phased out the natural gas production. In six months, we should begin to see a nearly identical return in profit margins," the Italian CEO replied.

"When you say nearly, do you mean temporarily or permanently?" Banner asked.

The African CEO said, "You may never see the astronomical profits you have become accustomed to in the past. We will be lowering the cost of power through new technologies. These technologies will be expensive in the beginning, as most are, but they will decrease as profits increase."

"I don't know if I can be involved in this change." Banner said. "I need more time to review the numbers."

Rebel said, "Wait a minute, sir. Any questions about the numbers will be verified for you today. As I have explained before, we have little time to waste! Please sit back down. We will answer every question with a detailed reply, sir."

Banner said, "Okay, okay. I understand, but you need to understand that I have been in business for nearly fifty years. I am not going to be pressured into just any deal. The numbers have to make sense for our shareholders."

"I will make this as clear as possible," Rebel replied. "You and the shareholders will accept less for the betterment of the planet and the employees. We are going to create a cleaner environment and a middle class that is worth bragging about."

Banner took his seat again.

A few hours passed. The questions were answered and Canter and Banner asked for a moment in private.

"We better just wrap this deal up and agree to these terms, Banner," Canter said.

"You heard what they said. We may never reach the record profits that we have in the past."

"We either join them or suffer the same consequences that our friends in the power industry did. I am too old to fight this battle," Canter said.

"And I am too old to start over!" Banner said.

"Come on, man. It's not like we're going to be starting from scratch. We will simply convert our investments from one energy source to the other. Those men will be doing all of the real work. We can't win this fight, but we can come out of this situation in one piece."

Banner remained silent for several minutes, but he ultimately agreed to join forces with the alternatives. The other CEOs were called back into the room. The deal was acknowledged, and Rebel dismissed himself to let them complete the deal.

After Rebel returned to base, the team gathered to discuss the outcome of the meeting. Over the next few days, the news reports explained how the alternatives would be taking the place of natural gas exploration. The responses were mixed. Most citizens were happy to see that the alternative-power resources were going to be put in place, but others were skeptical.

Nick was disappointed by the reports. He said, "I want to have a news conference to explain in detail the reasons why we must make these changes."

Grimaldi said, "It will not matter what you explain to our challengers. They are closed-minded individuals who will never understand what we are trying to accomplish."

Tony said, "Nick, you are doing what's best for this country. There are people who have a lot of money invested in the current infrastructure. Of course they will criticize you. All they care about is money. Don't ever question yourself!"

"I'm just happy we didn't have to blow anything up!" Maggie said.

Nick said, "I believe the results of the first mission influenced their decision. I also think we will gain more respect and strength with every endeavor!"

Grimaldi said, "I agree with all of you, but never underestimate the power of greed. We will anticipate a battle with every obstacle."

PHASE 18

Don't Drink the Water

The team gathered again to plan their next move. Grimaldi said, "The next phase in the revolution is to make sure that the water-purification system is run properly. I am not too concerned with the cost effectiveness of the water distribution as I am with the quality control."

"Look at this report." Maggie pointed to one of the monitors in the control room. "The governor of Kentucky has declared a state of emergency in Lexington. The water has been reported as being rusty with a terrible odor. Many of the citizens are becoming ill, and there is a large spike in emergency room visits over the past year. Test results are showing high levels of lead content in the water supply. The newly appointed city manager ordered the discontinuation of receiving Lexington's water from Kentucky's water source. In order to save money, he had the water division change over to the local city river water supply in Lexington. Oh my God! Those poor people!"

"This is unacceptable!" Nick said.

"I have seen scattered reports of issues throughout the country over the years, but this is extraordinary," Grimaldi said. "We have to do something about this immediately."

Nick stood up. "I will be paying the governor of Kentucky a visit."

"Calm down, Nick. We have to investigate these allegations first," Grimaldi said. "I have already hired several environmental-testing companies in each of the states throughout the country. They have been testing the water purification levels over the past few weeks. We should have the results soon."

Maggie said, "In the meantime, we will be mapping out a plan of attack for each state. We need to know where the filtration systems are housed as well as the exact city building that is responsible for the water."

By the end of the week, the details were being reported in the media. The team had completed collecting the information that was necessary to pursue the parties who were responsible for what happened in Lexington.

Nick called for the team to meet in the control room. "We have gathered the information and are prepared to engage the men and women responsible for these derelict acts of negligence."

"Look at the latest reports on the news," Maggie said. "'Latest discovery: An official for the G. A. automotive facility in Lexington, Kentucky, reported three months ago that they were experiencing corrosion to their parts from the recent water changes. Once the city manager was made aware of these issues he immediately took action to restore the manufacturing plant of the clean water source. Unfortunately, the city manager made no efforts to restore the clean water for the rest of the city. The latest results from the investigation show that all of this began in April 2014. Soon after, the citizens began complaining about discoloration in their water as well as its smell and taste. Test results revealed high levels of bacteria as well as the presence of a disinfectant byproduct, TTHM, which stands for Trihalomethane, a disinfectant. The standard purification process uses chlorine to disinfect the water, but this TTHM disinfectant is cheaper. Trihalomethane also caused the lead pipes to erode, leading to higher lead counts in the water supply. Six months later, a local pediatrician found high levels of lead in blood samples from the children of Lexington. When these reports were forwarded to Governor David Spader, he disputed the results. The state finally admitted that the test results were accurate when the news became mainstream. A spike in cases of Legionella bacteria in the Lexington area has been discovered as well, resulting in eighty-seven cases with ten fatalities.' This just keeps getting worse. We must act quickly."

Grimaldi said, “We have received the results from the independent testing companies. Apparently, nearly one hundred cities in the nation are testing poorly. Some have lead content, and others are just inadequately purified.”

Nick said, “I have contacted one of the most prestigious law firms in the country. This team led the initiative for people who are being poisoned by the gas corporations. They have begun an investigation in Lexington. The firm is preparing to send investigators throughout the nation.”

Grimaldi said, “We are prepared to take action. Rebel will visit the governor first. He is the one responsible for appointing the city manager.”

Tony said, “I saw him being interviewed the other day. He acted as though he was unaware of these processes in Lexington.”

Nick said, “He must have known what was happening once G. A. Automotive was affected. I have no doubt that Spader ignored the needs of the citizens of Lexington.”

“How do we handle this situation?” Joey asked.

“Very carefully. Rebel will pay a covert visit to the governor. You will enter his home in the late evening and explain that you know that he was fully aware of the irresponsible acts of his city manager. You will tell the governor that he should resign.”

“So you want me to scare him into resigning?” Nick asked.

“That is all you should do, Nick.” Grimaldi said. “I understand your anger, but we must not overreact.”

“I understand, sir, but he is a criminal,” Nick said. “I should shake him up a little.”

“He is as guilty as it gets,” Tony said. “He wouldn’t dare report Rebel for a little rough stuff.”

Grimaldi said, “He would—and he will. These guys will use any piece of evidence they can find to discredit Rebel. Keep your cool and deliver the message, Nick.”

“Okay.” Nick couldn’t wait to confront the governor.

Nick piloted Phantom-1 toward the governor’s mansion. The entire structure was gated and was clearly costing the taxpayers more than what they were receiving for their contributions. He found the security detail surrounding the residence. "Rebel to Control."

"Go for Control."

"I have two security men at the main entrance—two on the back grounds. What do you have inside the building?"

"I have one just inside the front entrance and one at the rear. You can drop down onto the balcony and enter the governor's study. He is working on his laptop."

"Copy that, Control. Moving in."

The Phantom hovered over the balcony, and Rebel lowered himself onto the balcony. The governor was watching the news on his laptop.

Rebel quietly slipped into the room. "Hello, Governor Spader."

"Who the hell are you?" Spader reached for his glasses. "Rebel? What are you doing here?"

"I'm here to take your confession," Rebel replied.

"Confession? I have no idea what you mean! You had better leave immediately—or I will call the police." The governor reached for the phone.

Rebel fired a grappling line at Spader's arm, "There will be no need for the police, Governor. I'm not here to sentence you. I am here to give you an opportunity to resign your position." Rebel pulled the governor toward the balcony.

"Are you kidding me? On what authority?"

"On the authority of the citizens of Lexington, Kentucky. Several petitions throughout your governorship have demanded your resignation. You are clearly for the corporations—and not the citizens of this state."

Spader said, "I will not resign my position. Follow the legal channels mandated by the state of Kentucky if you want to have me impeached."

Rebel released him of the line and clutched his fists.

The governor looked at the phone again.

Rebel drew even closer, covering him completely with his shadow. "You will resign! I will give you the opportunity to do the right thing, Governor."

"I refuse … to be … intimidated by … some terrorist."

Rebel clutched the governor by his shirt, lifted him, and tossed him onto a leather chair.

"People like you make me sick. You will resign—or you will suffer the consequences."

"Are you threatening me? I am the governor of Kentucky!"

"You are just a man—a man who cares little for the oath he took to uphold the Constitution of the United States of America and the citizens of this state."

There was a knock on the door.

Sweat dripped from the governor's brow. "I will do you a favor. Just walk out that door—and I will not report any of this to the authorities."

"Save your promises for the fools of this world. I will promise you this: if you resign, I won't return." Rebel made his way to the balcony as the security team broke through the doors.

The Phantom vacuumed him up and away.

Rebel returned to base, and Grimaldi said, "How did it go, Nick?"

"Not bad. He was afraid of my threats at first, but once he realized I was not there to physically assault him, he gained some confidence."

"What do you think his response will be?" Maggie asked.

"I had him on the ropes, but but once his men knocked on the door, his tone changed."

"You probably should have punched him a couple of times," Tony said.

"Believe me—I wanted to. The closer I got to him, the more tempted I was. Somehow, he knew I wouldn't harm him—and he answered like a politician."

Grimaldi nodded and said, "You did the right thing, Nick. The next move will be to deliver a new set of petitions to the media. We will advertise these injustices throughout the country. We have one hundred cities in a dozen states. We have already assigned the petitions to each senator, and we expect overwhelming results."

Maggie said, "Yes, we should be able to get enough signatures to present to the White House. Once we receive the final paperwork, Rebel will deliver the petitions to the city officials."

Rebel said, "If we want results, it will have to come from someone in power."

Rebel spent the next couple weeks fighting for the citizens of the neglected states. The efforts of the people, the law firms, and Team Rebel resulted in representatives being exposed and investigated. It was the first mission that directly influenced the political system.

Once Rebel delivered the petitions, he returned to Michigan. "I think we are going to strike some nerves up in Washington with this one."

Grimaldi said, "Oh, believe me—we have been ruffling plenty of feathers from the beginning!"

"Be careful what you ask for, Nick," Maggie said. "I hope the president doesn't find out about your visit with the governor."

Grimaldi said, "I don't think the governor is in any position to add to his problems. Besides, he would have already reported Rebel by now."

Joey said, "This is true. It definitely proves his guilt though."

Tony said, "I agree, Joey. He would have reported Rebel if he were not guilty."

Nick said, "We will have to keep an eye on this situation. I have a feeling we'll be revisiting this conflict."

PHASE 19

An Appointment with POTUS

The team gathered in the control room.

Grimaldi said, "Time to discuss the next phase of the revolution."

Maggie pointed to one of the monitors.

"This just in: Reports of the inadequate water quality across the nation are stirring up a negative response from citizens. Some of the people are asking for the impeachment of certain city officials who have been accused of extorting the money being saved from neglecting proper water purification. Certain groups have created a very precarious situation with these findings as well as gaining much-needed support for a progressive movement.

Nick said, "I feel that it is time to have a meeting with the president of the United States."

Grimaldi said, "Yes, it may be time to ask for a meeting with President Jackson."

Nick said. "I believe it is time to move into the job-creation phase of the revolution. I also feel that we will need the president's executive powers to increase the tariffs. As in the past, this will force manufacturing jobs to be created—starting with the Big Three."

Tony said, "We have an increasing population in this country, and we must have increased numbers of manufacturing jobs to support the economy."

Grimaldi said, "This is very relevant. We have witnessed the results of outsourcing, especially over the past ten years. The idea of a global economy has not been effective—as we now realize. When America is successful, the rest of the world benefits. Most of the countries that take on manufacturing are not awarded a living wage for the workforce. This results in cheap labor for corporations and record profits."

Tony said, "Thus far, we have not felt any resistance from the government. I feel that President Jackson is satisfied with the results of our efforts to date."

Maggie said, "I think we should create a website for the people so that they will be able to contact us to assist them with any concerns and issues they feel are important."

Nick said. "That's a great idea, Maggie! I want it tested carefully so the IP address can't be tracked back to us."

"I have already been working on that. As far as anyone tracking our IP address, I've taken care of that issue as well. I have secured servers throughout the globe that are nearly impossible to be found. They are in obscure locations and use mirror sites as well as a special program I designed. My program is designed to bounce the IP address from server to server infinitely. This will defend us against any hacking, shutdowns, or tracking. Last night, I put the finishing touches on our site by adding some features that will automatically steer any search engine that uses related words to our website. I think we should name it Rebel's Revolution."

"Great work, Maggie!" Nick said.

Grimaldi asked her to launch the website. She would double-check the site throughout the night. The next morning, she launched the website.

Mitch Whiner, the Speaker of the House of Representatives and highest-ranking member of the Republican-controlled Congress, was being hounded by his constituents. They were demanding the Speaker put pressure on the president for the actions of Rebel, and they wanted him to be stopped by any means necessary. Whiner arranged a meeting with the president. Whiner said, "The American people are outraged by the events that have transpired. The power corporations, gas corporations, and water districts have all been terrorized. Our inside sources have established that this Rebel character is responsible for these terroristic acts. This is both un-American and anti-capitalistic. Mr. President, if you are not willing to take action against this criminal, you may be found in contempt of the Constitution of the United States!"

Jackson said, "Let me remind you, Mr. Speaker, that Rebel has not been accused of breaking any laws by these corporations or anyone else. There is no proof of these allegations."

"I insist that you bring this criminal to justice immediately, Mr. President!"

The president said, "As far as I know, there was a massive breakdown of the power infrastructure. Furthermore, I have not received any reports of foul play from any source at this time. From where I sit, the American people have benefited from these changes. This has brought our dependence on fossil fuel so far out of the Stone Age. We should have been at this point twenty years ago! From my sources, the preliminary findings show that energy consumption is so low that it is unbelievable!"

The Speaker said, "Do you mean to tell me that you are not going to put a stop to this?"

"Put a stop to what?" the president asked.

"There will be a congressional investigation immediately!"

"That is your prerogative, Mr. Speaker. I believe this meeting is over. You may show yourself out."

"This is not going to end well for your friend, Mr. President!" Whiner stormed out of the room.

The president said, "I think you have it twisted!"

The president summoned his top aide. "I think it is time to have a face-to-face meeting with Rebel."

"Yes, sir. I will get right on that." He went on the Internet and typed "Rebel" in the search bar. He navigated the Team Rebel website and began to gain an insight into Rebel's mindset. A manifesto pointed out how Rebel wanted to restore the American dream, beginning with reforming infrastructure, to encourage the powers that be to realize the errors of their ways and discontinue the suppression of the innovative minds of the world. Instead, powerful leaders needed to use alternative ideas to create a better world for all of humanity.

The second major point was stopping the greed of the few at the expense of the many by creating new jobs that paid a living wage. This would return the middle class to greatness, thereby uplifting the entire country and, eventually, the world. Thirdly, the site reflected the goals of putting an end to the corruption and influence of money on political, social, and financial changes in our country.

The aide found many positive responses to the revolution. He learned that there were two ways to send a message to Rebel—publicly through the boards or privately via e-mail. He sent a private message and requested a meeting with the president at a secret location.

The team convened in the control room to discuss their options.

Maggie said, "Nick, it looks like you have another fan. This e-mail just arrived. This is from the president of the United States. 'It is very important that we meet, Rebel. I have recently received requests from certain powerful representatives of Congress about current events that allegedly involve you. I am concerned with their outrage, and I am not sure how they are going to respond. You and I should open a line of communication concerning any future developments. I feel that it is of the utmost importance that we meet as soon as possible.'"

"Wow! The president of the United States wants to meet with me? What do you think?"

Grimaldi said, "Well, this could go two ways: either he supports our efforts and is attempting to work with us or he is feeling the pressure from the right-wing establishment and is going to attempt to detain you by force."

Joey said, "Do you really believe they would attempt to detain Rebel?"

Grimaldi said. "Never put anything past a politician. President Jackson will cover his ass before any other."

Maggie said, "If they attempt to arrest you, Nick, how would you react?"

"I don't believe that it will come to that. However, if it did, I would fight my way out. No one will come between us and the revolution—not even the president of the United States!"

Grimaldi said, "That is exactly why I chose you, Nick. You are a man of integrity, a man who will not fold under the pressure of his enemies—not even the most powerful man in the world,"

Nick said, "Accept the meeting, Maggie. I will be prepared for whatever needs to be done."

Rebel piloted Phantom-1 to a hidden bunker near Washington. Rebel approached an obscure location near the mountains and used his surveillance equipment to look for the hidden bunker. The Phantom cruised the area thoroughly, but he could find no sign of a structure. "Rebel to Control."

"Go for Control."

"Looks like the area is clear of any extracurricular activity. I'm landing at the meeting sight."

"Copy that, Rebel. Watch your back," Maggie said. "They better not try any funny business."

"I agree with Nick. I feel that the president is on our side," Grimaldi said.

Rebel exited the Phantom and ordered it to hover over the site. Suddenly, a bunch of vines on the mountainside began to move aside as a hidden doorway appeared. The door opened, and two Secret Service agents escorted Rebel into the mountain. Once they were inside, the door slammed closed behind them. Rebel turned to be sure no one was approaching from behind. He felt that the slamming door was a bit much, but he kept his cool. They walked up to the end of the hallway, and one of the agents put his hand on a bio scanner, which opened a hidden elevator door. Both agents entered the elevator, and Rebel followed. They descended for a couple minutes.

When they arrived at the next destination, two more agents were waiting behind bulletproof glass. The agents put Rebel through a full body scanner. As Rebel's suit was being scanned, it fluoresced through its full spectrum of color changes like an alien cephalopod, including a complete cloak. Once the agents were done scanning Rebel, the suit changed back to platinum.

The agent who was monitoring the scanner said, "I thought the system showed Rebel disappearing for a second there?"

"That wasn't a glitch. He did disappear. I am going to explain what happened to the president before we let Rebel have his face-to-face meeting."

While the agent briefed the president, Rebel waited calmly.

When Rebel arrived in the meeting room, the president was in a steel enclosure with a ballistic viewport and an intercom.

Rebel walked up to the intercom, introduced himself, and said, "I hoped you and your detail would understand that I am not here to hurt you. I'm only attempting to support your agenda with my actions, Mr. President. I really thought you could show a little more trust here."

President Jackson put his hands up and said, "I am sorry for the formalities, but, as you know, the Secret Service has its policies. They are only following protocol, Rebel. I do believe that you are here to help." The president pointed to the door, and one of his agents opened it. The president walked up to Rebel and shook his hand. "I want to thank you for taking care of some of the more challenging issues of our time. I would have loved to been able to implement the alternatives myself, but the politics of this nation have become very … well difficult!"

Rebel said, "How do you feel about the decline of the middle class over the past ten years?"

"I believe that we will return our middle-class workers and wages to where they were before my predecessor took office," President Jackson replied.

"What is your plan to do so?" Rebel asked.

The president said, "I am very happy with the results of this revolution, but I have chosen to govern to the center. You don't understand the pressure I am under to make everyone happy, Rebel. The corporations that supported my second campaign are very powerful."

Rebel said, "If we are to change corporate America's agenda, we would like you to exercise your executive powers and increase the tariffs. The tariffs are currently at 2 percent, and your democratic predecessor had increased them to 25 percent. As you know, the 25 percent tariff forced much more job creation and a higher-wage job market. This also increased the number of union jobs, regenerated the middle class, and revitalized the economy. Without a strong middle class, this country is weak!"

President Jackson frowned. "I understand exactly what it is you're talking about, but I was reelected with the support of these corporations. They would be very upset if we increased the tariffs."

"From what I understand, you took no money from these corporations while running for your first term, but you did take contributions from them in your second campaign. Correct?"

"Yes, I did, which I now regret. I had decided to govern from the center in my second term."

"I understand that most high-ranking politicians accept money for campaigns, but that should not mean that you are beholden to these corporations," Rebel said. "I have been led to believe that you are constitutionally obligated to everyone, an equal representative to the working-class and the poor, who voted you into this office as well. I understand that you make promises as a part of your campaign, but does this mean that you give personal promises to those who give you the largest sums of money?"

"Well, no, it does not. I have passed many legislative bills and helpful programs to assist the lower-class and middle-class citizens of this nation."

"Unfortunately, not the one thing that could have increased middle-class incomes. As long as these tariffs are not increased, it will take a full-scale revolution. All the citizens of this country who are struggling will be reduced to raging in the streets to force the corruption from politics." Rebel pointed toward the exit. "You do not want that, do you, Mr. President?"

President Jackson said, "I believe that you are sincere in your convictions and that you want to create change for the betterment of our country, but people will fear these changes—and that will put us in danger. I need some time, Rebel."

"Mr. President, when a politician asks for time, that usually means years—at the very least. The time is now! You can choose to be a great leader or you can choose to be like most others, a man who came and went with no legacy worth remembering. I will give you another week to use your executive powers and increase the tariffs. As for the dangers you have mentioned, do not worry about the threats. I will take care of them. In one week, I will begin to execute the next phase of the revolution—with or without your support, Mr. President!"

The president said, "I am a fan of yours, Rebel, and I assure you that I will give my best effort to support you. However, I must warn you that this will be very dangerous. I hope I have your support as well!"

"Some of your largest contributors have already tried to kill me, sir … unsuccessfully. You should have the utmost confidence in my resourcefulness, as I have proven myself thus far."

Rebel thanked the president, shook his hand, and was escorted back to Phantom-1.

The Rebel website was getting flooded with requests for help with all kinds of environmental and political issues.

Maggie said, "I've been reviewing the website for hours. I knew there were plenty of problems in this country, but this is ridiculous!"

Nick said, "The concerns of the citizens will help us in terms of support with the revolution and our efforts to create positive change. How many requests came in today?"

Maggie replied, "So many that it is overwhelming. Listen to this one. 'I am writing to ask if Rebel could please do something about the layoffs in our state. My husband has worked in the automotive industry for fifteen years, so we thought for sure that we would be able to afford to buy a home by now. Unfortunately, he is laid off from work nearly as much as he works. We have been evicted from three different rental properties over the past four years even though we pay our rent every month. The landlords are taking our money, but they are not paying their mortgages. They claim that they have lost their jobs and cannot afford to pay their personal mortgages.'"

"This is an issue all over the country." Nick shook his head. "Corporate greed effects everyone."

Grimaldi said, "Yes, it does. People don't realize that almost every problem in this world is created by greed."

"Listen to this one," Maggie said. "'I was an engineer at Freeland

Motors for more than twenty years. Back in 2004, they began layoffs in my department. They were mostly outsourcing engineering positions to India. Last year, there were only ten engineers left from a team of one hundred. On the first of the year, all of us were let go. They decided to completely phase out the entire American workforce. They brought in a small group of Indian engineers to replace us. We have dedicated our futures to engineering, and we have loans, mortgages, and families to feed. I was reduced to taking a job at a pizzeria for ten dollars an hour. Please help us to regain our livelihoods, Rebel.'"

"Unbelievable!" Tony said. "It's bad enough when they outsource our blue-collar jobs, but when they advertise promotions and supreme lifestyles, encouraging these people to go deep into debt for their education and then put them out on the streets for cheap labor, it's inconceivable."

Nick said. "We will put an end to this. I promise."

A week later, the team gathered. Grimaldi said, "Can you please pull up the news report from this morning, Maggie?"

"Sure. Here it is." She pointed to one of the monitors.

"Just in. The president has called for an emergency congressional gathering this morning. He has signed an executive order that will increase the tariffs on trade. Corporate America and the Republican Party have answered with great displeasure. The backlash has begun. The White House is receiving tremendous pressure from corporations and investors. The Speaker of the House has scheduled a meeting with the president."

PHASE 20

A New Adversary

The team worked feverishly to research each of the Fortune 500 corporations from the top to the bottom. They found that less than 10 percent were actually treating their employees fairly, paying them well, and refusing to automate or outsource jobs to foreign countries.

Nick said, "From what I have learned, many of these corporations pay huge sums of money to Washington lobbyists, who pass these dollars to congressmen and senators. These politicians then vote in favor of the outsourcing legislation, which creates a global economy and spreads manufacturing jobs throughout the world. Unfortunately, most of these laborers in other countries do not organize as we have done here. This results in them receiving much less than our minimum wages. The corporations make all of the money by creating this system, which results in lower wages in America as well. When wages decrease, people lose their homes. In addition, fewer taxes are collected, resulting in loss of police and fire departments, educators, and government municipalities—weakening the economy of America and the world."

Tony said, "When the American economy is strong, we travel to foreign countries, spreading the money through tourism, unlike when the manufacturing is done elsewhere."

Grimaldi said, "This is all true. We definitely have our work cut out for us. There is so much abuse in the job market today and neglect in the environment. We should begin with the automotive industry. They will have no choice but to agree to our terms. The plan for the Big Three is to decrease the automating and outsourcing of American jobs, reduce production of gas-operated vehicles, and increase alternative-vehicle production. We will also inform them of their options. They may invest in the alternative companies that have established battery-manufacturing plants as well as power-source research to stop the suppression of these technologies. These batteries can be used for vehicles and infrastructure. When the wind is not heavy enough to generate power in the windmills or the sun is not bright enough for the solar panels to generate energy, the batteries will recharge the system."

Nick said, "Maggie, please set up an appointment with General American Automotive."

"I'm on it, Nick," Maggie replied.

Rebel would meet with the George D. Grump, the CEO of G. A. Automotive, the largest automotive manufacturer in the world. It was a personal issue for Nick because they were responsible for mistreating his uncle and the state of Michigan. G. A. Automotive, Freeland Motors, and Christy Motors were responsive for the economic plight in Michigan over the past ten years. Nick would not rest until they agreed to his demands.

Team Rebel began surveillance of the main headquarters of G. A. Automotive.

Maggie hunched forward and studied the data from the security footage. "Oh, boy."

"What?" Nick leaned over her shoulder.

"I think we have a problem, babe," she said. "The bastards at G. A. Automotive plan to fight the president's executive order. Grump contacted the other two CEOs, and they also spoke of plans to kill Rebel when he shows up. These men want Rebel dead—and they have no plans to involve the police."

"I want it this way, Maggie. Due to the legal ramifications that we may incur. If the automotive corporations report me to the authorities for forcing them to change their policies and manufacturing practices, I may be branded a terrorist."

"That makes sense," Grimaldi said. "That's why they would be reluctant to report Rebel to the authorities. I believe they are afraid of having to deal with a backlash. Citizens would realize that Rebel was confronting them for a good reason."

"Grump is in his office as we speak," Maggie said.

"Let's review the blueprints of G. A. Automotive headquarters one more time," Nick said.

Rebel looked down on the mammoth structure. The building was made up of five towers, standing at least thirty stories tall. Its stainless-steel exterior could be seen for miles. Rebel activated his cloak mode and landed on the highest tower.

Nick unbuckled from the pilot's seat, imagined his mask, and exited the fighter. He glanced to his right and saw three men taking aim at him. He quickly ducked behind a secure structure. They rushed Rebel with a grenade and rapid rifle fire. Instinctively, Rebel flipped behind a large generator, avoiding the explosives. Rebel reached into his backpack and threw a disc toward his attackers. The weapon slid across the floor, stopped between two mercs, and exploded.

In the confusion, one of the hired guns panicked and began to fire, accidentally shooting his partner. Rebel rushed the man, grabbed him by his military vest, and threw him several feet in the air. "Rebel to Control."

"Go for Control."

"The merc who was injured has been hit with a few shots to his leg. Fortunately, he is wearing a Kevlar vest, and his wounds are not fatal."

"Copy that, Rebel."

Rebel placed his tranq-gun on the man's shoulder and said, "This is for the pain, man." He put the merc out of his misery.

The third merc snuck up behind Rebel and fired at him with a grenade launcher. The grenade landed directly in front of Rebel, exploded on impact, and created smoke and debris.

When the dust finally settled, Rebel was motionless.

The man began to laugh. "I knew I could finish you, you freak!" The merc touched Rebel's suit, and the suit became defensive—causing the enemy to bleed. The suit changed colors, surprising the predator.

Rebel clenched his fist and threw an uppercut at the man's jaw, knocking him unconscious. Rebel flipped to his feet and said, "Hope Grump didn't spend too much money on you boys!"

In the executive offices, three more mercs were to challenge him. One of the men broke through the wall, jumped on Rebel's back, and put him in a headlock.

Rebel grabbed the man's torso with one hand and threw him through a couple of partitions. Before the merc was released, he was able to drop a grenade at Rebel's feet, which exploded, causing the floor to give way. Rebel lost his balance and fell to the floor.

The second man jumped on Rebel, unloading his submachine gun into Rebel's chest. When he reloaded his weapon, Rebel got up onto all fours, threw a reverse-sweep kick, and took out the man's feet. The gunmen landed on his side, and the magazine slid across the room. Rebel flipped to his feet as the third enemy quickly approached from behind, firing at him from close range with an assault rifle. Rebel turned to confront the attacker, and the second merc began to fire at Rebel. Both men ran out of ammunition and rushed Rebel. They grabbed Rebel's arms, attempting to bring him to the ground. They pulled out knives, stabbing at Rebel from all directions. The knives could not penetrate the armor, and the suit began to pulsate, building up a surge of energy.

Rebel thrust his arms out, shocking the men and knocking them unconscious. He had little time to contemplate his newfound ability. "Rebel to Control. How many more enemies are left?"

"That's all of them. Looks like you can approach the CEO!"

Rebel saw Grump and said, "Why all the security?"

"Why don't you just die!" Grump yelled.

Rebel said, "Why don't you just cooperate. I'm bringing an end to the right-wing new world order. Embrace the replacement of the current regime of the few by the compassionate masses that embrace the needs of all. You and your associates are done practicing business in a pre-Depression manner, like during the times of the robber barons when people were used as slave laborers!"

Suddenly, an explosion ensued. The ceiling tiles began to fall. A large piece of machinery dropped from the ceiling and landed on top of Grump. Rebel jumped back and gathered his senses.

Grump's image was flickering. All of a sudden, it vanished.

Rebel realized he was speaking to a hologram. He turned his attention to the object that had dropped from above. Rebel stared at a combat-military robot that stood seven feet tall on a tripod. The machine had a triangular caterpillar track for each foot with a rear-stabilizer foot shaped like a steel ball swivel for balance and support. In the center-mass position, there was a six-barrel electric mini-gun. On each side, the creature had two articulating machine guns with grenade launchers. An armored triangular-shaped shell covered the top of the robot, and there was an optical sensor in the center of its body.

The robot targeted Rebel, firing from both sides. Rebel pulled out both guns and blasted the enemy with a volley of concussion rounds, hoping to distract it long enough to give him the time to load one of his mini-rockets. The concussion rounds seemed to confuse the robot slightly. It stopped within five feet of Rebel and began to scan the area.

Rebel avoided the line of fire, rolled toward the robot, and pulled out both pairs of titanium nunchucks. The enemy attempted to hit Rebel with rapid fire, adjusting to the difficult angles that Rebel was creating. Rebel attacked the robot's weapons system on the left side, destroying its gun. He jumped on the robot, and jammed the nunchucks into the robot's optical sensor.

The robot bucked Rebel into the air, spun toward hum, and began to fire from close range. Rebel's suit protected him from the onslaught. He was able to find cover in a nearby storage area. The robot scanned the area and waited for Rebel to return.

Rebel threw a smoke bomb at his adversary, distracting the creature just long enough to rush it. He reached into his backpack for a bomb and threw it over his shoulder. As smoke consumed the area, the robot began to fire in Rebel's direction.

Rebel sprinted toward his enemy, and some of the ammunition was absorbed by the suit's force field. Once Rebel regained a visual on his enemy through his thermal vision, he extended his arms, and fired his grappling hooks into the robot's chest. The hooks latched onto its armor. Rebel came to a screeching halt. Pulling as hard as he could, to sent his attacker into a frontward somersault. The robot landed on its chest.

Rebel planted a C-4 pack on the back of the robot, flipped out of the blast ratio, and destroyed the robot.

When the smoke cleared, Rebel did not detect any further threats. He took a few moments to inspect the robot's scattered pieces. "Dead."

Maggie said, "Control to Rebel."

"Go for Rebel."

"Not a great idea, taking that attack head on, Rebel! Be more tactical in the future!" Maggie said.

"Yes, that was slightly taxing. I'm fine though!" Rebel said. "I didn't exactly have time to map out a plan."

Two more robots began to target him. Rebel dropped smoke, distracting them long enough to make his way to the center of the room, and readied himself for battle.

Just as the smoke began to clear, the assassins acquired their target. Their mini-guns began to spin, firing at Rebel. However, it was too late. Rebel had already drawn his weapons. He locked in on the robots with his rockets, and destroyed the metal menaces. "Rebel to Control."

"Go for Control."

"Do you have a location on Grump?"

Maggie said, "I've been searching for him this whole time. Unfortunately, it appears as though he was never in the building. The hologram was being transmitted from a remote location."

"Unfortunately, my work is done here. I'm on my way back to base," Rebel said.

The team assembled on the launchpad, and Rebel said, "I'm very upset that there were no negotiations with that greedy bastard. Compared to the previous missions, it looks like we are in for a huge battle with Grump. After all we have accomplished over the past few months, I anticipated some type of bargaining. This guy is pure evil and should be dealt with as such!"

Grimaldi said, "I understand your frustration, but there is a line that is not to be crossed if we are to keep the support of the president, Nick."

Joey said, "Nick, I think we need to visit the armory before you go on the next mission."

"Yeah, I know what you mean," Nick replied.

Nick said, "How should we handle this situation?"

Grimaldi said, "You should visit the other two automotive corporations and convince them to agree with our terms. Perhaps this will force Grump's hand when the others cooperate."

The team agreed with Grimaldi.

Maggie turned to Nick and asked, "Are you okay to continue?"

"I'm fine. It's more my ego at this point."

Maggie said, "By the way, while you were under attack, you barely touched that one man before he flew into the air. Does the suit really give you that much strength?"

"Yes, the suit does give me great strength, but that was something different. When I became infuriated by the one merc, the suit fed off of my anger. A burst of energy flowed through the suit, transferring into an electric charge. The power surge exited my hands in a burst of focused energy. That's why you saw the man fly into the air. In the second instance, it was as though the suit felt that I was in danger. All of a sudden, I felt a stronger surge of energy. I felt no anger or fear though. The suit must have its own defensive mechanism to protect its wearer. When the mercs were attempting to stab me, I went to shake them off. A burst of energy threw them across the room. That's the only way I can describe it."

Grimaldi said, "We are only scratching the surface of what this suit is fully capable of. In time, you may evolve into a self-sufficient weapon, Nick. You may even be able to fly one day."

"That wouldn't surprise me. I remember being able to jump up a couple of stories during our training and landing from even higher distances."

Tony said, "This is surreal. I cannot believe what I'm seeing. You're becoming a weapon, Nick!"

Grimaldi said, "Maggie, please set up an appointment with Freeland Motor Corporation."

Maggie set up the appointment and reviewed the blueprints of Freeland's headquarters with Nick.

Joey stepped into the control room. "Are you guys almost done in here?"

"Just finishing up. Let's go, Joey," Nick replied.

The men went in the weapons vault. Joey said, "I was in the control room, watching the attack from the combat robots. We need to upgrade you to some armor-piercing ammo." Joey opened a case of ammunition and took out one of the bullets. "Each of these bullets contains a center-explosive gel charge. These should be able to penetrate any armor. Once the armor is penetrated, there will be a miniature explosion—like an armor-piercing artillery shell. This should, at the very least, slow down any further attacks from these robots."

"Good idea, Joey," Nick said. "As the mission escalates, the competition gets wealthier."

PHASE 21

Gaining Ground

Maggie said. "I spoke with the assistant to the CEO of Freeland Motors, and they agreed to the meeting. The CEO is Clay Edsel Freeland."

"Thanks, Maggie. We need to be sure that Freeland is actually at the headquarters before I leave."

Maggie pointed to one of the monitors. "I have his office up now. Let's do this!"

"There he is," Nick said. "I'm gonna head out immediately."

"Be careful," Maggie said. "Keep your cool. I love you."

"I got this—and I love you back."

Rebel was surprised to find a modest structure as he landed on the rooftop. He entered the CEO's office, avoiding detection, and introduced himself to the assistant.

"Can I please have your autograph Rebel?" she asked with a smile.

"Thank you, but I'm not here for that. I'm just here to help."

The assistant called the CEO, and Mr. Freeland asked her to show him in.

"Please follow me, Rebel."

Maggie said, "Can I *please* have your autograph, Rebel?"

"You have nothing to be jealous of, Control," Rebel whispered into his microphone.

Rebel carefully entered the office, but there were only a couple of security guards with Freeland.

Rebel said, "Hello, Mr. Freeland. My name is Rebel."

The men shook hands.

"You have nothing to worry about here, Rebel. There will be no fighting. At the same time, I will not be dictated to when it comes to running my business!"

Rebel said, "I'm not here to run you out of business, sir, but there will be little compromise in the negotiations."

Freeland said, "There needs to be change. I am being pressured by some of my associates. They're demanding that we not give in to the changes you're asking of us."

"You and your colleagues' business practices will be replaced by the alternatives—sooner than later. Climate change is real, and if you continue with your current practices, there will not be much of a planet left to leave behind for your grandchildren. You are destroying our planet with these oil-producing products."

"Wait a minute, Rebel. Here at Freeland, we operate under the guidelines of the law."

"Oh, you mean the corrupted regulations? The citizens of this country are fed up with the disparity of wealth between you and your colleagues. The foreign auto companies are manufacturing more alternative vehicles that have better fuel efficiency and higher-quality, longer-lasting products that do not pollute the environment. They also are paying higher wages to their employees. I implore you to discontinue the automation and outsourcing of jobs. Create a realistic number of jobs if you want to continue doing business in America!"

"Sounds to me like you're not asking!" said Freeland.

Rebel replied, "I have several corporations that are willing to invest in alternative-manufacturing operations. They are ready to join my revolution, replacing you and your antiquated practices. I will use my influence with the citizens to encourage them to use these alternatives."

"These alternatives are very expensive to produce. Most of the community will not be able to afford them," Freeland said.

"Yes, this is true. When you and your colleagues manufacture these alternatives, you overcharge the citizens, but my investors are willing to take less profit in order to save the environment, Mr. Freeland."

"I wish them luck in their endeavor—they're going to need it," Freeland said.

Rebel said, "Also, within the next few years, we need to eliminate all gas-fueled vehicles."

"Is this even possible?" Freeland asked.

"Take a trip to Brazil, Mr. Freeland. We can grow sugarcane here in the States, so that may be an investment you should look into for the production of ethanol fuel."

"I understand what you are referring to with the Brazilian ethanol fuel. I believe we may have some interest in these fuel sources, but the oil corporations will never allow the replacement of traditional gas-fueled vehicles."

"I realize that the greed of the oil corporations outweighs their foresight and that they intend to use every drop of oil possible before giving in to the alternatives. Unfortunately, we cannot afford to go along with that plan. If they do, they will destroy this planet! Don't worry about the oil corporations. I will handle them."

Freeland said, "I believe that your intentions are legitimate, Rebel. I also believe that we must change the manufacturing model, if not for the planet, at least for my grandchildren's future. I also believe that I am ready to move forward with you!"

"Very good, sir. That's all I wanted to hear from you. I promise that you will not regret your decision. One day, you will be looked upon as a savoir!"

The men shook hands, and Freeland said, "Okay, Rebel. I promise to move forward with you."

"Thank you, Mr. Freeland. We will be in contact by the end of the week."

Rebel returned to base and said, "I feel that we've made very good progress with Mr. Freeland."

"I agree. He seems sincere about the changes that are necessary," Grimaldi replied.

"I will not be convinced about anything these men say until I see it in writing!" Tony said.

Joey pulled out a hammer from his tool belt. "Most of the time, it takes brute force to deal with a tyrant!"

Nick said, "That is exactly what Rebel is here for. Without the threat of force, we would not have achieved anything at this point!"

Maggie said, "I have set an appointment with Chrysty Motors. You're scheduled to meet with Reginald C. Dodge in two days at their corporate headquarters."

Rebel thanked Maggie, and they viewed the blueprint of the building.

Rebel landed on the rooftop of Chrysty Motors and was disturbed by the outlandish surroundings. Rebel exited the Phantom and made his way to the meeting place. Maggie had done some research. She found that Chrysty Motors had merged with an Italian company, Fuego Motors, six months earlier. Since the Italians were in a foreign country, they feared a war on American soil. Fuego decided to use attorneys to deal with Rebel. It was a first for Rebel. He would prefer to fight it out with a handful of mercs.

Rebel approached the assistant's desk. "Hi, I am here to meet with Mr. Dodge."

The assistant put her hand up to her mouth and whispered, "I am a huge fan of yours, Rebel!"

"Thank you, miss," Rebel replied.

Once she had announced Rebel, the assistant asked him to enter the boardroom.

The room was filled with people. "Hello, my name is Rebel. Wow, this is a large group!"

Mr. Dodge introduced himself and said, "We merged with an Italian company recently. This is the CEO of Fuego Motors, Mr. Diablo, and these lawyers are here to represent our mutual interests."

Rebel decided to hear them out.

The lead attorney said, "Rebel, this is quite simple. You have no contractual agreement with Chrysty Motors. We are aware of your demands, but we are in disagreement."

Rebel smiled and shook his head. "Due to the climate changes that we have been experiencing around the world over the past decade and the corruption your clients have participated in, along with the majority of corporate America, there must be an immediate transformation of procedure."

"We are sorry to hear about that. How is this our problem though?" the attorney asked.

Rebel said, "I'll tell you how. Your clients pay billions of dollars to corrupt politicians through lobbying instead of just passing on a portion of that money to their employees, creating a copacetic work environment. Instead, your employees have had their wages stagnated or decreased tremendously over the past ten years. Your clients treat their employees unfairly. All the while, the cost of living increases every year, including the cost of their products! Your clients really have no choice but to comply—or else there will eventually be a revolution that will not allow them to keep their wealth or even possibly, their lives."

The lead attorney stood up and said, "Are you threatening our clients with this revolution?"

"I'm not threatening anyone. I am promising that the citizens of this country are sick and tired of these conditions that have been created, and they are going to revolt. When they see someone like me taking action, they will be encouraged and empowered by my movement because they with have more than a fighting chance with me in their corner. I will not stop fighting for the citizens of this country until we have changed the culture of corporate America, have reversed climate change, and have restored the American dream!"

"You have no legal rights to dictate to our clients how they should or should not run their corporations. You should leave now—or we will be forced to call the police and have you arrested for trespassing!"

Rebel turned to the CEOs and said, "Is this how you want to proceed?"

Dodge and Diablo looked at each other for a moment.

Dodge said, "I think we should come to some type of compromise here."

The lead attorney said, “Please, sir. Let us handle this.”

Rebel said, “This is the problem with the corporate mentality. You have middle management and corrupt lawyers who want to protect their perks. You are the equivalent of medieval monarchs, and your employees are the peasants.”

“We have been hired to do a job, Rebel.”

“You have no right to stop the CEOs from negotiating with me, do you?” Rebel asked.

Diablo said, “Please allow us to negotiate with Rebel.”

The lead attorney said, “Who do you think you are, Rebel, dictating to us how to run this business. You are nothing more than a terror.”

Diablo motioned for the attorney to sit down and asked Dodge for a recess. He and Dodge excused themselves for a few minutes.

Diablo said, “I believe we should come to some compromise with Rebel.”

Dodge replied, “I am not convinced that we are going to maintain current profits with these alternative lines. We also will have to deal with the backlash from Big Oil.”

“I am aware of the oil corporations, but they are nowhere near as dangerous as Rebel or the threat of a revolution. I have seen this country’s resolve throughout history. With Rebel leading the American citizens, it will be nearly impossible to defeat them.”

Dodge said. “Let’s set up a meeting for next week. That will give us some time to crunch the numbers with our team.”

When the men returned, Diablo said, “We are willing to set an appointment to discuss the terms.”

Rebel said, “I will have the contract delivered to you tomorrow by the end of the business day. I will also contact the regional union president and his committee to attend our next meeting as well.”

The CEOs agreed, and an appointment was set for the following week.

When Rebel returned to base, Grimaldi said, “I believe that we are making progress with Chrysty Motors.”

Maggie asked, "Does anyone here believe that these men are going to hire an expensive team of lawyers and then just give in to us?"

"You didn't see the look in their eyes, Maggie!" Nick explained.

"We were watching. I believe we have their attention," Grimaldi said.

Maggie pointed to one of the monitors. "Look at the latest reports: 'This just in. G. A. Automotive has reported the recent damage to their headquarters as a malfunction with some robotic units that were being tested for automation.' Obviously, Grump does not want the public to find out that Rebel was involved in the policing of his business."

Nick said, "I think these reports are a sign that Grump may be scared of the bad press that he will receive if the truth comes out about my visit."

Grimaldi said, "Yes, I think we have Grump right where we want him."

Maggie said, "I believe we should give a one-on-one interview to a lead reporter from one of the national media sources. Rebel should take the credit for the changes we have brought to the forefront."

"We would also be taking credit for the destruction of the infrastructure," Grimaldi said.

Nick said, "No. Maggie is right. We should take the revolution to the people. We can reveal the whole truth, ending all speculation. This may put even more pressure on the corporations."

Grimaldi said, "You both may have a point. I'll set it up."

The following day, the team prepared to answer questions from the media.

Grimaldi said. "Nick, I agreed to a live broadcast so they will not be able to edit any of the conversation. Please do not be baited into answering any personal questions. Stick to business. That is what you are going to be there for."

Nick said, "Of course. I'm prepared to emphasize the information on our website. As far as any future plans, they will have to wait and see."

"Are you going to talk about any of the previous missions?" Maggie asked.

"I don't see how that could be a problem," Nick said.

"That is fine," Grimaldi said. "Just keep it short. We do not need to answer too many questions at this point."

Rebel met with one of the national news outlets in Atlanta. Security led him to the newsroom. The building was full of people, and everyone was excited to see Rebel.

Drake Trapper, the lead anchor, said, "Thank you very much for taking this interview, Rebel."

"Thank you for having me, Mr. Trapper."

The men walked over to the set, and the cameras were ready to roll. The room was buzzing with anticipation, and the employees could not keep quiet. The set director asked for a microphone to pin on Rebel, but the device would not attach to his suit. He asked for a microphone that was mounted to a stand, and the assistant hurried to retrieve one.

Trapper said, "Are you ready?"

"Yes, sir. I am."

The director asked for silence, putting up his hand. "Four, three, two, one."

Trapper said, "We are joined here today by the man who calls himself Rebel. Thank you for joining us. As you must know, the people have so many questions."

"I understand, Drake. It's nice to be here. I would like to let everyone know that I have a website that is active to the public. If they have any questions or concerns, I will receive them."

"The website is being shown at the bottom of your screens," Trapper said. "Let me ask you, Rebel, are you from another planet?"

"I would like to answer that question, but I'm afraid it would distract from the real issues here. In time, I will explain where I am from—just not until the revolution is won."

"So you are not denying the possibility?" Trapper asked.

"I need to make this clear without offending anyone. I am here to save this country from climate change and to address the declining middle class. The corruption in this country has reached catastrophic levels. I have witnessed corporate greed and neglect for far too long. I realize there has not been an organization to deal with these threats."

"So, will you take credit for the destruction of the power grids?" Trapper asked.

"Yes."

The crowd in the studio began to chatter again, and the director threw his hands in the air to quiet them.

Rebel said, "I attempted to negotiate with the leaders of the power corporations, but they decided to lure me into a trap. I was forced to defend myself … as anyone would. They lied to me—just as they have lied to the public for years. These corporations overcharge for their services and pollute the environment with fossil fuels. I had the alternative infrastructure aligned to supply the citizens of this nation with clean, sufficient energy. Now we are showing improvement in air quality and keeping the cost as low as possible. Lower rates will come." Rebel looked proudly at the camera.

"So, you're not concerned with any repercussions, now that you have decided to take credit for your actions?"

"This is a revolution, Drake. I will do what is necessary."

"Are you working alone?"

"No. I have enlisted several companies to assist me in the transformation of the infrastructure and with any future investments that may be needed to support the revolution."

"I am sorry. I meant like a team."

Rebel said, "No. I have used an alias to contact the companies who have assisted with the revolution."

"Are you willing to divulge the company names to us?" Trapper leaned in closer.

"Sorry again. They would like to remain anonymous at this time."

"So what is next, Rebel?"

"I'm currently negotiating with the automotive industry. We are close to an agreement."

"What are the issues with the automotive corporations?"

"Pollution through traditional gas-guzzling vehicles must come to an end as well as outsourcing jobs, which have created a minimum-wage state," Rebel replied.

"How will you get them to agree with these demands?" Trapper asked.

"I have explained to them that several companies are willing to step in and create the alternative manufacturing that is necessary to reverse climate change and support employees across the nation. These companies are willing to take less profit and increase the compensation of their employees in time."

"It could take years to develop these manufacturing plants," Trapper said.

"Actually, there are thousands of empty manufacturing plants that were closed by the automotive industry in the bailout of 2008. These plants were ordered by the government to be liquidated in the bailout. They are ready to be bought and prepped for production. We are ready to take over this industry. The current industry will be replaced—sooner rather than later!"

"What is the goal?" Trapper asked.

"I will not map out my entire plan for you, Trapper. That would be detrimental to the revolution. I will leave you with this—there is a lot of work to be done, as all of you know. I will take on the polluters and leaders. I will not rest until this planet has been saved and the American dream is restored!"

The crowd cheered.

"When is your projection for the revolution to be completed?" Trapper asked.

"There is no time frame. I will do my best to complete this revolution efficiently. I would like to thank all of you for your support. Thank you for this opportunity, Drake, and good day."

Trapper thanked him for the interview and continued to address the nation.

Rebel made his way back to base. "So what did you think?"

Maggie said, "I think you did very well."

"I agree," Grimaldi said. "You stuck to the game plan. Very good, Nick."

"Well, it's official. You're a celebrity, Rebel," Joey said.

Nick laughed. "Easy, killer. I would rather not have done that interview, but the citizens deserved some clarification."

Grimaldi said, "Enough with the celebrity talk. Let's get back to business."

"Agreed. I'm ready to pay a second visit to G. A. Automotive," Nick said.

Rebel drove the ATV to the headquarters and entered through the parking structure. Rebel secured a grappling line to a steel beam, jumped over the opening, and reeled himself down to the front entrance.

The people on the street looked on with surprise as he entered the building through the front door. "Hello. My name is Rebel. I'm here to see Mr. Grump."

"Okay, sir. I will let him know that you are here."

Grump was meeting with his board of directors. "I am not interested in giving in to this terrorist, but I am aware of the progress he has achieved with my colleagues."

One of the most experienced directors said, "The deal that Rebel proposed to our competitors and us is fair to all parties. We will be able to stay in business and invest with the alternative companies in battery manufacturing, leading to future investments with the alternatives, including utility production. We also may invest in future technologies that will be very profitable looking forward."

Grump said. "I understand all of that. Unfortunately, I have paid millions of dollars for lobbying. It kills me just to give in to this bastard!"

Another director said, "If we were to go to war with this thug, we could not afford to halt production in any of our facilities. It could put us into bankruptcy. We cannot survive a stoppage of work in this economy."

Grump agreed to meet with Rebel and explained his feelings.

Rebel replied, "How do you think your former employees feel about their plight due to the outsourcing you have implemented? How do feel about the millions of former middle-class families being oppressed by a system put in place to service your greed while you and your family have never sacrificed a day in your lives? I'm here to put an end to the corruption. If anyone tries to extort money from you for any wrongdoings, contact me through my website. I will deal with them for you personally!"

Grump said, "All right, then. I am in."

"You won't regret this, sir," Rebel said.

That evening, the team gathered to celebrate the victory. Grimaldi cracked open a bottle of champagne. "Here's to perseverance and hard work paying off."

Maggie turned on the news to see what was being reported.

David Steele said, "A press release has been issued by the three automotive giants, confirming that the superpowers are negotiating a new contract with the UAW. These negotiations involve discontinuing outsourcing and automated jobs, reduction of the manufacturing of traditional-fueled vehicles, a substantial increase in alternative vehicle production, and investment in battery-manufacturing companies and ethanol fuel sources. One of our reporters is standing by at the Main Headquarters of G. A. Automotive. Andrea, what have you found?"

"An alternative source says that the revolutionary who goes by the name of Rebel probably had something to do with these events, but the automotive corporations are denying any association with him."

"Thank you, Andrea. We're going to speak with another one of our reporters who is standing by at UAW headquarters. Who exactly put this meeting together, Jim?"

The reporter said, "The official with whom I spoke earlier said that Rebel was responsible for the negotiations, and the union was just recently notified of the occurrence."

David replied, "So your source has verified that Rebel has initiated these negotiating—not the union?"

"Correct. But any time there is a negotiation in terms of the automotive industry, the union must be notified and assumes the leadership role, representing the labor force."

Team Rebel was pleased to hear the news reporting something positive for a change.

Nick wrapped his arms around Maggie and gave her a big kiss.

Grimaldi said, "Until the contract is signed and the changes begin, our work is not complete!"

"I feel the momentum of the revolution shifting into a celebratory moment," Nick said. "However, this battle is nowhere near over"

Tony said, "These men are not to be trusted to keep their

word—regardless of any contract. These CEOs have teams of lawyers who look for loopholes in contracts that will allow them to break the agreement."

Grimaldi said, "This contract will be written with a group of lawyers that Rebel will retain through one of the alternative companies I have been conferring with for many years. The CEO of this alternative company has no affiliation with the military—so there will be no tying him to the revolution or to us. Rebel, you will explain the terms to the lawyers, and they will draw up the contract with your final approval. They will supervise the contract negotiations. We will not move to the next phase of the revolution until we are confident with the results!"

PHASE 22

Fight to the Death

The following week, Rebel met with the CEOs from the three automotive corporations and their lawyers at a conference center in Detroit. Rebel made sure that the union committee and his own attorneys were in attendance. Rebel's lawyers presented their version of the new contract to the union committee a few days prior. The union committee also added a few suggestions to the contract. When both parties were satisfied with the contract, the lawyers for the corporations received their copies.

Jack Offner, one of the attorneys, said, "There must be more time allowed in terms of the ceasing of the outsourcing."

"We request a reasonable time frame," Team Rebel's counsel, James Figner, replied.

"This should take two years—minimum," Offner replied.

"We will allow a maximum of a six-month period. We understand the terms you have contracted with your business partners overseas. You must give them a six-month notice before pulling any jobs from their manufacturing facilities."

In a recess, Rebel said, "There will be no compromise on this issue. It is crucial to our efforts that we stop any further outsourcing within the six-month time frame!"

The lawyers went back to the table, arguing back and forth with the opposing counsel for an hour.

Rebel stood up, faced the CEOs, and said, "Do you gentlemen recall our agreement from last week?"

The CEOs looked at each other and asked for another recess.

Freeland said, "Grump, we are willing to agree with the terms of this contract. Just swallow your pride so we can move on."

Grump was not willing to give in to the terms.

The three men debated for fifteen minutes before taking a vote. Freeland and Dodge agreed to give Rebel the contract, but Grump refused to sign it. He stormed out of the conference room.

Rebel said, "Where are you going, Mr. Grump?"

Grump rushed down the stairs and jumped into his limousine.

Rebel returned to the meeting to find that Freeland and Dodge had agreed to the terms of the new contract. He shook hands with remaining CEOs, the lawyers, and the union committee. "Let's give Mr. Grump some time to reconsider our terms. Meanwhile, we will begin to implement the new contract for Chrysty and Freeland Motors."

Rebel returned to base. "I'm very disappointed in Grump!"

Grimaldi said, "We have to convince him that we are not playing games here!"

Maggie said, "What are we going to do other than dangle him upside down by his legs from the top of his huge building?"

"We must use force with this one!" Tony said.

"I will pay Grump another visit—very soon," Nick said. "Meanwhile, we need ears and eyes on him immediately. We will gauge his emotions. Once he realizes that the contract is actually in effect and the other corporations are fully engaged, he will be furious!"

Freeland and Dodge attempted to contact Grump but received no reply. Team Rebel would use surveillance to monitor Grump. They discovered him speaking on the phone and making plans with the military division of G. A. Automotive to bring in more sophisticated weapons to kill Rebel.

The team gathered to contemplate their options.

Grimaldi said, "Grump is not replying to our e-mail request for another meeting. I'm afraid that we are not going to get anywhere with him. Rebel must visit Grump again and convince him that his operations will be phased out eventually. Once we've implemented the alternatives, his practices will soon be obsolete."

Nick said, "We all knew this would happen, but Grump believes corporate America will prevail. He does not understand the powers that he is up against. I'll visit him again tonight and convince him that it will not matter what he throws at me. I will fight to the death—even if it means his!"

Maggie said, "Nick, are you thinking what I think you're thinking?"

"I'm done negotiating with him!"

"Please keep your cool, Nick!" Grimaldi said.

"I promise I will, but I'm only giving Grump one more chance to comply. If he doesn't agree with our terms, I may have to go old school and get a little physical with him!"

"It's about time you begin to muscle some of these billionaires," Tony said. "This will send a strong message to the rest of them!"

Maggie said, "I have something new from Grump. This e-mail says that Grump is ready to have a meeting within the hour at the headquarters of G. A. Automotive." She quickly pulled up the surveillance footage. "I have Grump at his headquarters right now."

Nick quickly suited up and rushed to Phantom-1 for his visit with Grump.

Rebel landed on the roof in cloak mode.

"Control to Rebel."

"Go for Rebel."

"There are two guards inside the entrance."

Rebel used his special powers. "I have their heat signatures through the wall. I'll draw them out here and take care of them."

Rebel fired a tranq-dart into the door.

The men heard the noise and came out to investigate.

Rebel dropped down on one of the men while firing a concussion bullet at the other. He put the second man into a chokehold, leaving him unconscious.

"Looks like you're clear until you get to Grump's office. He has two more guards with him."

"Thanks, Control. I'm en route to the office!"

Before Rebel could get to the office, he encountered two humanoid-like-robots. The 'bots were much more sophisticated than the previous ones. They had heads, arms, and legs and were athletic. They also had machine guns mounted to their arms.

One of the bots found Rebel in its sights and began to fire its machine guns. The other picked up a desk and threw it in Rebel's direction. Rebel back-flipped through a plate-glass wall, shattering it. He landed in an office, avoiding the desk and the gunfire. Rebel worked his way around to the other side of the building and was able to split up the two bots.

Rebel made his way up to the next floor through the staircase. He used his X-ray vision to track one of the attackers. He stomped on the floor to draw its attention. The bot sensed the noise, and it jumped through the ceiling.

Rebel set his pistols for armor-piercing rounds and began to fire into the center of its chest. The ammunition barely slowed it down because it wasn't able penetrate the advanced armor. It fired on Rebel with both arms extended.

Rebel jumped through the ceiling and dropped down on the robot. Rebel pulled a pair of nunchucks out of his suit, wrapped the chains around the bot's throat, and choked it. The metal menace began to twist and buck as its counterpart entered the room and launched a rocket at Rebel.

Maggie yelled, "Jump!"

Rebel jumped through the hole in the ceiling as the rocket destroyed the other robot.

The second robot leaped through the hole in the ceiling and chased after him. Rebel pulled out his other pair of nunchucks and attacked with both pairs flailing. Before the bot could fire on him, Rebel disabled its weapons system.

The robot had no weapons and rushed at Rebel.

Rebel put his nunchucks away and struck with a double jab, an inside leg-kick, and his right hand. The robot was able to keep its footing and countered with its right hand, knocking Rebel back a few feet. Rebel countered with another combination of strikes—a lead jab kick, a right-knee lunge, and a left-hook kick to the head—knocking it to the ground.

The weakened bot was able to get back to its feet and attacked Rebel with its right hand.

Rebel slid behind the bot, putting it into a chokehold. The robot could not escape Rebel's strong hold. Rebel kicked out its legs, pulled out one of his pistols, and fired several armor-piercing rounds into the robot's skull. At such close range, the ammunition penetrated and exploded internally, dropping the assassin to the floor.

"Control, do you still have Grump in the building?"

"Yes, he is still in his office. It looks like he is not aware of you. He is just casually working at his computer. I'm not sure why or how, but it seems like he is very relaxed."

"Maybe he feels a little too confident with his new toys. I'm on my way to his office."

Rebel kicked in the door, and Grump's two security guards ran out of the rear exit, leaving him alone and unprotected.

Grump screamed, "How the hell did you get past my robots?"

"I warned you before that there is nothing you can do to stop me, Grump!"

Grump said, "What are you going to do, Rebel? Kill me? That is not your style. You are supposed to be *so* righteous, but you're just a common terrorist! You may have fooled the people of this country, but you haven't fooled me!"

"I'm not going to kill you, but I wouldn't be very righteous if I couldn't deliver on my promise to the people!" Rebel grabbed the CEO and raised him off of his feet. "You are going to sign that contract, or—"

One of the bots came from behind and fired in the room. The robot was able to recover from the armor-piercing rounds because its internal CPU was in its central core, surrounded by advanced armor. The robot's targeting system was not aiming accurately.

Rebel consumed the barrage of ammunition, protecting Grump from the attack. They were thrown through the wall and into the next room. Rebel said, "Are you okay?"

"Yes!" Grump said.

"Stay down! I'll take care of your mess," Rebel said.

The impaired robot was able to reacquire his target. It entered through the damaged wall, firing in Rebel's direction. Rebel was concerned for Grump's life, and he took on the attack aggressively.

The bot sent Rebel tumbling across the room.

Grump stood up and ordered his assassin to cease-fire. Its voice command was damaged, and the bot would not comply.

Rebel gathered his senses and drew his pistols. Unfortunately for Grump, the metal menace fired again. Its attack targeted Grump instead of Rebel. Rebel's suit began to change colors dramatically. Rebel turned to the bot and rushed through its hail of bullets. He grabbed the robot and delivered a powerful surge of energy.

The robot flew across the room.

Rebel made sure the bot was destroyed and threw it through the wall.

Rebel approached the bot to confirm its demise. The robot did not respond.

Rebel then went to check on Grump. Unfortunately, he was dead.

Maggie said, "Rebel, get out of there now! The police are on their way!"

Rebel rushed to the rooftop before the police arrived.

Once he returned to base, the team had an emergency meeting.

Nick said, "I'm very concerned about how this is going to look to the public!"

Grimaldi said, "We have video footage that is going to be leaked to the media within the hour. This footage will show that the robot killed Grump."

Maggie said, "It may not matter because the corporations are going to claim that Rebel had no business being there!"

Tony put his hand on Nick's shoulder and said, "Let's keep our cool. Here is how we are going to handle this. Rebel will go to the authorities to explain what happened. Give them a copy of the e-mail invite. They will understand the state of mind that Grump was in and how he clearly ambushed you."

Joey said, "Maybe we should just wipe out the camera footage!"

Grimaldi said, "No. The footage shows the bots attacking Rebel—as well as Grump's death. That would not be advantageous."

Nick said, "We have to leak that footage immediately so the public can see the unedited truth. They'll realize I have nothing to hide—and then I will go to the authorities to explain what happened."

Grimaldi asked Maggie to put the footage on the Internet.

Nick and Maggie turned on the news. The footage was being shown across the world. The media speculated about the attack. The investigation was underway, and the police wanted Rebel to come in for questioning.

Grimaldi walked into Nick and Maggie's living room. "I have contacted the attorneys from the automotive negotiations. They want to meet Nick at the district attorney's office in two hours."

"I'm ready. I'll just tell the truth!" Nick replied.

Grimaldi said, "Explain the situation to the attorneys—and then follow their directions. Worst-case scenario is that you get booked and bailed."

"I hope it doesn't come to that," Maggie said.

The board of directors at G. A. Automotive convened to discuss their next move. "I want to make it clear that I will be choosing a replacement for Grump within the week," the president said. "Also, I have the board's blessing to end this war with Rebel and sign the contract with the union so the corporation can move on with business."

The vice president said, "Are we going to let Rebel get away with his actions?"

The president said, "You heard the board's decision. We are in the middle of a media nightmare. We cannot afford to have our business policies revealed to the whole world any further. Sales are down due to the bad press we are receiving. Do you have a problem with that?"

The vice president said, "Rebel is responsible for Grump's death!"

The president said, "Grump is responsible for his own fate. He could have taken the deal on the table. Instead, he insisted on killing Rebel. Now he is dead—and we are left to deal with the consequences of his actions, which have made all of us appear to be tyrants!"

The vice president sat down without replying.

Rebel met with the attorneys and explained what had happened.

Figner said, "So, you did have an appointment with Mr. Grump?"

"Absolutely. Here is a copy of the e-mail." Rebel handed Figner a flash drive.

Alysia Carnaggi, the district attorney, said. "I believe you, Rebel, based on the documented e-mail and video footage I have reviewed. However, I do not understand why Grump would have a meeting with you so late at night."

"I believe he did not want any witnesses to the attack that he had waiting for me."

"Did he threaten you in previous encounters?" Alysia asked.

"He was very irrational in previous meetings. Of the three auto CEOs, he was the only one who never fully accepted the alternatives. The other CEOs came to an agreement with the transformation and encouraged Grump to be reasonable."

"Did you threaten him at any time?"

"As you will see in the video footage, I was attacked by Grump's army at the headquarters last night. Once I eliminated the threat, I tried to convince him to agree to the terms of the new contract. When Grump refused to comply, I attempted to rough him up a little—using a different approach. Suddenly, one of his robots began firing at both of us."

Alysia said, "On the surface, it makes sense, but I will still have to conduct a formal investigation."

"I understand completely," said Rebel. "Do not hesitate to contact my attorneys with any more concerns, Ms. Carnaggi."

"How do we get in contact with you?" she asked.

"I have established a website, and you may leave me a personal message."

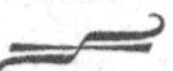

Rebel returned to base, and Maggie said, "That was a close call. I thought they were going to arrest you. I'm so glad they didn't!"

Nick said, "I think that went better than any of us could have imagined, but I'm still disappointed, that Grump went to such extremes, sealing his own fate. I did not want it to end up this way, but I hope the new CEO will be more reasonable."

Grimaldi said, "Whoever takes Grump's place should have the fear of Rebel in him and make the right decision!"

Tony walked up to Nick and gave him a hug. "I am proud of you, son. You did what you had to do for the good of the country!"

"You've got balls, Nick," Joey said. "I don't know if I would have walked in to the district attorney's office like that. I was nervous for you, man."

"Thanks, Joey. I was nervous, but I have all of you with me. Your support means the world to me."

By the end of the week, Lindsey A. Grammer was appointed CEO of G. A. Automotive. In Grammer's press conference, he agreed to the terms of the new contract with the union—just as the other automotive corporations had.

The next few months were spent supervising the execution of the new contract. Rebel would not move on to the next phase of the revolution until this was completed to the letter. A few more months passed before the changes were completely implemented. Rebel was patient with the process and was involved in every phase of the restructuring. He did not trust the corporate heads.

When the contract was incorporated, Rebel met with the union leaders. “Make sure you keep me informed of any problems you encounter in the future, Mr. President!”

The president of the union thanked Rebel and said, “If you ever need anything from the union, do not hesitate to ask, Rebel!”

“This revolution is not over, sir. If I need anything from the union, I promise to call. Thank you very much for your bravery!”

The president asked, “What is the next step in the revolution, Rebel?”

“I can’t say at this time. Just keep watching the news. I will put an end to corruption in this country, and I believe you will be satisfied with the results!”

The men shook hands, and Rebel returned to the base.

PHASE 23

The Big Boys

The West Coast location was breathtaking, with a foundation built on the edge of a mountain as well as a beautiful ocean view. The Phantom launch area had two options—one off the mountainside and the other leading into the Pacific Ocean from beneath. The location would be perfect for Team Rebel. They tested the weapons and vehicles to make sure that everything was ready for the revolution.

Nick called a meeting to plan the next phase in the revolution.

Grimaldi said, "Now that the changes to the utilities and the automotive corporations are underway, the next phase should be geared toward health care."

Nick said, "I'm concerned that, with the new health care program just beginning, we might give the program a year or so before intervening."

Maggie said, "Our website is receiving many requests regarding the health care program. Also related are the GMOs that are being used to create two-thirds of our so-called food."

"These issues have to be addressed eventually," Grimaldi said.

"Yes, but that is a war in itself. I feel that we should hold off with that phase of the revolution," Nick said.

"Yes, you may be right," Grimaldi replied.

Nick said, "We should work on the oil corporations next. They're like the final piece in the related utilities and automotive operations."

"Good point, Nick. Yes, first and foremost is the pollution they have been creating for over a century. Also, they need to be regulated to stop the manipulation of oil prices."

Maggie said, "Part of the work has already begun with the automotive hybrids and electric vehicles that we have encouraged in prior missions as well with the technical advances in battery manufacturing."

Nick said, "The portable hydrogen creator will contribute to changing the mentality of this industry for the betterment of this country and the rest of the world,"

Grimaldi said, "The plan in terms of the oil corporations will be for the reduction of unneeded exploration and extreme price fluctuations. There may always be a need for oil, but if our plan works, it won't be anywhere near the current rate. We will consequently put an end to all importing as well. Just as with the previous missions, we will hire the oil workers in alternative replacements. I have been in constant contact with Professor Miejer, and he was able to adapt his machines to power massive ships, trains, and tractor-trailers without polluting the environment."

Tony asked, "Where has this technology been hiding?"

Grimaldi replied, "It has been in research and development for more than ten years. This technology works on the same principle as thc portable version, but the waste oxygen will enhance the combustion in the engines."

Maggie said, "Amazing! When will it be ready for mass production?"

"Professor Miejer has informed me that production has already begun. We will join him in the manufacturing phase immediately and put the people to work as soon as possible."

Grimaldi said, "There are five oil corporations to negotiate with here in the States. Surveillance will begin on these corporations right away!"

Nick said, "We will be giving the oil corporations the option to invest in the hydrogen manufacturing. If they are smart, we shouldn't have much resistance."

Maggie said, "Being smart has nothing to do with it. Their greed will outweigh any intelligence."

Nick smiled and high-fived her. "Sounds like we're ready to move to the next phase of the revolution!"

"Exx-Oil is the largest oil producer in America. They're based in Dallas. The CEO is Tex W. Bitterson."

"Maggie, please make an appointment with the CEO so negotiations can begin," Nick said.

As Rebel approached the headquarters of Exx-Oil, the headquarters looked like a resort butting against the coast. There was even a golf course on property.

"Rebel to Control."

"Go for Control."

"I knew that this building was large, based on our blueprint review, but this is ridiculously enormous! It's the size of a small campus. I hope Bitterson's ego isn't equally immense."

"I wouldn't be surprised if it were, Rebel," Maggie said.

Rebel landed on the rooftop, entered the building, and approached the CEO's office. There was no assistant standing by. Rebel knocked on the door, but there was no answer. Rebel decided to walk into the office.

Mr. Bitterson was a tall man, with a bald head, and a large belly. His suspenders barely held up his dress pants. "I demand an explanation for why you have walked into my office unannounced!"

"Why did your assistant make the appointment if you weren't willing to meet with me, sir?"

"I saw the appointment scheduled on my calendar, but I didn't realize that it was with you," Bitterson replied.

"I'm not here to play games, sir. I will get straight to the point. Your company, Exx-Oil, along with the other American oil producers, has ignored the decay of our planet for far too long. The time is now for serious change. You have also been taking advantage of the American people. The price gouging and manipulation of the citizens of this country must come to an end."

The CEO said, "Where are you from, Rebel?"

"That is not important, sir. What is important is for you and your industry to restructure immediately."

"Relax. I understand that you are sensitive about your background.

Some people wonder why you are so secretive. You have disrupted this country's way of life, and we don't even know who or what you are."

"Again, that is not important at this time. I will reveal who I am when the time is right, Mr. Bitterson."

"You're asking us to trust you when you're not willing to return that trust. Seems unfair, don't you think, Rebel?"

"I'm here to help the world. You have no reason for suspicion. The citizens of this country have supported me throughout the revolution."

"Well, the citizens are not running this country now, are they?" Bitterson replied.

"I'm sure you've read the news about our agreements with the utilities and automotive industries. The time has come for your industry to invest in change for the future. We are suggesting that you and the rest of the industry begin to shift toward alternative sources of energy as well."

"Yes, it is time for change. Please schedule an appointment with my assistant for Monday. We will negotiate the terms once I have a chance to crunch the numbers with my board of directors."

"Thank you, sir," Rebel replied.

Rebel returned to base.

Grimaldi scratched his head and said, "I don't believe him at all! Bitterson and his corporation come from some of the oldest money in this country, and they will not accept our proposal without a fight!"

"I couldn't believe it, either," Nick said. "We're going to have to keep a close eye on him."

Maggie continued her surveillance of the CEO. "I'm on it. I scheduled you an appointment with P. B. Oil. You are set to meet with Dudley Roberts tomorrow at eleven."

"Thanks, Maggie," Nick said.

Rebel arrived at the headquarters of P. B. Oil. "Rebel to Control."

"Go for Control."

"There are several buildings connected to each other with bridges. This twenty-story tall structure has five acres all to itself—and extravagant landscaping!"

"Stay focused, Rebel," Grimaldi replied.

Nick landed on the rooftop and made his way to the CEO's office. He approached the assistant's desk and said, "Hello. My name is Rebel. I have an appointment with Mr. Roberts. Would you please let him know I am here?"

"Yes, sir." She called the CEO to announce Rebel's arrival.

Roberts was a tall, skinny man who was much younger than Bitterson and wore jeans and a T-shirt.

"Have a seat, Rebel" Roberts said. "Would you like a drink?"

"This is not a social call, sir. I will make this clear for you. Your corporation, along with the other oil producers have been taking advantage of the American people for long enough. It's time for serious change. With all of the climate issues we are experiencing, you must rethink your place in the world for the future of mankind!"

"What do you propose we do to change these issues?" Roberts asked.

"Well, as you have witnessed over the past several months, we have been making great progress with the utility and automotive corporations. We have already reduced energy consumption by considerable amounts and have lowered the carbon footprint in the United States, benefitting the globe. The numbers are still decreasing."

"I'm not sure how those changes apply to my industry."

"This is what I propose for you and your competitors. You are going to move in an alternative direction by investing in wind, solar, and battery manufacturing. The latest innovation is the hydrogen converters, which are going to revolutionize the infrastructure. You're up to bat." Rebel pointed at the CEO. "Now is the time for you to restructure—just as everyone else is."

"There should be no problem in converting operations within the year," replied Roberts.

"I need an effective date!" Rebel said.

"Please schedule an appointment with my assistant so that we may negotiate the terms."

"Would you be willing to meet with the other CEOs for a joint conference?" Rebel asked.

"Sure, why not? I will have my assistant contact them today," Roberts said.

Rebel headed back to the base. "I get the feeling that all five of these corporations have been preparing for this day since we destroyed the power grids. They claim to be willing to meet with me as a group."

Grimaldi said, "I don't believe they're willing to change their philosophies—not for one minute!"

Tony said, "These bastards are the same type of scum as the automotive CEOs—if not worse. They are greedy and untrustworthy. I think they're going to try to kill you, Nick."

Nick said, "I believe you both are correct, but I also believe that getting them to agree to a meeting—whether it is an actual negotiation or a battle—does not matter to us. Either way it plays out, we will afford them the opportunity to join the alternatives. No one will ever be able to claim that we forced them out of business because we will give them every opportunity to do what is just. In the end, the people will understand."

Maggie said, "Thank you for clarifying your thoughts with us, Nick. I was beginning to think you were crazy."

Grimaldi said, "Please confirm the appointment with all five corporations as soon as possible, Maggie."

She sent an e-mail to confirm that the corporations were all in touch with each other and to be sure that Roberts held up his end of the bargain.

Grimaldi called a meeting with the team. "Maggie informed me that we still do not have a confirmed date for an appointment with the oil corporations. It's been a couple of days now. We must prepare for another battle. My gut feeling is that they are going to try to kill you, Nick. Don't be surprised if the oil tycoons spend huge dollars on the most sophisticated weaponry. Otherwise, we would have already received confirmation of a meeting by now. They definitely are stalling."

Nick said, "I'm not worried about their plans. I have my own backup—Phantoms 1 and 2—and I will be ready for anything those jokers throw at me!"

Maggie said, "We need to do something."

"We have to be patient, Maggie," Grimaldi said. "We cannot act too fast. We will give them a little more time."

Maggie said, "There is still no meeting set."

Nick asked, "Have you picked up any type of conversation through surveillance?"

"Nothing yet. I have everything covered: cell phones, e-mail transactions, satellite-tracking systems, and security feeds from their homes and offices. We have eyes and ears everywhere!"

Grimaldi said, "We will give them twenty-four hours. Then it's go time!"

Maggie looked down at her monitor. All the CEOs were heading somewhere. "Nick, look at this. They're on the move. You should follow them immediately."

Nick suited up and hurried to the Phantom. "I'm on my way." Rebel took to the air, blasting into supersonic speed. "Rebel to Control."

"Go for Control."

"I'm close to the projected area. Ready for the coordinates."

"I've tracked the CEOs to an airport in Oklahoma City. Phantom-1 will take the controls."

"Copy that, Control," Rebel saw a private jet. "Rebel to Control."

"I see it, Rebel. The CEOs have arranged to be picked up by a limousine at the landing strip."

Rebel waited as the planes landed on the private airstrip.

"Control to Rebel."

"Go for Rebel."

"I have hacked into the limousine's computer system. I've got the GPS and audio feed in the limo, but it seems as though they are not speaking to each other. I'm not receiving any audio—just movements."

"Good work. Continue to track them. I'll follow in cloak mode," Rebel replied.

Maggie checked the system. "Control to Rebel."

"Go for Rebel."

"The CEOs are heading to a warehouse about twenty minutes west of the airport. That building happens to be owned by Nash's private security corporation. There is a great chance that these men are using Nash's building to plot against you. I'm unable to find a surveillance system in the warehouse. It seems to be abandoned—or maybe it is purposely off the grid for situations like these."

"I'm on their tail," Rebel said.

"They're entering the warehouse, Rebel."

"I'm here!" Rebel landed and used the surveillance equipment in Phantom-1 to recon the meeting. To his surprise, the sensors were coming up blank. There were no images, sounds, or heat signatures. He decided to launch a tiny recon drone from the roof.

The drone used a laser to cut through a ventilation duct and infiltrate the building. Once inside, the drone used its audio and thermal sensors to zero in on the meeting.

"Rebel to Control."

"Go for Control."

"This building has a barrier of some kind. I'm not receiving the transmission from the drone. We will have to review the recording once the meeting is complete."

"Copy that, Rebel. Standing by," Maggie replied.

Within minutes, Rebel observed the five CEOs leaving the warehouse in the limo. The drone returned to Phantom-1.

"Rebel to Control."

"Go for Control."

"The meeting is over. I will transmit the recording to you now."

Back at the base, the team observed the transmission. As the drone made its way through the building, it entered a short hallway with three doors. The drone hovered in front of the nearest doorway, scanning for audio. It heard noises and made its way to a bookcase for cover.

With video rolling, Bitterson explained, "I have contracted some of the most sophisticated, state-of-the-art military weapons technology. These top-secret weapons are currently unused. Where everyone else has failed, we will destroy this terrorist once and for all. Our stock has plummeted ever since the automotive industry signed that damn contract. We must put an end to this revolution—or else our way of life will be destroyed."

Dudley Roberts, the CEO of P.B. oil asked Bitterson for details. "I will not explain it here and now, but you will find out soon enough. I must have your commitment though." Bitterson handed each of them an envelope with a paper that listed the amount of cash he would need to acquire this technology. "There will be no compromising with this terrorist. Rebel will be eliminated at all cost."

Roberts opened his envelope and said, "For this kind of money, you better be right."

"I have been assured by my expert that—whether Rebel is from another planet or whether he has the most sophisticated government technology—our newly acquired weaponry is the best in the world. I have been given a money back guarantee that this will kill him!"

The other CEOs opened their envelopes.

Bitterson said, "We will win this war!"

Back at the base, Grimaldi said, "I am very concerned about putting Rebel in a situation against all five of these corporations'!"

Nick said, "I'm concerned as well. I think I will be ready—no matter what they throw at me. I'll have Phantoms-1 and 2 with me for backup. The alternatives will have to be in place in case we have to disable the oil rigs."

Maggie said "Do you have any idea of what they are referring to?"

Grimaldi said, "I am not aware of any technology that is more sophisticated than our suit, but there may be some new advancements that are beyond my top-secret clearance. I the oil corporations have access to the top-of-the line mercenaries."

Nick said, "These men have chosen a side, and this is a revolution. They are not Boy Scouts. I will do what I have to do. Are the alternatives ready to go?"

Grimaldi said, "Yes. I will make the arrangements while you and Joey prep Phantoms-1 and 2 for a battle.

PHASE 24

Down But Not Out

Team Rebel received e-mail conformation of the meeting with the five corporations.

Nick asked, "Where do they want to meet?"

Maggie brought up the stadium on one of the monitors. "At the football stadium in Houston."

"I think that's good" Nick replied. "The Astrodome is an open stadium. The Phantoms will be able to enter from the center if need be."

Grimaldi said, "In a stadium so large, you could be caught at the center of the field. You will have no cover!"

Maggie said, "The meeting is set for the center of the stadium!"

Joey said, "If they attack you in the center of the stadium—with no cover and no place to use your grappling hooks—you will be vulnerable."

Nick said, "I understand the situation, but I'll find a way to make it work. I am trained for combat!"

Team Rebel devised a plan of attack. They were looking at a schematic of the stadium and a map of the surrounding area.

Joey said, "We should have Phantom-2 standing by for backup—over on that tall building to the west."

"Yes. Very good idea, Joey," Nick said.

Maggie had checked the security system and the camera feeds in the stadium. She tried to access the system for nearly an hour. "I'm being blocked by some type of military scrambler."

Nick said, "Please keep trying to break through that firewall. I would like to have that surveillance for this mission. It may be our most difficult battle yet!"

Maggie started back to the control room and turned back toward Nick. "Please abort the meeting if I can't get into the system."

Nick took her hand. "While I was in the Black Ops, we would enter combat situations without surveillance all the time. I'm prepared to deal with anything they throw at me, Maggie. I need you to trust me!"

Maggie began to cry.

Nick held her in his arms. "I promise to be careful, Maggie. I'll have the Phantoms for backup. I would never go into a suicide mission. I would never do anything to hurt you!"

She grabbed his arms. "I am begging you, Nick. If I am not able to access the system, please do not go on this mission!"

Nick said, "This is a revolution, Maggie! It must be completed for the sake of all of our futures!"

Maggie pulled it together and returned to the control room to work on breaking through that firewall.

An hour later, Nick went up to the control room and kissed Maggie. "Everything will be fine, babe!"

"I know you will be." She sighed. "I just feel so helpless right now."

"Keep working on the system—and do your best," Nick returned to the launchpad to prepare for battle.

Grimaldi brought up a schematic of the stadium on the monitor. "Let's review the plan of attack one last time."

Nick said, "Okay, Mr. G."

Grimaldi said, "If you lose radio contact with us, you know what your options will be."

"I got it." Nick turned to Grimaldi. "Thank you for everything, Mr. G. No matter how this ends, I will never have any regrets—and I do not want you to have any either."

Nick hugged and kissed Maggie. "I love you. Don't worry. I'll be back in a couple of hours. Be ready to celebrate!"

Maggie smiled and said, "I love you too, babe. You better come back in one piece!"

Nick hugged Tony and Joey, and the team stepped back as the fighters lifted off.

Rebel hovered over the stadium. "Rebel to Control."

"Go for Control."

"Do you have eyes in the stadium yet?"

Maggie said "Negative. I haven't been able to break through that firewall, but I'm still working on it. I think you should wait until I crack it before you enter the stadium."

"Don't worry. Joey and I have this covered." Rebel held his position and launched a swarm of recon drones toward the objective. Four of them took positions on the corner rafters, overlooking the field. Four more drones covered the north, south, east, and west entrances. One drone covered the loading dock, and six more drones monitored the stadium from top to bottom.

Maggie said, "I've received the transmissions from all of the recon drones. Thanks for that, boys! I'm still going to crack that firewall. Damn it! I'm picking up about fifteen thermal signatures inside the stadium."

Rebel hovered over the edge of the roof in cloak mode. The Phantom's hatch opened and Rebel dropped onto the rooftop—ordering the fighter to hover over the stadium in cloak mode—and grappled his way to the rafters. "Control, I'm on the south side of the building. Do we have any enemies hidden up here?"

"I can't say for sure. The drones haven't swept that area yet!"

Rebel scanned the area and found a sniper hiding behind the field lights. Rebel carefully approached the sniper, using the stealthy powers of his suit to blend in with the rafters. He approached from behind and tranqed the sniper. Rebel feared that the sniper would fall to his death, but the gunman and his weapon were secured by a safety harness.

Maggie said, "We have a sniper on the opposite side of the stadium, Rebel!"

"Copy that, Control." Rebel fired a line across the rafters, swung from beam to beam, and camouflaged himself again. Rebel fired a dart at the merc, but it had no effect on him. He shot another dart, but the sniper turned toward Rebel and fired at him.

Rebel flew back and fired a grappling line to the rafters to save himself from falling. *This must be a new advanced robotic unit.* Rebel secured himself to another beam, cloaked himself, and made his way to a better vantage point above the sniper. He dropped down onto his target and disarmed the sniper. He snapped the sniper's weapon in half and dropped it to the catwalk.

The enemy detached his harness and leaped two stories to the catwalk.

Rebel followed the assailant to the catwalk.

The merc clutched Rebel's shoulders and pulled him into a knee strike to the torso, followed by a combination of punches to the head. With incredible speed and power, the merc knocked Rebel to the platform.

Rebel popped up and fired a grappling hook at the enemy. The hook entangled the merc's arm, throwing him over the edge of the platform. He dangled from the line, helpless.

Rebel fired a line to the roof and released the merc from the line just below the rooftop. Rebel secured himself to the rooftop and lured his foe upward, attempting to bring the battle far away from the others to avoid too much attention from below.

The adversary jumped from beam to beam, drawing closer to the roof.

Rebel pulled out his nunchucks to challenge the threat.

The powerful foe punched Rebel's head.

Rebel slipped the attack and struck his enemy with a combination of strikes from both pairs of nunchucks. The attacker's arms were bleeding. *Maybe the gunman is a man after all—on some type of physical-enhancement drug.*

The merc jumped up to his feet and rushed Rebel again. He attempted to take down Rebel with a wrestling charge, but Rebel kneed him in the head and struck again with an elbow to the back of it.

The opponent was not fazed by the attacks.

Rebel tossed a proximity disc toward the merc's feet, and it exploded in his path.

The man's flesh was torn from his forehead, revealing a silvery metal skeleton, but he continued to advance toward Rebel. *This must be a cyborg—combining the skills and stealth of a mercenary with the power and durability of a robot.*

Rebel pulled out his nunchucks as the cyborg swung at Rebel. He avoided the strike and sent a flurry of nunchuck combinations at the cybernetic unit, striking high and low. The foe finally was slowed down by a damaged arm and leg. The cyborg persisted in attack mode and would not give up. Rebel backed to the outer edge of the rooftop and drew the aggressor closer to the edge. The metal tyrant ripped a steel pipe from a fence that bordered a generator on the roof and charged at Rebel. The cyborg gripped the object with both hands, raising it over its head to strike Rebel.

Rebel doubled up his nunchucks to block the pipe, but he was forced to the ground.

The cyborg attempted to spear Rebel with the pipe, but Rebel rolled to his side, causing his opponent to miss.

Rebel pulled the pipe out of the surface of cyborg's grasp, and the cyborg lost its balance. Rebel threw the cyborg and the pipe over the edge of the roof. It exploded midway through its descent. Rebel had stuck a magnetic frag-grenade on the pipe before dispensing of his enemy.

Rebel said, "Control, I removed two of the threats, but I'm going to need you to send a drone to be sure this cyborg is disabled before I move on."

Maggie said, "I had a drone watching the battle the whole time. It was definitely a cyborg. After the explosion, I surveyed the area. All we saw were pieces of flesh and a metal skeleton. No sign of any threat left, Rebel. I'm not finding any hidden threats. It looks like you're clear to approach the CEOs."

Rebel said, "I'm counting fifteen men on the field. I can see the CEOs and their security detail in full military gear."

"Are you ready, Rebel?" Maggie asked.

"Ready, Control."

Rebel fired a line to a fence post, securing himself to some generators. He rappelled from the roof to an outside entrance. He walked slowly toward the center of the field, carefully surveying the scene.

Maggie said, “I have the feeds from the drones. I am reading fifteen thermal signatures as well.”

“I’m making my way to the center of the field, Control.” As he got closer, he said, “Something isn’t right with the CEOs!” Rebel zoomed in on the them and realized that the five men in cowboy hats were not the CEOs. Instead, they were actually cyborgs! Rebel signaled for Phantom-1, while he continued toward the center of the field.

Once Rebel came within firing range, the cyborgs took aim. Suddenly, Phantom-1 descended upon them through the opening of the stadium roof. Rebel turned and ran for cover. The mercs fired on Rebel, and the cyborgs concentrated their efforts on Phantom-1.

Maggie ordered the fighter to target the cyborgs. The cyborgs fired on the Phantom with their machine guns as the rest of the army pursued Rebel.

Rebel quickly activated his jet boots, ascending for cover.

Trapdoors opened on the field, and two cyborgs emerged from the openings. They took aim on Rebel, firing missiles at his jet boots.

Rebel crashed to the turf. He quickly removed the boots and stood up to collect his senses.

The mercs charged him again, firing their weapons. They threw him into one of the trapdoors, and it slammed shut. The cyborgs and the mercenaries guarded the trapdoor. Rebel was confined in an underground room.

Phantom-1 was dropping smoke and firing all over the field. The fighter destroyed one of the cyborgs, but the other four were able to escape through the tunnel area.

Rebel said, “Phantom-1, drop concussion grenades on my attackers—now!”

Phantom-1 dropped a cluster of grenades on the mercs.

Maggie said, “Phantom-1, drop knockout gas cartridges on the threats—now!”

The fighter was able to neutralize the human threat, but four of the top-floor suites opened and shot missile at Phantom-1. Each launcher was equipped with an energy-disruption emitter that was capable of going through hundreds of frequencies per second to disrupt electromagnetic energy fields. Phantom-1's defense system warned it, and it evaded the missiles. A missile flew into one of the restaurants and exploded, destroying the area.

Maggie targeted the suite that had fired on Phantom-1 and sent the coordinates to its targeting system. Phantom-1 rushed toward the launcher, firing its own missile into the suite and destroying it.

Two other missile launchers locked in on the Phantom and fired, sending it crashing to the field. Maggie ordered Phantom-1 to retreat, but it could not respond.

Rebel said, "What the hell was that?"

Maggie said, "Rebel, they just took down Phantom-1. You need to find a way out of there—now! I'm sending in Phantom-2 immediately!"

"No! Wait until I can clear the way for Phantom-2!"

"Are you crazy? I'm sending in Phantom-2 now!"

"Trust me. I'm okay. Just give me some time before you send in Phantom-2!"

Maggie yelled, "Hurry!"

The remaining cyborgs split up. Three of them stayed on the field, and three of them went to the underground level.

Rebel pounded and kicked the walls, but he could not break through any of them.

Maggie said, "Rebel, there are three cyborgs heading to the lower level. They are going to try to box you in. You only have a couple of minutes before they will have you surrounded."

"I got this!" Rebel placed a strip of plastic explosives on the wall, moved to the opposite side of the box, and triggered the explosive. It blew out a hole large enough to escape, and Rebel worked his way back toward the tunnel. He heard the cyborgs approaching and secured himself inside a ventilation shaft in the ceiling. He looked through the shield and watched the cyborgs rushing past him.

The cyborgs reported that Rebel had escaped. Two of the cyborgs reached down and ripped open the trapdoor. Two C-4 packs exploded as the door opened, sending the cyborgs hurtling through the sky.

The four remaining cyborgs split up.

Rebel dropped out of the ventilation shaft and made his way to the vending area. He saw one of the cyborgs approaching and ducked into a restaurant. He knocked over a table as to draw the menace toward him. Rebel went into the kitchen and knocked a pan to the floor.

When the cyborg entered the kitchen, Rebel attacked with combinations of strikes from his titanium nunchucks, tearing the flesh of the cybernetic combatant while exposing glimpses of its titanium skeleton.

The enemy was able to withstand the attack and struck back with a combination of punches, knocking Rebel back a few feet.

Rebel struck back with another combination with his nunchucks. One of the cyborg's arms flew across the room as it was knocked to the ground. The cyborg reached over to a countertop and lifted itself up. It rushed him again, striking with a dropkick.

Rebel grabbed its leg and used a double-legged dropkick to throw his opponent across the room. He held its leg and ripped it from its socket. The cyborg landed in a pile of broken dishes, and wires dangled from its arm and leg. Sparks popped out of the creature's damaged limbs as it attempted to rise again. Rebel grabbed the enemy by the head with both hands and ferociously twisted its head, decapitating the metal menace.

Rebel picked it up by the torso, slammed it against the wall, and ripped off its chest plate to reveal the main processor. He told the core to send a message to the corporate leaders: "You're finished! Now I will destroy you all!" Rebel ripped out the cyborg's brain and slammed it on the ground.

Another cyborg rushed to the scene, but it could not find Rebel.

Rebel came out of his cloak mode and fired thirty rounds of armor-piercing ammo at the cyborg.

The target flew behind a concession stand.

Rebel holstered his weapons and leaped over the counter to finish off the cyborg. The hail of exploding bullets had damaged it so severely that the left side of its head had no remaining tissue. Where the cyborg's left eye had been, there was just a gaping hole. Its legs were riddled with holes and resembled Swiss cheese. Its right elbow was damaged and useless. However, the cyborg's reinforced, armor-plated chest had not been penetrated.

The cybernetic nuisance made its way to its feet, reached out with its good arm, and fired.

Rebel dodged the ammunition, finding cover, but he lost his balance. An uppercut sent him flying into the walkway, and he crashed to the floor.

The cyborg fired at Rebel with an assault rifle that was strapped over its shoulder.

Rebel avoided the barrage and jumped into a service hallway. He planted a C-4 pack in the microwave and severed one of the gas lines from a deep fryer.

As the cyborg scanned the area, the microwave oven exploded, creating a huge fireball. The blast threw the assassin to the ground.

Rebel entered the main hallway as the cybernetic skeleton rose from the flames. Its flesh was completely burned away from its skeleton, but it would not give up. The cyborg rushed at Rebel, but Rebel had already targeted it with a mini-rocket. The cyborg was destroyed.

Rebel retreated to the other side of the stadium to avoid another attack from the remaining cyborgs. "Control, I think I saw something in the higher-end suites. There may be an ambush waiting for Phantom-2. I'm going to sweep the upper levels. Do not send Phantom-2 until I clear the way."

"There are three automated missile launchers in the top-level suites, Rebel. Phantom-1 destroyed one of them before it was taken down by two of the others."

"I'm going to take out those missile launchers!" Rebel fired his grappling line at the ceiling trusses and made his way to the top floor of the stadium. He used his X-ray vision to make sure there was no more than a single cyborg in the area.

"Rebel, just around the corner, in Suite 100—there's one of your three targets."

"Copy that, Control." Rebel approached the suite and found the missile launcher on a tripod. He camouflaged himself in cloak mode, slid open the door, and tossed an explosive onto the missile launcher—destroying the missile and the suite.

Rebel then would move on through the halls to find the remaining threats.

He found another missile launcher in a suite on the other side of the stadium. He tossed an explosive onto the missile, but he forgot to cloak—and the missile was able to detect him. The tripod spun around and launched a missile at Rebel.

Rebel leaped out of the line of fire, and the missile struck the adjacent suite. The floor caved in, and Rebel crashed to the level below.

Rebel quickly gathered his senses and moved on. He was sure not be to be caught by both cyborgs at the same time.

"Control to Rebel."

"Go for Rebel."

"Are you okay?" Maggie asked.

"I'm fine."

"Please be more careful, Rebel."

"Copy that, Control. On my way to the next target."

Rebel found the last missile launcher, unfortunately, one of the cyborgs was guarding the entrance. He decided to enter the suite below and plant a C-4 pack on the ceiling. He then grappled his way to the top of the above suite from the balcony.

The explosive went off, but the floor did not cave in.

The cyborg made its way to the lower level to investigate, and Rebel used his X-ray vision to track his target. Once the cyborg began to move away from the entrance of the top suite, Rebel entered the suite in cloak mode. He tossed another C-4 pack at the missile launcher and ran out of the blast area as the missile was destroyed.

The explosion left a hole in the floor. Once the smoke cleared, the cyborg surveyed the upper level and pursued Rebel. Rebel used his thermal vision to search for the cyborg in the smoke and flames and ran at his enemy before it could find him. Rebel dropkicked it out of the suite. The cyborg crash down to one of the mid-level suites. It took a huge fall, lying motionless on its face.

"Control, do you have a visual on the cyborg?"

"Yes. According to my readings from one of the drones, its vitals are flatlined."

"I've destroyed the missile launchers in the suites. I'm going to finish off the last cyborg!" He made his way to the field. "Control to Rebel."

"Go for Rebel."

"No luck in finding this last cyborg. I think we're clear for Phantom-2's approach."

"Negative, Control. I'm not sure if we're out of the woods just yet. I have to go. I've found the last cyborg!"

"Where are you—and what are you going to do?" Maggie asked.

"I'm at the center of the field. I'm going to destroy this piece of junk!" Rebel replied.

Maggie said, "Wait for Phantom-2 to back you up. It can be there in seconds!"

"Finish scanning the rest of the stadium with the drones before you send Phantom-2 in here!" Rebel said while in pursuit of the cyborg.

The cyborg scanned the stadium and attacked.

Rebel pulled out both pairs of nunchucks, inviting the cyborg to engage.

The cyborg charged at Rebel, firing his assault rifle. Rebel began to spin his nunchucks like helicopter blades, deflecting the bullets. The enemy fired until it finally ran out of ammunition.

Rebel moved in for the kill. He began to throw combinations at the cyborg with his nunchucks. The strikes from his nunchucks seemed to be effective at first, but this cyborg was much more agile and resilient than the others. Rebel struck his opponent with a lead right foot, but the cyborg slipped the attack and grabbed him by his other leg, swung him around a few times, and hurled him through the air.

Rebel crashed through several rows of seats, destroying everything in his path. He quickly returned to his feet and reset his nunchucks. He unleashed another barrage of combinations on his enemy.

His foe struck with a right hand, but Rebel dodged and trapped one of its arms with the nunchucks. He leaped into the air, swinging up and over the cyborg's head, and both legs locked around the opposite arm. He ripped the arm from its socket and sent it flying into the cheap seats. Sparks sputtered from its shoulder. It tore the skin off from its chest plate, and blood ran down its body. A missile emerged from its chest and it took aim on Rebel.

Rebel rushed to loaded a mini-rocket, but the cyborg across the stadium emerged from its unconscious state with miniature missiles and specially hardened tips that were equipped with energy-disruption emitters—just like as the launchers in the suites. The cyborgs beat Rebel to the draw. The first missile struck Rebel, but his force field protected him from the explosion. The second missile disrupted his energy field long enough to catapult him through the air.

The cybernetic brutes were finally breaking down Rebel. As the cyborg made its way toward Rebel, Phantom-2 swooped into the stadium and fired a missile at the cyborg across the stadium, demolishing it.

Maggie yelled, "Phantom-2, destroy that last cyborg!"

As the last cyborg locked in on Rebel again, Phantom-2 swooped in. It fired a grappling hook at the cyborg's leg, catapulting it away from Rebel. The metal menace dangled upside down on the line.

Rebel got back up to his feet and found his gun on the stairs. He fell to the ground and reached for his gun. It flew into his hand.

As Phantom-2 ascended, Rebel said, "Drop the cyborg in the center of the stadium!" He locked onto it with two mini-rockets. Rebel blasted the last cyborg to pieces of meat and metal.

Phantom-2 vacuumed Rebel up from the stands. As they left the stadium, Rebel looked down on Phantom-1. "Rebel to Control."

"Go for Control."

"How bad is Phantom-1?"

Grimaldi took the microphone and said, "It's far too damaged to risk towing back to base and being slowed down. Let it go, Rebel."

Rebel said, "Let's tow Phantom-1 out of here before we leave."

Phantom-2 descended onto the field, hooked Phantom-1 with a towrope, and flew to the nearest body of water. "Control, can you program Phantom-1 to self-detonate?"

"Not sure if it can receive. Hold on. Yes, it is receiving the transmission. You have one minute until detonation, Rebel."

Phantom-2 released the towline and dropped Phantom-1. It exploded just before hitting the water. Rebel made sure that there was no trace left behind. "Rebel to Control."

Maggie cried, "Are you okay?"

"I'm okay!"

"Get back home!"

"Prep the MRI!"

When he arrived at the base, Maggie jumped into his arms. "Please put an end to this revolution!"

"Please calm down and help me over to the MRI." Nick winced in pain.

Maggie and Tony helped Nick onto the machine.

When Nick removed his suit, the pain immediately increased.

Grimaldi ran the scan, and the test results showed that there were no broken bones. However, the scan did show some torn ligaments that would have to be rehabilitated.

Nick grabbed the suit and returned it to his frame as soon as the test was complete. "I need to put the suit back on. The pain has increased tremendously since removing it."

"Is that better?" Maggie asked.

"Leave the suit on if you must," Grimaldi said. "Obviously, the suit is acting as an anti-inflammatory agent, reducing the swelling and pain. Leave the suit on for at least the next twenty-four hours." He put his hand on Nick's shoulder. "I'll sent the test results to Dr. McKenzie."

Once Nick had the suit back on, he said, "I feel better already." He had virtually no pain in a matter of minutes. "Can you get me one of those hyperbaric chambers to speed up the healing process?"

Grimaldi said, "We have them at Grimaldi Industries. I'll have one delivered immediately."

"Thank you. I need to take every precaution to be sure I'm able to get back into the game as soon as possible."

Grimaldi said, "Maggie, are you okay?"

She ran out of the room.

Nick said, "Just let her go. Uncle Tony, please bring me some food, water, and an ice pack."

"You got it, Nick." Tony rushed to the kitchen.

"I'll feel better in a couple hours. I just need to rest," Nick said.

Grimaldi knocked on Maggie's bedroom door, but she refused to answer. He said, "I'm worried about Maggie, Nick."

"She'll be fine. Let her cool off for a few hours. *I could have prevented this injury if I had just listened to her. I need to apologize.*

Grimaldi said, "Are you feeling any better?"

"I'm feeling fine as long as I have the suit on. I think it'll definitely help me to heal faster."

"That makes perfect sense. Take it easy for the next twenty-four hours—and then we'll see how you feel."

PHASE 25

Plan of Attack

The next morning, Nick woke up with the suit on. He rose slowly to his feet and discovered that he was able to walk fine. He began to jog in place, finding only a slight discomfort. He was able to remove the suit to shower and prepare for the day. Once he dressed for breakfast, Nick began to feel some increased pain in his leg. He immediately reached for the suit.

Tony had prepared breakfast in the kitchen. "How are you feeling today, Nick?"

"I feel much better."

"The suit is fantastic!" Tony replied.

Grimaldi walked into the kitchen and said, "The suit has healing powers."

"For sure."

Grimaldi said, "We will have to respond to this attack with great malice!"

"How can we destroy the oil rigs without spilling the oil into the sea?" Nick asked.

"Do you remember that huge oil spill from 2010?" Grimaldi said.

"I do. The news reported that the oil corporation could have stopped the spill much sooner."

"The news reports claimed that blowing up the rigs at the core would have stopped the spill immediately. Instead, the corporation allowed the oil to spill for more than ninety days because the rigs would have been shut down permanently. Their greed caused devastating pollution, and many businesses and employees lost their livelihoods as well."

"Yes, I remember that report," Tony replied.

"I researched a company that builds the oil rigs." Grimaldi put a diagram on a monitor.

"If we destroy the rigs at the core, they will be permanently inoperable because they cannot be repaired at those depths. We could have the drones programmed and ready by tomorrow!"

"I'll be ready to go by then," Nick said.

"What about Maggie?" Joey asked. "We need her."

"Let me talk to her." Nick went to her door and knocked. "Maggie, are you in there? Please open the door." Maggie would not respond.

The next morning, Grimaldi said, "How are you feeling, Nick?"

"I feel much better today. I'm walking without any pain." Nick went over to the heavy bags and took a fighting stance. He threw a jab and then a lead kick. He waited a moment—no pain. He repeated the combination more quickly. "No pain again." He attacked with a four-strike combination, "Yes! I'm ready."

Grimaldi said, "You look as good as new. That suit is phenomenal!"

Nick said, "I'm so grateful for these powers. We need to get back to business. We must use the other Phantoms to destroy the rigs—just like we did with the power corporations."

Grimaldi said, "Joey, I will be bringing in the other Phantoms within the hour. I have already ordered a replacement for Phantom-1. It will be delivered this afternoon. We need to have all of them ready for attack within twenty-four hours."

"I only need one hour," replied Joey.

Grimaldi said, "You're going to need a little more than an hour. I need you to run a full test on the new fighter, especially its cloaking capabilities, before the next mission. This is very important. Program it to respond to Phantom-5."

"Do you want me to program Phantom-2 as Phantom-1, Phantom-3 as Phantom-2, and so on?"

"Exactly!" Grimaldi rushed to the vault to gather the drones for the next mission. He set up on the table and began programming them. These deep-submersible kamikaze drones were used for undersea operations.

The following day, Grimaldi called for a meeting with the team, but Maggie refused to answer her door again.

Grimaldi said, "Can you please speak with Maggie, Nick? We need her back in the mission!"

"I'll go to her in a minute." Nick knocked on her door. "Maggie, I'm fine. The suit has healed me. According to Dr. McKenzie's report, I should not be able to walk for another week. I feel much better. Leaving the suit on has sped up the healing process."

"I'm very upset with you, Nick!"

"Please open the door, Maggie."

Maggie opened the door and walked past him in her workout gear.

"Where are you going, Maggie?"

Maggie made her way to the heavy bag area. She geared up and began to vigorously throw combinations at the bags.

After a round, Nick said, "Maggie, please talk to me."

"I can't lose you—not for the revolution, not for anything!"

"I'm fine. We must move on, Maggie!"

"I'm not sure I can, Nick."

"I'll give you some more time. I love you, Maggie."

The team gathered without Maggie.

Grimaldi said, "I had a private investigation company research the oil corporations for six months. The investigators recorded every drop of oil produced and delivered from these suppliers. They discovered that these corporations have been stockpiling a small percentage of oil each month. The investigators have been able to find inside sources from the storage locations. The sources confirmed that the stockpiling has been going on for at least ten years. These five corporations have enough oil to supply the United States for the next decade without producing another drop of oil."

"I'm not surprised at all," Tony said. "They always have something up their sleeves."

Grimaldi said, "This does not include the strategic oil supply of the United States, which is meant only for military use. Once we destroy the rigs, they will claim that they must import oil and increase its price due to the importing cost to compensate for the 70 percent of production we will destroy. If we leave them with 30 percent of their production—and with the alternatives we have brought to the forefront—there will eventually be no need for more than 10 percent of the current production. The oil corporations will not be able to take advantage of the people by claiming that there is not enough oil left. We will leak this investigation to every media outlet in the world, exposing the oil industry for their attempted deception."

Nick said, "You're brilliant! With this information, we should have enough ammunition to counter the propaganda of the right-wing establishment!"

Tony said, "I hope the American people are wise enough to see through the lies of these corporations and understand that we are here to rescue the American Dream and the planet!"

Grimaldi said, "This mission will be similar to the attack on the power corporations. The northern region of the country produces approximately 30 percent of the oil, and the southern region produces the other 70 percent from offshore drilling. We will use our DSV kamikaze drones to destroy the rigs in the southern region. This will leave just enough oil production for the transition period and keep us independent from foreign oil. We will make sure the employees at the power and oil corporations are first in line to be hired at the alternative companies."

Joey double-checked the ten drones and loaded them on the Phantoms. Joey loaded Drone-1 and Drone-6 on Phantom-1, Drone-2 and Drone-7 on Phantom-2, Drone-3 and Drone-8 on Phantom-3, Drone-4 and Drone-9 on Phantom-4, and Drone-5 and Drone-10 on Phantom-5.

Once the plan was ironed out, Nick approached Maggie again.

She opened the door and walked toward the bed.

"We need your help," Nick said. "We can't complete the attacks on the rigs without you. Please help us finish what we started, Maggie!"

Maggie turned and said, "You're not invincible, Nickolas. The suit was not able to withstand that last attack. If it weren't for Phantom-2, you could be dead right now. Please quit while we're ahead—and you're still alive!"

"I'm fine, Maggie! The suit has healed my wounds. How could we justify coming so far just to quit now!"

"How do you think I will feel if something happens to you. I will never be able to forgive myself!"

"You're not forcing me to do anything. The revolution is bigger than you and me!"

"I cannot live without you, Nick. I love you more than anything in this world. We could go somewhere far away from these evil people and live a happy and safe life together!"

"No matter where we go, evil people are everywhere. Running is never the answer. No matter how far we run, corruption will be waiting. It's everywhere, Maggie!"

Maggie said, "You're right, Nick. There is nowhere I can think of that's perfect. I'm just so afraid of losing you. I'm letting my emotions get the best of me. I will help you finish this mission, but if something happens to you, this revolution will mean nothing to me!"

"I understand. I guess I have been so absorbed by the revolution for so long that I've had tunnel vision. I love you more than anything in this world! Next time, I will call for help sooner!"

"There will not be a next time because I will do it for you, Nickolas," Maggie said. "Grimaldi wanted to send in Phantom-2 as soon as you neutralized that last missile launcher, but he respected your wishes. If we are truly a team, you must learn to respect our wishes as well!"

Nick said, "You're right. I was being a macho ass. I now realize I'm not invincible. I promise that this is the last time I will act like I'm indestructible!"

The couple embraced and exchanged a passionate kiss.

Maggie said, "Remember your promise!"

They went to the control room.

Grimaldi gave her a hug and said, "You had us worried there for a while."

Nick suited up, loaded his weapons, and joined the team in the control room.

Maggie asked, "Why are you geared up, Nick?"

"I have to finish this mission, Maggie!"

Maggie said, "You are in no condition to fight!"

"I need you to trust me, Maggie. If there is a fight, we will be underwater. I will not have to rely on my physical strength as much."

Grimaldi said, "Nick is right, Maggie. He should be present for this mission. We must be sure that the drones are deployed into the rigs safely. You never know what they might run up against."

Maggie held her tongue.

Grimaldi said, "The Phantoms must be in cloak mode for this entire mission. Nick, you will deploy with Phantom-1 at the same time as the other four Phantoms seek out their targets and engage the rigs. Once the perimeter has been secured, submerge to the bottom of the rigs, survey the area for any threats, and deploy the DSV kamikaze drones into the targets. Once they have successfully secured their positions, move to your next objective."

PHASE 26

The Final Countdown

The team gathered on the launchpad to give Nick their best wishes.

Maggie hugged Nick and said, "Remember your promise."

"I will, Maggie. Please don't worry. I have learned my lesson." He kissed her.

The team headed up to the control room.

Grimaldi said, "Maggie, please deploy the Phantoms."

She programmed the order, and the Phantoms headed out for attack.

Grimaldi said, "How does everyone think the CEOs will respond once the rigs are destroyed?"

Maggie said, "I don't even want to think about that!"

Joey said, "I really don't care how they feel, but I am going to love how the people feel!"

Tony said, "I wish I could see the look in their eyes when the rigs are destroyed!"

Just then a message came in from the oil tycoons.

Maggie said, "Control to Rebel."

"Go for Rebel."

"We have a message from the CEOs. They want to make a deal!"

"I know they're just stalling again. We can't believe anything they say. It's just a ruse. They're not to be trusted, Maggie. We will destroy the rigs as planned, and they will have to negotiate with the alternatives for a piece of the pie!"

Grimaldi said, "Nick is right. They cannot be trusted. We will proceed as planned."

Tony said, "You need to remember who we're dealing with, Maggie. They're pure evil!"

"I know, but I'm worried about what they will have waiting for Nick!"

"Trust Nick. He was born to do this!" Tony said.

"I do trust him. I trust all of you. I just don't want anything to happen to him!"

Grimaldi said, "He is trained to complete this mission. He is the best man I know!"

"I know. I know!" Maggie held her head up and took a deep breath. "Let's do this!"

At Exx-Oil headquarters, Roberts said, "I think we should have negotiated with Rebel when we had the chance. He means business!"

"This is America! Have you forgotten about capitalism? We are free to do business in any way we see fit!" Bitterson said.

Roberts said, "Of course I know what you are talking about. I also know that we have ignored this revolutionary who was willing to negotiate with us and allow us to continue to invest in the future. Instead, we tried to kill him. He is pissed off! Do you think he is going to allow us to invest in the alternatives now?"

Bitterson said, "I think it is far too late for negotiations. Rebel is not responding to our request. We must protect the rigs and our investments. You need to contact your security managers immediately to make sure they are secured!"

The other CEOs agreed.

Rebel and the Phantoms arrived at the first five rigs. Each was the size of a large production facility, housing its workers while on duty. The DSV kamikaze drones were ready for attack.

Grimaldi said, "Make sure the Phantoms are in cloak mode near the rigs."

"Rebel to Control."

"Go for Control."

"It appears as though the standard security guards are patrolling the surface of the rigs. Entering the water."

"Copy that, Rebel."

As Drone-5 headed to the bottom of the rig, it ran into a single-manned military diver-propulsion attack vessel with harpoons that were tipped with explosives. The DPAV looked like an underwater motorcycle with an enclosed cockpit.

The mercenary in the DPAV fired at the drone, barely missing it.

Maggie said, "We have to be careful when firing on the enemy. We cannot fire in the direction of the oil rigs!"

As the DPAV moved in for another attack, Phantom-5 positioned itself for a clear shot on the enemy. The Phantom zeroed in with a torpedo and fired, splitting the vehicle in half and killing the mercenary.

Drone-5 was clear to continue its objective. The Phantom continued to survey the scene. The main valve was secured behind a steel barrier. The drone made its way to the target, lasered a hole in the wall, and made its way into the valve. When Drone-5 was successfully positioned, Phantom-5 headed to its second phase.

The next three drones encountered no resistance. They were successfully deployed onto their assignments, completing the first phase of the mission as well. The Phantoms made their way to the second phase.

Phantom-1 submerged and deployed Drone-1 to its target.

Maggie said, "Rebel, look to the northwest corner of the rig. You have company!"

"Copy that, Control." Rebel defended the DSV from the threat, but a second DPAV approached from behind.

Phantom-1 fired a torpedo at the DPAV, sending it to the depths of the ocean. The second DPAV fired on Phantom-1.

The defense system warned Rebel of the attack, and he spun out of the line of fire. Rebel fired another torpedo, destroying the vessel, and directed his attention at Drone-1. One of the harpoons had partially damaged the drone.

Grimaldi said, "Well, it looks like we have crossed a line from which we cannot return. I am sorry we had to take lives here, but it couldn't be helped in this case."

Maggie said, "I think my conversation with Nick finally convinced him that the threat is more dangerous than he is powerful. He will be more focused now than ever before. If he isn't, he will lose what is most important to him … us!"

Rebel retrieved Drone-1 and returned to the Phantom to access the damage. "Rebel to Control-3. How serious is the damage to Drone-1?"

Joey said, "Take its back shield off for inspection."

Rebel opened his toolbox, took out an Allen wrench, and removed the bolts. "The optical sensor is damaged."

Joey said, "Drone-1 has no video. You will have to load him into the rig yourself, Rebel."

Maggie said, "You can't go inside that thing! Why did you tell him that Joey?"

"I can do this—no problem, Control," Rebel said. "Once I get inside, you can just guide me to the target."

Rebel moved toward the rig to deploy Drone-1, and it lasered through the barrier within minutes. Rebel pushed the metal inward. "We're inside. Which way to the target?"

Maggie said, "Make your way down to the bottom. You will see a large structure that looks like a giant valve. Set Drone-1 on the valve, and it will do the rest."

Rebel placed Drone-1 on its target, and the drone magnetically attached itself to the valve. Rebel made his way back to Phantom-1, departing for the next phase.

Grimaldi said, "Maybe we should have the nearest Phantom return to base. I think I should get in this fight. I didn't anticipate this much resistance."

Joey said, "No way, Giovanni! We can't afford to lose you! I will do this!"

"Control to Rebel."

"Go for Rebel."

"Control-1 would like to join the party via Phantom-5."

"Negative, Control-1—not recommended!" Rebel said.

Joey said, "Control-3 to Rebel. I will join you. I'm prepping more drones to assist with the mission … just in case."

"Very good," Rebel replied.

Tony said, "Are you sure about this, Joey?"

"I'll do whatever it takes to complete the mission!" he said.

Maggie commanded Phantom-5 to return to base.

Joey grabbed scuba gear, oxygen tanks, and underwater weapons.

Grimaldi said, "We need to be more cautious in the second phase of the mission. We cannot allow any altercation to damage the rigs and spill the oil!"

Rebel said, "The Phantoms must scan the areas carefully and draw any other attackers away from the rigs before setting the drones back into action."

Maggie said, "We don't have all night."

Rebel said, "I understand. We will scan the surrounding areas carefully and then proceed."

Grimaldi said, "Maggie, program the new directive into the Phantoms."

Phantom-2 arrived at its target and scanned the area, but nothing out of the ordinary showed up on the radar. Phantom-2 proceeded to the bottom of the ocean to release Drone-7 to its objective. Drone-7 was able to access the enclosure undetected.

"Rebel to Control."

"Go for Control."

"I suggest that you have Phantom-2 assist Phantom-3 with its next objective."

Maggie quickly keyed in the orders. "Copy that, Rebel."

Grimaldi said, "We should program the Phantoms to back each other up once they complete their objectives."

Rebel said, "Sounds like a plan!"

Maggie pointed at her watch.

Grimaldi said, "I am aware of the time, Maggie, but we must be cautious."

Phantom-2 and Phantom-3 finished the second phase of the mission.

Maggie said, "Sending Phantom-2 and 3 out to back up Phantom-5."

Grimaldi said, "How are you doing, Control-3?"

"I'm picking up a vessel on radar," Joey said.

"Wait for Phantom-2 and Phantom-3 to join you before approaching the rig," Maggie said.

"Okay, but they'd better hurry before someone picks up on me out here," Joey said.

Phantom-2 and Phantom-3 arrived at Joey's location within minutes.

Maggie said, "Control to Phantom-3. You're clear to enter the water along with the other Phantoms. You have all of the backup drones, but you need to allow Phantom-2 and Phantom-3 to eliminate that vessel. Avoid battle."

He replied, "Copy that, Control. I see something by the northeast corner of the rig."

Maggie programmed Phantom-2 and Phantom-3 to attack the threat.

As the Phantoms approached the target, Maggie decided to draw the enemy away from the rig. She programmed Phantom-3 to hover uncloaked near the rig. The vessel was able to detect Phantom-3, drawing the enemy away from the rig. The enemy vessel took the bait and pursued the Phantom. Maggie commanded Phantom-2 to target and destroy the vehicle from behind. Just as Phantom-3 was given the order to cloak and dive, Phantom-2 fired a torpedo at the vessel, destroying it in a tremendous explosion.

Maggie said, "Control to Control-3. You're clear to release Drone-10 into the water."

"Copy that, Control." Joey released the drone, following closely behind with Phantom-2 and Phantom-3 in order to protect it from another attack. Two vehicles began to close in on Drone-10, and Joey said, "Control, we have multiple contacts on sonar approaching Drone-10!"

"Copy that. Stand by, Control-3." Maggie programmed Phantom-2 and Phantom-3 to attack.

Joey stayed close to Drone-10 to defend it. The DPAVs fired harpoons at Drone-10 and barely missed, but one of the harpoons was sucked into the engine intake of Phantom-5 and exploded on impact. This destroyed its internal composition, disabled one of the engines, and caused an electrical fire. "I'm hit. I have an engine-failure warning! I smell something burning!"

Grimaldi said, "Pull the emergency-extinguisher lever on your center control panel!"

Joey deployed the extinguisher, barely escaping explosion. "Oh, shit. I lost my cloak! I'm visible! Where's that backup, Control? I'm a sitting duck out here!"

Just as the enemy vehicle was lining up another shot at Joey, Phantom-2 approached out of the murky depths. It fired a torpedo a second after the enemy fired an explosive-tipped harpoon, altering the enemy's trajectory enough to miss its target. The harpoon crashed to the depths of the sea.

Maggie said, "Control to Control-3."

"Go for, Control-3," Joey replied.

"Is Phantom-5 operable?"

Joey said, "The system has a glitch. I can't keep control of it! I'm gonna to have to abort!"

Maggie said, "Gather the backup drones and make your way to the bay area. Phantom-2 is ready to retrieve you now!"

Phantom-2 approached the damaged aircraft, and Joey was able to secure the drones and exit through the bay door. He worked his way up to the belly of Phantom-2 with the drones as Phantom-5 sank deeper.

Maggie said, "Control to Rebel."

"Go for Rebel."

"Can you get over to Phantom-5's location?"

Rebel said, "Phantom-4 completed phase 2 of its objective and just arrived at my location. We're in a time-sensitive situation. Joey is too far out for us to make up the time, Control. Does he have the situation under control or not?"

Joey said, "Control-3 to Rebel. We have this under control. Finish your objective!"

Grimaldi said, "Rebel, do not worry about Control-3. He can handle this!"

With Phantom-2 and Phantom-3 securing the area, Drone-10 made its way to the bottom of the rig.

Joey said, "Drone-10 has completed phase 2!"

Grimaldi said, "Maggie, please program Phantom-2 and Phantom-3 to join Rebel for backup. Once they are clear of Phantom-5, set it to self-detonate. We can't leave a trace of evidence behind because it might be traced back to Grimaldi Industries!"

Phantom-2 and Phantom-3 exited the water and orbited the area to be sure that Phantom-5 self-detonated.

Maggie was able to engage Phantom-5's self-detonate command, leaving no trace of evidence.

Joey made his way to Rebel's location.

Rebel scanned the surface of the final rig, and Phantom-4 backed him up.

Maggie said, "Control-3 is en route. He will be at your location within ten minutes, Rebel."

Rebel said, "Everything looks clear on the surface, Control. We're submerging to survey the scene below."

Phantom-1 entered the sea just south of the rig, and Phantom-4 entered from the north. Phantom-1 detected two single-manned military DPAVs, and Phantom-4 discovered two more DPAVs in its quadrant.

Maggie said, "Looks like you have four enemies guarding the rig, Rebel. Wait for backup before you engage!"

"Copy that, Control."

Grimaldi said "Maggie, how much longer before Phantom-2 and Phantom-3 arrive to assist Rebel?"

"I can speed that up!" She programmed the Phantoms to climb to a safe altitude above sea level.

Phantoms 1 and 4 were outnumbered and decided not to risk an attack. Instead, they waited for Phantom-2 and Phantom-3 before approaching the threat.

Rebel said, "We'll stand by until the other Phantoms arrive, Control."

"Control to Control-3."

"Go for, Control-3." Joey said.

"Prepare for Mach 1."

"Okay." Joey took a deep breath and closed his eyes. The Phantoms entered Mach 1, and Joey held his seat belt tight with both hands.

Once the Phantoms returned to cruising speed, Maggie said, "Can you read me, Control-3?"

Joey said, "We're here, Control."

Within minutes, the Phantoms arrived.

"How's that for speed?" Maggie said.

Tony and Mr. Grimaldi nodded.

Once Phantom-2 and Phantom-3 arrived, Rebel said, "Are you okay, Control-3?"

Joey said, "I think so. I haven't puked yet!"

Rebel said, "I have a plan. I want Phantom-2, Phantom-3, and Phantom-4 to spread out, submerge as low as possible, and attack from under the DPAVs. Once the threat is eliminated, I will deploy Drone-6."

"I'm not sure that Control-3 should engage the enemy again," Maggie said. "I think Control-3 should stay on the surface with the backup drones and monitor the overall area as the eye in the sky to secure your objective. You should attack with Phantom-3 and Phantom-4 and release Drone-6 once the threat is eliminated."

Grimaldi said, "I agree with Control. We should go with her plan!"

"Copy that, Control. En route," Rebel said.

The Phantoms submerged in cloak mode to a depth that the DPAVs were not capable of reaching. Phantom-3 worked its way underneath two of the DPAVs and slowly released floating proximity mines. The mines ascended toward their targets.

On the other side of the rig, Phantom-4 approached a third DPAV, positioned itself directly below its target, and took aim.

In Phantom-1, Rebel approached on the opposite side of the rig from below. "I have sights on the fourth target. Fire on my mark!"

Control said, "We are finding activity on the rig from the eye in the sky!"

Rebel said, "That'll have to wait, Control. Three, two, one … mark!"

Phantom-1 and Phantom-4 fired their torpedoes simultaneously, obliterating the targets.

The two enemy targets above Phantom-3 were alerted to the attack and shifted into high gear. One of the proximity mines found its target, destroying the DPAV. Seconds later, a second proximity mine eliminated the second DPAV.

"Control to Rebel. The eye in the sky has reported four Zodiac boats with armed security on the surface. There are a couple of divers in each of the boats!"

Rebel said, "Affirmative, Control. Those divers are not capable of reaching these depths without a submersible."

Maggie said, "You're clear to deploy Drone-6."

Nick reached his objective within minutes. "I'm releasing Drone-6 to the rig!"

"Copy that, Rebel.

Drone-6 was nearing its destination when it exploded suddenly.

Rebel said, "We have had a major malfunction down here, Control!"

Maggie yelled, "That was no malfunction. Phantom-3 detected a torpedo on sonar. There must be a sub down there! Take evasive action immediately!"

Rebel made his way deeper into the abyss with Phantom-3 and Phantom-4. "What trajectory was that torpedo coming from? We need to follow it back to its origin."

Maggie said, "It came from the north quadrant. Concentrate your search in that direction for now."

Rebel and the Phantoms moved in the direction of the attack.

Phantom-3's defense system alerted it to an approaching torpedo. Phantom-3 accelerated in the opposite direction and dropped proximity mines. The torpedo closed in on Phantom-3, but the mines neutralized the threat.

Rebel said, "What the hell is out here? How are they able to detect us while we're in cloak mode?"

Maggie said, "You and the other Phantoms have your searchlights on. They can't see you, but they can see the lights. I turned them off. Search with your thermal sensors and sonar instead!"

Rebel replied, "How dumb of me. I forgot about the lights. Going dark!"

Maggie said, "You're going to have to keep in constant movement, Rebel. I have already programmed the Phantoms to move in evasive patterns!"

Phantom-4 detected a thermal-heat signature among the rocks on the sea floor. It was coming from the direction of the previous torpedo attack. The enemy approached from behind the object while Phantom-4 used its night-vision camera to capture an image of a deep-sea submersible.

Maggie and Grimaldi studied the image for a moment.

Grimaldi said, "I thought those subs were still in the experimental stage. I didn't know they were operational. This one is a single-man DSAF. Vessels like this are capable of reaching depths that most other underwater vehicles cannot. They have the maneuverability of an undersea jet fighter and the weapons of an attack sub. Be very cautious with this vessel, Rebel. I have seen this sub in action as a prototype. Subs like this one are smaller and more maneuverable than the Phantoms. We have no idea what they are fully capable of. You must work with the other Phantoms as a team to win this battle!"

Rebel said, "Copy that, Control-1."

Phantom-4 fired a torpedo at the DSAF, successfully hitting its target and exploding the enemy. The explosion drew the other DPAVs out of hiding.

Rebel said, "I'm sure there are more where that came from. We must eliminate the threat before sending out any more drones!"

Four more DSAFs emerged from the depths of the sea.

Rebel said, "I see two more vessels approaching. They are too close to the rig. We cannot fire on them. We're going to have to split up and draw them away from the rig before we attack!"

"Copy that, Rebel." Maggie programmed the Phantoms to follow Rebel's directions. They would head away from the rig since the enemy would use sonar and thermal sensors to track the Phantoms.

Rebel slowed down to draw one of the DSAFs toward a huge boulder. He circled the boulder, leaving a proximity mine in its path. Once Rebel had circled the boulder, he picked up an explosion on his sonar. He circled again to confirm that the enemy was eliminated. The target was destroyed.

"Rebel, Phantom-3 is under attack!"

"I'm on my way, Control!"

Phantom-3 took evasive actions. As the fighter locked in and fired, the Phantom's defense system automatically released countermeasures and was able to neutralize the torpedo.

Another fighter had fired on Phantom-3, clipping one of its wings and sending it spiraling out of control.

Rebel engaged the attacker, locking in on him and blasting the enemy with his own torpedo. The torpedo struck perfectly, sending the vessel crashing into a sunken ship. Just as Rebel was relishing his win, the second attacker targeted him. It had trouble locking in on Rebel, and he avoided the attack.

Maggie programmed Phantom-4 to track the DSAF that was pursuing Rebel. The Phantom approached the enemy from behind and locked in on him.

Rebel said, "I can't shake this one, Control. I need some help over here!"

The fighter fired a torpedo at Rebel.

Control said, "Head toward the surface! Get in the air!"

Rebel climbed as fast as he could, using full power to evade the attack.

"Faster, Rebel!" Maggie said. "You only have five seconds until impact!"

Just as Rebel was about to exit the water, he saw an enemy boat. He emerged within inches of an attack boat that was patrolling the surface. He flew over the boat and drew the torpedo to its new target. The torpedo missed him and blew the boat to smithereens. Rebel took a deep breath and looped back into the water on the other side of the explosion.

The DSAF went back to secure the rig, but Phantom-4 fired a torpedo at him, obliterating the vessel.

"Control to Rebel."

"Go for Rebel."

"Phantom-4 has just destroyed another vessel."

"Copy that, Control," Rebel said. "I'm gonna check on Phantom-3."

Maggie said, "Rebel, I've programmed Phantom-1 to zero in on Phantom-3's location!"

"Is it okay?" asked Rebel.

"So far, yes. I think it's fully functional. It was just clipped by the torpedo and lost control momentarily. While I'm finishing the diagnostics on it, you need to back it up—just in case. Looks like it's fully functional, Rebel, but there are two enemy fighters remaining. Take evasive action!"

The Phantoms searched for the last two fighters.

Joey said, "I think it's time to get back in this fight, Control. We're running out of time!"

Control said, "Hold tight, eye in the sky. We need the area secured first!"

Rebel said, "Control, have Phantom-3 and Phantom-4 come from opposite sides of the rig. Just as they are about to cross paths, have them turn their searchlights on. They should draw the enemy on their trail, and I will attack them from below. Once I have them targeted, kill the lights on the Phantoms and have them disperse!"

"Got it, Rebel. I'll program all three of the Phantoms to intersect. Once you have your shot, take back the controls. I will redirect the other Phantoms to engage."

"Copy that, Control. You have command."

Maggie programmed the order, and the Phantoms moved into position. When the Phantoms were about to cross paths, she activated their lights, luring the DSAFs into the trap.

Maggie said, "The Phantoms are being targeted, Rebel."

Rebel disengaged his autopilot and rushed toward the fighters. "Now!"

Maggie commanded both of the Phantoms to kill their lights, evade, and reengage.

One of the enemy fighters was able to lock in on Phantom-4 and get off a shot, striking Phantom-4 with a direct hit.

Control lost remote-function immediately, and Phantom-4 began to sink.

Rebel zeroed in on one of the fighters and fired a torpedo, destroying it. "Which one of the Phantoms was hit?"

"Phantom-4. It's bad, Rebel."

"How bad is the damage?"

"It's out of the game, Rebel!"

"Can you program it to self-detonate?"

"Hang on," Maggie said. "Yes, it's receiving partial commands!"

Rebel said, "Command, Phantom-4 is to engage its self-destruct sequence and detonate on my mark!" He waited for the fighter to be sure that he wasn't detected. The enemy fighter approached Phantom-4 to confirm its destruction. "Control, three, two, one, mark!"

Maggie sent the command to Phantom-4 to self-destruct, taking the enemy with it.

Rebel said, "I believe that was the last fighter, Control. I'm surfacing to retrieve the backup drones."

"Looks like you're clear for approach," Maggie said.

Rebel began to make his way to the surface.

Joey said, "Hold your position, Rebel. I'm en route to the rig."

Control said, "Negative, eye in the sky. Wait for Phantom-1 to pick up the drone!"

Rebel ascended to the surface in cloak mode and aligned Phantom-1 with Phantom-2.

Joey released Drone-11 into the water for Rebel.

Rebel secured the drone and made his way back to the bottom of the rig.

Control said, "I'm not detecting any further threats through Phantom-3's sonar. Looks like you're clear for deployment."

Rebel surveyed the entry point. "Looks clear to me, Control. I'm releasing Drone-11 now."

The drone took position and began to laser into the rig. Phantom-1 and Phantom-3 stayed close for protection.

As Drone-11 was nearing entry, a DSAF charged toward it and ripped the drone off of the rig.

Rebel said, "We have another attacker, Control. He is too close to the rig to fire. He's using the drone for cover. I have to handle this myself!" Rebel exited Phantom-1 and used the jet boots to close in on the vessel.

The DSAF drilled through the center of Drone-11, rendering it useless.

Maggie said, "Be careful, Rebel. You're not 100 percent!"

Rebel replied, "Don't worry, Control. I'll be okay. No matter what happens, do not allow the Phantoms to fire in the direction of the rig!"

Grimaldi said, "We cannot allow there to be a blowout of the well. If there is, the mission will be a failure!"

The enemy fighter stayed close to the rig for cover, but Rebel grabbed the vehicle's water-propulsion jet. Rebel attempted to clear the vessel from the rig.

The pilot tried to buck Rebel from the hull, reversing throttle toward the rig and attempting to crash Rebel into it.

Rebel focused his energy on attacking the vessel with the powers of the suit. He mustered all of his strength and used his powers to strike the DPAV with a bolt of energy. The pilot lost control, and the vessel began to sink. When the vessel was motionless on the sea floor, Rebel used one of the tips of his hardened pitons to punch the wounded vessel's canopy, forcing the high-pressure seawater into the vessel. It imploded and sank to the bottom.

After returning to Phantom-1, Rebel said, "Program the Phantoms to complete one last scan of the area. Once cleared of any threat, deploy Phantom-2 for the release of Drone-12."

Control replied, "Affirmative, Rebel!"

"It's about time I get back in the game!" Joey said.

The Phantoms circled one more time to search for other threats.

Control said, "All clear, Rebel. Phantom-2 is on approach."

Phantom-2 reached the bottom of the rig, and Joey deployed the last drone.

Rebel said, "Control, program the Phantoms to set their backs to the drone—and be ready to fire on anything that moves!"

Maggie moved Drone-12 into position, and it fused itself to the wellhead to secure its position.

The second phase was completed, and the drones were all in place for detonation. The Phantoms ascended to the surface.

Rebel said, "Phase 2 is complete!"

Maggie said, "Copy that, Rebel … engaging final phase."

Rebel said, "We're clear of the blast area. Blow the rigs!"

Just as she was about to engage, Maggie looked at Grimaldi and motioned for him to press the button.

Grimaldi said, "This one is for every person who has been oppressed by these savages." Grimaldi invited Tony to press the button.

Tony walked up to the keyboard and detonated the explosives.

Maggie checked the systems of all ten security feeds on the rigs. "The mission objectives are complete. The superstructures are intact, and the wellheads have been imploded—with no visible signs of blowout!"

Rebel screamed, "Yes! We did it!"

The team embraced.

When the CEOs received the news from their security managers, they looked at each other in shock. Their investments were useless.

Bitterson yelled, "What the hell? I am going to make a call to my source in the White House. This is unacceptable!"

Roberts said, "I told you we should have negotiated with Rebel. Now we're screwed!" He stormed out of the office.

At the White House, the president was awakened in the middle of the night. Republican congressmen and senators flooded the president with e-mails and phone calls. They were being pressured by their big-money supporters to take action immediately.

The president's cabinet convened for an emergency meeting. They were concerned that the destruction of the wells was too extreme and that Rebel's actions would definitely come with major consequences from the contributors of the president's campaign.

President Jackson's top advisor said, "This can go two ways, Mr. President. Either the price of oil goes through the roof—and the public wants to know what we are going to do about Rebel—or the alternatives are a success and Rebel is a hero. For now, all we can do is wait and see, sir!"

The president said, "Get me a meeting with Rebel first thing in the morning!"

Rebel returned to base with Joey.

Maggie ran down to the launchpad to meet Nick. She hugged and kissed him. "Are you okay, Nick?"

"I'm fine, Maggie. With a little rest and rehab, I'll be as good as new!"

Maggie said, "The president is not happy, Nick. He wants a meeting with you first thing in the morning!"

"The president is going to have to wait until I'm ready! This revolution has just begun. There is still a lot of work to be done, but the only place we are going for now is on vacation!" Nick extended his arms to Tony and Grimaldi in celebration.

The team embraced each other with great emotion, looking forward to the future.

THE END

Printed in the United States
By Bookmasters